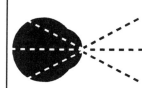

This Large Print Book carries the
Seal of Approval of N.A.V.H.

RASPUTIN'S DAUGHTER

ROBERT ALEXANDER

WHEELER PUBLISHING

An imprint of Thomson Gale, a part of The Thomson Corporation

Detroit • New York • San Francisco • New Haven, Conn. • Waterville, Maine • London

LIBRARY OF CONGRESS CATALOGING-IN-PUBLICATION DATA

Alexander, Robert, 1952–
 Rasputin's daughter / by Robert Alexander.
  p. cm.
 ISBN-13: 978-1-59722-467-3 (pbk. : alk. paper)
 ISBN-10: 1-59722-467-7 (pbk. : alk. paper)
 1. Rasputin, Grigori Efimovich, ca. 1870–1916 — Fiction. 2. Russia — History — Nicholas II, 1894–1917 — Fiction. 3. Rasputina, Mariia Grigor'evna — Fiction. 4. Fathers and daughters — Fiction. 5. Courts and courtiers — Fiction. I. Title.
 PS3576.I5118R37 2007
 813'.6—dc22
                 2006038709

Published in 2007 by arrangement with Viking, a member of Penguin Group (USA) Inc.

Printed in the United States of America on permanent paper
10 9 8 7 6 5 4 3 2 1

FOR MARLY RUSOFF

AUTHOR'S NOTE

All dates in the book are Old Style, as the Julian calendar was in use until 1918, when the Gregorian calendar was instituted. The original Russian spellings of proper names have also been maintained. And for purposes of clarification, a chronology of events and a complete glossary are located at the end of the book.

In the beginning of the twentieth century
Russia found itself at a *rasputiye,*[1]
When all of a sudden there appeared a
   rasputnik[2]
And Russia became mired in a *rasputitsa.*[3]

— M. Tarlova

[1] crossroad
[2] debauched person
[3] season of horribly muddy roads

Believe me, I'd tell you if I knew. But I really have no idea how Rasputin was introduced to the former imperial family, and I will swear to my death that I took no part in it. I've heard rumors that he was eager to penetrate the palace, that he did so via dubious means, and that he was assisted by one of the former grand duchesses — I think the one from Montenegro. It seems quite possible, but of all that I have no firsthand knowledge.

No, I didn't become involved in the plot to murder Rasputin until much, much later.

PROLOGUE

Petrograd, Russia
April 1917

It wasn't clear who had betrayed me.

As I was dragged through the ransacked halls of the Winter Palace, a silent armed soldier on either side, I wondered who had been spying on me, who had leaked word of my return to the capital. How had these two young militants known to come searching for me at our apartment on Goroxhovaya? Who had ordered them to break down my door, chase me through our rooms, and carry me off?

"Let me loose!" I screamed, after they'd caught up with me in the kitchen. "You can't do this!"

Only one of the soldiers spoke, the tall one, who was at best only a year or two older than me. He waved a signed and stamped piece of paper right before my face and barked the darkest words that could be said in Russia.

"By order of the Thirteenth Section!"

I fell silent, not simply out of fear but because now it was perfectly clear. There was no escaping the all-powerful Extraordinary Commission of Inquiry for the Investigation of Illegal Acts by Ministers and Other Responsible Persons of the Tsarist Regime. Of course I had nothing to do with politics. But I knew very well why I was of interest to the Thirteenth, which had been charged with the gravest of revolutionary duties, "investigating the activity of the Dark Forces."

Sandwiched between the two guards, I was led through the palace, which was no longer glowing and regal but filthy, littered with broken furniture, muddy carpets, shredded curtains, and torn portraits. I started crying. Where had all this hatred come from? What poison had killed our love of tsar and country and, far worse, of one another? Were the newspapers right? Could one person have ruined so much? Had Papa really been that almighty?

My eyes darted about for hope — a familiar face, a sympathetic smile, an easy escape. Instead I saw only a whirl of chaos, room after room destroyed by a landslide of rage. As I was dragged into a gallery with dark red walls, I gazed up and saw scores upon scores of portraits of war heroes staring down on me. Finally, the soldiers kicked open a pair of regal doors and shoved me into St. George's Hall, the main throne room of the tsars, including that of our very last, Nikolai II.

But the silver throne no longer sat upon the dais.

Instead it had been smashed, hacked to pieces and thrown aside, and the royal canopy above it ripped away. Likewise, a red velvet panel with the enormous double-headed eagle had been cut from the wall. At that moment I knew, despite the chaos of these days, that this revolution had been a stunning success: There was no going back, not now or even in the decades or centuries to come. The monarchy was gone from Russia forever.

Without slowing, the two young soldiers pulled me through the vast room with its columns of white marble. There at the far end, just to the side of the ravaged dais, sat a man reading something — a report, I assumed. As we approached, he looked up and rose to his feet. He was dressed in military garb, though I couldn't tell his rank. The closer we came, the more certain I was that I knew this man with the wavy

15

hair, the narrow puffy eyes, the thin lips. But where had I seen him before?

"Matryona Grigorevna Rasputina?" he asked, his eyes all over me like a painter's.

I could tell he was searching for family resemblances. And of course he found them, he couldn't miss, for I had my father's long dark hair and his sharp blue eyes, broad forehead, and small chin. The man before me made no attempt to cloak his shock and revulsion, and under his disapproving eyes I started to shake.

Though I was on the verge of crying again, I tried to hold myself proudly. Here in the capital I was known by a far less provincial name.

"You may call me Maria."

"Age seventeen?"

"Eighteen."

He dabbed a pen in an inkpot, wrote something down, and then waved the pen like a scepter at the soldiers. "Leave us."

Their tight grasp on my upper arms had been like tourniquets; now, released, I felt a sudden rush of pleasure. The boy soldiers turned, not in unison, and sauntered away, leaving me with this strange man. He alone couldn't represent the much-feared Thirteenth Section, could he?

As I watched, he carefully placed the sheaf

16

of papers he'd been reading in a folder. With a bold stroke of his pen, he made a notation on the cover.

"What's that?" I inquired.

"A report."

"A report on what?"

"On someone I just interviewed."

"Are you going to throw them back in prison, or are you —"

"I will ask the questions and you will answer them," he snapped. "To start, tell me why you've returned to the capital."

Just then I heard a strange noise. Looking toward the dais, I saw a large fancy grate in the wall. Were looters having their way in the next room?

Carefully measuring my words, I said, "I've returned to Petrograd to find a friend."

"Who?"

I wanted to say, *Someone I desperately need to see, someone I once loved.* But I had to be strong. I dared not let my interrogator see how much I hurt inside, let alone betray the information I was carrying. There was not a doubt in my mind that if the Thirteenth Section knew what I did, I'd be tossed directly into the Peter and Paul Fortress. Perhaps I'd even be shot. It was for these very reasons that my mother back in Siberia had begged me to stay home.

17

"For whom are you searching?" he demanded.

"A friend who . . . who has been imprisoned."

"I see," he replied, as if he'd already heard that story a hundred times, which I was sure he had. "And do you know why you are here?"

Desperate to move on, I said, "There are many things I don't understand, especially why two young *xhama*" — rogues — "would break down my door and drag me from my home."

That long mouth with the thin lips drew itself into a tight pinch of . . . amusement? No, of course I wasn't what he expected.

Containing his humor, he said, "Be seated. My name is Aleksander Aleksandrovich, and I mean to ask you about your father."

That was all it took, just his first name and patronymic. There was not a girl with any brains in the capital who was not in love with this man. Yes, of course I knew who he was, and my entire body trembled. For years I had cherished his beautiful words as much as his beautiful photograph.

As forcefully as a priest, I chanted:

"To sin shamelessly, endlessly,
To lose count of the nights and days,

18

And with a head unruly from drunkenness
To pass sideways into the temple of God."

My would-be interrogator was suddenly blushing. "I wrote that."

"Of course you did." It simply sprang from my mouth. "You're Aleksander Aleksandrovich Blok, and that was my father's favorite poem. I recited it to him the very night he was killed. . . . In fact, your words were practically the last I spoke to him."

The color rushed from his face and he turned as pale as snow on a moonlit night. His own heavenly images of sinful Russia had touched the heart of the devil incarnate? His motifs of heartache and remorse were the last blessing the evil one had heard before meeting . . . death?

I'd never hated a man so much before. Sitting before me was not only Russia's most romantic poet in more than a century, not only our greatest gift since Aleksander Pushkin, but the person who'd once been both my savior and my inspiration. When I, a peasant girl from the distant countryside, had landed in the Steblin-Kamensky Institute, a school for daughters of good home and breeding, I was like a *reeba bez vodii* — a fish without water — lacking in friends, stylish clothing, courtly manners, a fancy

19

home, personal maid, or anything else that a girl of good society took for granted. But I did have this poet's images and words, and they had helped transform me from a clumsy *derevenschina* into a worldly young woman.

My voice quivering as if I were hurling hate on a deceitful lover, I gasped, "Why in the name of God did you bring me here? What do you of all people want from *me?*"

Blok stared straight at me. "I need to know what happened the night of December sixteenth, the night your father was killed." He paused. "Allow me to explain, Maria Grigorevna. I was drafted into the army and now serve the Provisional Government. As secretary of the Extraordinary Commission, I have been present at most of the interviews with former ministers and those closest to the former imperial family."

"Oh, really?" I said, mocking him. "I've wondered where you were and what you were doing. I haven't seen any new poems from you in quite some time. Is that why?"

He glared at me. By the depth of the furrows creasing his forehead, I knew I'd hit not only a sore point but probably a sore truth. I couldn't have been more pleased.

Pressing on, I said, "So you've found something more interesting to do . . . such as gathering gossip?"

"Maria Grigorevna," he said, as sternly as a commandant, "it's my job to take the stenographs from the interviews and edit them into readable form. As I've been going through the endless pages on your father, however, I find that not only is Rasputin more a mystery than ever but the truth of his murder is more and more unclear."

"Of course it is. After all, both monarchists and revolutionaries have proved equally adept at twisting both my father's life and his death into political legend."

"They say that first your father was poisoned, next shot, then stabbed. But still he lived, and frantic to kill him, they finally threw him through a hole in the ice and —"

Bitterness stinging my tongue, I interrupted. "Don't you know better than to believe the stories told by a man's enemies?"

"Yes, but . . ."

As his words trailed off, I could see it in his eyes, his fascination with my father, which wasn't surprising, since the entire Empire had been obsessed with him — or, more correctly, with the myths about him. And yet, as I stared at Blok, there seemed to be more. Could he be one of the few who admired my father, who saw Papa as the ultimate revolutionary, the peasant who'd climbed from the lowest rung to the very top and done what no terrorist had ever been able to do, overturn our entire society?

Suddenly I blurted out the truth. "If you really want to know who murdered the mysterious Rasputin and how, I can tell you. I can tell you exactly what happened on the night of December sixteenth because I was there and saw it all with my own eyes. First, though, you must realize one thing: I was and am a devoted daughter. I loved Papa, and he . . . he loved me."

The tears came then, and there was not a thing I could do to stop them. Staring blankly ahead, I simply let the large salty drops roll one after another down my cheeks. But I was not crying because I loved my father. I was crying because I felt so guilty.

"What is it, Maria?" Blok asked, with surprising softness.

I swiped at my eyes. What could I say about my father, the greatest of all Russian enigmas?

"You have to look at the final days of his life," I said, my voice quivering. "I learned everything I know about Papa during that last week."

"Then you must tell me every detail of those days, right up to and including the night of the sixteenth, when he was lured to the Yusupov Palace."

"Yes. . . . But since when has anyone in Russia been interested in honesty, let alone truth?"

CHAPTER 1

December 1916
One week before Rasputin's murder
It was past eleven in the evening when the telephone rang in our apartment, which wasn't that unusual because people were always in need of Papa's help, and in our city, the city of Peter, clocks had never made sense. Though we were fast approaching the lowest point in the year and the day's light had been barely more than an indifferent blink, sleep for all of us was elusive.

Still wearing my favorite blue dress, I was sitting on the bed, Pushkin's *Evgeni Onegin* and Bely's *Peterburg* by my side. But instead of reading these famous poets, I was captured by a new one, Marina Tsvetayeva, who a few years earlier had achieved my dream of publishing a book when she was just eighteen. Several of my small pieces had already been set in type, but would I ever write enough poems to fill an entire book?

As the phone rang a second and a third time, I glanced at my young sister, Varvara, who was dozing fitfully on the other half of the bed we shared, her head buried beneath a lumpy down pillow. When the telephone continued its shrill noise, I pushed aside my books and in my stocking feet hurried from our small bedroom into the hall. Where was our maid, Dunya, and why wasn't she answering? Many people assumed that because of our royal connections, we lived a grand life, rich in material goods and waited on hand and foot, but that was not so. Our third-floor apartment at 64 Goroxhovaya Street, just a block from the Fontanka River, was, to the surprise of many, a mere five rooms — our salon, the dining room, Papa's study, his bedroom, and Varvara's and my room — that was it besides the bath and the kitchen. And none of our rooms in this five-story brick building was grand. Even our neighbors were rather ordinary. Katya, who lived upstairs in Flat 31, was a seamstress. There were also a clerk and a kind masseuse, Utilia, who often complained that Papa bothered her for affection.

When I came into the hall, I was, as usual, greeted by music and loud voices. Papa loved Gypsy music — particularly the Mazalski Gypsy Choir, so lively and full of fun, just like Papa's heart — but tonight he had a lone balalaika player in the salon. From somewhere I heard my gregarious father's laugh rise with delight. I also heard the giggle of a woman — no, I realized, *women* — but I had no idea who they were. Every day seemed to bring scores of desperate strangers into our home. From morning to night there was a queue outside our door and down the three flights, a line of princes and paupers, bankers and bakers, lawyers and factory workers, waiting their turn to see Papa and beg his influence or have him heal them.

Rushing to the black phone on the wall, I picked up the heavy earpiece, cupped it to my ear, and spoke into the mouthpiece. *"Ya Vas slushaiyoo."* I am listening to you.

"This is the Palace operator. One moment, please."

My heart immediately speeded up. Despite the late hour, I assumed it was the Empress. The very next moment, however, there was a click and I immediately recognized the voice of the Empress's only close friend, the person many were calling the second most powerful woman in all the Russias.

Speaking with the slight lisp that always made her sound as if she had a mouthful of porridge, Madame Vyrubova uttered the most commanding phrase in the nation: "I'm calling on urgent business from the Palace."

She begged to know if my father was home, and I assured Anna Aleksandrovna that he was. Then I lowered the earpiece and let it hang from its long cord. It was good fortune that my father was indeed here, I thought as I hurried down the hall, for often toward midnight he would go out. Just the night before, Honorary Burgess Pestrikov had treated him to quantities of wine and food at the Restaurant Villa Rode; it was four in the morning when Papa had stumbled into the apartment and collapsed on the sofa, where he slept until ten. The night before that, he'd stayed out all night with Madame Yazininskaya, presumably at her flat, for he did not return until lunch the following day.

Passing through our dining room, I swerved around several cases of sweet red wine a councilor had just brought, a gift that particularly pleased Papa because of the Dry Laws the Tsar had decreed soon after the start of the war. I then skirted our brass samovar, its fire gone out, and the heavy oak table, which was laden with a basket of flowers and plates of biscuits and sweets, nuts, dried fruits, cakes, and other delicacies that appeared day in and day out for our stream of guests.

By the sounds from the salon, I assumed that was where I would find Papa. In fact, he was not there. Rather, I found the lone balalaika player, strumming the melancholy tunes of our land, and two women, both huddled on the floor. One was our eternally loyal maid, Dunya, one of Papa's earliest disciples, who'd followed us from Siberia and who was, I couldn't help but notice, getting fatter by the week. The second was Princess Kossikovskaya, a young beauty of the best society. The princess had a number of diamonds sparkling in her rich brown hair and hanging from her ears, while strands of huge pearls drooped from her neck, but right then and there, hunched over on her knees, she didn't look so elegant. She was quite drunk.

And when I heard the beauty retch, I understood why Dunya, who was holding a basin to the young woman's smeared lips, hadn't answered the phone.

"Dunya, where's Papa?" I demanded.

"Back in his study," she said, with a quick wave over her shoulder.

I bit my lip, for it was not without some dread that I hurried out of the room and down the hall. Reaching the door of Papa's room, I raised my hand to knock — but hesitated. We were never, ever supposed to interrupt when Papa was healing someone . . . and yet if he was being summoned by the Empress, wasn't that more important? Absolutely, I thought, and I knocked firmly, albeit hesitantly.

A moment later came his gruff reply. "*Da, da.* Please enter at once!"

His study was small and narrow, with an icon and its oil lamp in one corner, an old oak desk, and, of course, his pathetic leather sofa, which was nearly rubbed bare. Perched on a chair in front of the sofa was Papa, wearing loose black pants, tall black leather boots, and a lilac *kosovorotka,* a shirt buttoned at the side of the collar. Every day any number of women begged for Papa's attention, but I had no idea how he treated them. Peering in now, however, I saw my father leaning forward and holding his visitor, none other than Countess Olga Kurlova, by the knees. The countess, wearing a pink Parisian silk dress that appeared loose, perhaps even unbuttoned in the front, was one of the great beauties of the Empire, with thick blond hair and cheeks that were high and distinguished. She was from Moscow, I knew, and though her family was neither so very noble nor, from what I heard, so very rich, she was a favorite in the capital, sought after by society for her seductive looks and keen wit.

As if I had walked in on a pair of lovers, Countess Olga gasped and clutched at the top of her dress.

"What are you doing here?" Papa asked with a scowl. "I thought it was our other guest. You know you're not supposed to bother me when my door is closed."

Averting my eyes, I said quietly, "There's a call of urgent business . . . from the Palace."

"What's that you say? Speak up, child!"

"There's a call from the Palace. . . . It's urgent, Papa."

All but forgetting about me, my father turned to the luscious countess and bragged, "Ah, Mama needs me. Mama needs me at the Palace."

Horrified that a peasant would refer to so lofty a personage in such coarse terms, the countess stared at him in shock. While some members of the court were permitted to address Her Majesty by her first name and patronymic — Aleksandra Fyodorovna — her lowly subjects were supposed to refer to her either as the Tsaritsa or the Empress. Never, ever, as Mama.

31

"I don't need them, I can just go back home to Siberia," my father boasted, holding up a sloppy finger to make a fine point. "But they wouldn't last six months on the throne without me! Really, not six months!"

"The phone, Papa!" I reminded. "You're wanted on the telephone!"

"Of course . . . yes, the telephone."

He kissed his right hand, then used that same hand to massage Countess Olga's right knee. The countess, though, was none too pleased and jerked back, whereupon the back of the old leather sofa fell off. The visiting beauty uttered a stifled scream.

"Ah, now, don't you worry, my tasty dish," muttered Papa, as he slowly and drunkenly pushed himself to his feet. "One of those fat sisters from the women's monastery slept on that sofa last week and broke it."

Almost without effort, Papa bent over the countess and lifted the heavy piece into place with one hand. Swaying slightly, he then leaned down and patted his guest on her head.

"We'll continue our purification later."

"Papa!" I insisted.

He stretched one hand toward me and called weakly, "Yes, yes. Come help me, *malenkaya maya.*" My little one.

Understanding that he'd drunk too much,

his "little one" was not eager to go to his side; I would have preferred simply to leave the room. But my mother in Siberia had long ago forgiven Papa his excesses, grateful for the three children he had given her, not to mention the finest house in the village and a field to till. So, as the oldest Rasputin female in the Petrograd household, I had no choice but to overlook things also.

Looking down at the countess one last time, Father made a drunken sign of the cross over her and intoned one of his favorite sayings: "Remember, great is the peasant in the eyes of God!"

As I helped him from his study, I stared at this terribly plain, even homely man, who was nothing less and nothing more than a *muzhik* — peasant — from Siberia. He was not dashing and debonair like the fathers of my classmates, many of whom were princes or counts. Instead, here was a person of only medium height, a semi-illiterate ox of a man who had toiled in the fields for years. He had light blue eyes, the kind that made people feel uncomfortable, his nose was long and slightly pocked and his skin wrinkled beyond his age, while his lips were thick and ripe with color. One look at him and anyone could tell he was from the wilds, for his long hair was dark and parted down

33

the middle like a crooked dirt lane, and his beard, which was thick like an ancient forest, had a dark reddish-brown hue.

No, my father was not a handsome man, nor was he charming or witty or devilishly tall, as so many wrote. But he did have an extraordinarily magnetic presence. He could enter a palace room and, though at first all the nobles would stare down on this ugly peasant, within moments they would be listening to his every word.

And he did have amazing physical strength. Never had I seen anyone able to grow sober so quickly, which he did just then. Oh, he leaned on me as I walked him into the hall, and he slurred a few words on the phone with Madame Vyrubova as she begged him to come to the palace, saying a motorcar had already been sent. But he pulled himself together in short order, for he was the Empress's favorite, the one on whom she depended most deeply, the one whom she loved as no other. No, my father had not lied, Aleksandra Fyodorovna could not exist without him. She knew it all too well, as did I.

Dunya left Princess Kossikovskaya vomiting to the sad twang of the balalaika player, and together we pulled Papa into the washroom, where we wiped his face with a damp cloth, changed his soiled shirt, and attempted to comb his unruly hair. As I pulled several strands aside, I hit the little bump on his forehead, a bump like a budding horn that he was always trying to conceal.

"I'll do it!" he shouted, trying to grab the comb from me.

"No, Papa, let me!" I said, slapping away his hand.

Cowering like a little boy, he bowed his head and let me continue; unfortunately, when I was done he looked no better than a roadside waiter. Meanwhile, Dunya had slipped away to the samovar, to return with a tall lukewarm glass of tea loaded with so much sugar that the granules floated this way and that like snow in a lazy blizzard. This was Dunya's medicine, which she dispensed not only when the barometric pressure changed, and half the city suffered from headaches, but also for colds, kidney aches, and, naturally, hangovers.

"Drink this all the way to the bottom, Grigori Effimovich," ordered Dunya, handing him the *podstakanik,* the metal frame holding the warm glass.

Father did as commanded, downing the entire glass of sweet tea as easily as a shot of vodka.

As I watched him drink, I thought of all

the horrible rumors about my father that floated like a black fog across town. The most persistent and most damning, of course, was that he was one of the *Khlysty* — the Whips — a peculiar and very secret sect that had evolved hundreds of years ago in Siberia. Whether or not their name was a derivation of *Xhristi* — the Christs — no one was sure, but according to rumor the *Khlysty* were a strange blend of paganism and orthodoxy and, it was whispered, were not afraid to sin. Because of all the nasty rumors — it was said they gathered deep in the forest, where in the dark of night they had big orgies and even ate the breasts of virgins — I was certain my father had never had anything to do with them.

Suddenly there was a heavy pounding on our front door, and Dunya scurried off. No sooner was she gone than Papa snatched the comb from me and threw it on the floor. I immediately retrieved it, for if one of my father's visitors found it tomorrow the comb was likely to end up being sold and resold. Indeed, there were many souls, desperate for a miracle, who would pay great sums to run Rasputin's comb through their own hair — what better way to bring God's blessings down upon them? Just a few months ago I'd caught a baronessa picking up Papa's fingernail clippings so she could stitch them into her dress and "be protected by his shield."

"Dochenka maya." My little daughter, he said, clasping both my hands in his massive grasp. "I had the same vision again. Earlier this evening I saw it all, quite clearly so."

"Papa, please, I —"

"No, I'm quite certain of it. Soon I'll be crossing over, soon we'll no longer be able to see each other."

In the last several years, fearing that he'd lost his powers, Papa had grown severely depressed. More recently, however, his gifts had seemed to return. Last week he'd healed a babushka who'd been as bent as a twisted branch with arthritis, and not long ago he'd foreseen a doubling of the cost of a single egg. But the return of his second sight wasn't so very reassuring. I simply hated this talk of his own death, which he'd been grousing of more and more.

"I'm not afraid, and you must not be either, *dochenka maya.*"

"But —"

"Don't worry, once I've crossed over I will send you a sign. I will signal you from the hereafter, and you will have proof that I am well and live on. Promise me you won't be afraid. Promise me you'll be strong!"

I hesitated before lying. "I promise."

"Good," he said, as he examined me with his piercing blue eyes. "Now listen to me. When I am dead you must hurry to the Palace and warn Mama and Papa that their lives are in danger. Promise me this too!"

"Yes . . . of course."

"I see it as the truth, and Mama and Papa must be warned!" said my father, his sluggish face now beginning to dance.

"But —"

Dunya came hurrying back, my father's extravagant thousand-ruble sable coat — a gift from the widow Reshetnikova — and beaver hat in hand, and said, "The motor is downstairs waiting, Grigori Effimovich. You must come quickly!"

Father looked at Dunya as if he couldn't remember what was happening. Pulling away from me, he shook his head and stumbled. I rushed to his side.

And he said, "Yes, Mama needs me. I must hurry."

Roused from his drunken stupor as if from a mere nap, Papa grabbed his heavy fur coat and hat from Dunya and started briskly down the hall toward the front door. As I watched him hurry off, I couldn't help but be swept with worry. All this talk of violence. All this talk of murder. I wanted to dismiss it as simple paranoia, but how could I after the disaster that had struck us not so very long ago?

"Dunya, where's my cloak? My muff?" I shouted. "Oh, and my shoes — where are my shoes?"

CHAPTER 2

There was no doubt about it, the horrible events of two years ago had been largely my fault.

My father had left Sankt Peterburg to visit a monastery and then return home to our village in Siberia. Varya and I, accompanied by Dunya, followed a week later, taking the train to Tyumen, where on a warm July day we transferred to a riverboat for the last hundred versts. Not long after we'd left the dock, the small cabin in which the three of us were packed became unbearably hot and stuffy.

"I'm going up top for some fresh air," I said, rising to my feet.

My sister didn't even look up, for she was already engrossed in a novel, her head propped on one of our bags. But Dunya, whose only duty was to guard us as carefully as a Cossack, immediately dropped her knitting into her lap.

She muttered a hasty, "But —"

"You'd better stay here," I interrupted, knowing she was loath to let us out of her sight. "It wouldn't be a good idea to leave Varya here alone."

"Very well, but be back in thirty minutes — no more!"

Before she could say another word, I slipped out. It was only within the last two months that Papa had permitted me to travel the streets of the capital without an escort; Varya, because she was younger, was still not allowed to go farther than the corner store. And relishing my new freedom, I scurried down the narrow corridor of the steamer, out the door, and up the steep stairs to the top deck, which was totally empty.

All at once I was intoxicated by the magic of my Siberia.

Grabbing hold of a side railing, I peered over the edge at the flat, dark waters of the River Tura, which gave way to the churn of the boat. Gazing upward, I breathed in as deeply as I could, filling my lungs with the rich scents of the endless pine forests on the left and, off to the right, the loamy soil of the wild steppes. I was glad to be going home, glad to escape the capital with its endless buildings and incessant gossip.

41

Here, where the nobility had never held land and so serfdom had never existed, everything was free and open, a nearly endless expanse of opportunity that existed nowhere else in my country.

Suddenly a lyrical voice sang out in the language of my heart:

"I have outlasted all desire,
My dreams and I have grown apart;
My grief alone is left entire,
The gleanings of an empty heart."

I had thought I was quite alone, yet when I turned I saw a young man with long brown hair and a short beard, half chanting, half singing the words of our greatest writer. He had a smooth dark complexion and wore clothes that were suitably clean but by no means new. I supposed him to be four or five years older than I. In his hands he held a book; I stole a glance at his trim, clean fingers.

When he turned his rich brown eyes upon me, I couldn't help but call the next verse back to him:

"The storms of ruthless dispensation
Have struck my flowery garland numb —
I live in lonely desolation

And wonder when my end will come."

I was immediately taken by his smile, kind and small. Moving along the railing toward me, he opened his mouth as if to ask me a question, then gazed down at the open book in his hands. He didn't know the poem by heart, as I did, yet he recited the last lines beautifully, not only as a literate man but with passion, his voice rising and falling.

"Thus on a naked tree-limb, blasted
By tardy winter's whistling chill,
A single leaf which has outlasted
Its season will be trembling still."

When his voice trailed away and was replaced by the churning of the steamer's boiler, I said, "Of Pushkin's earliest poems, that is my favorite."

"Mine too." He bowed his head to me and said, "They call me Sasha."

"Maria."

"Where are you coming from?"

"Sankt Peterburg. And you?"

Though he said he was a native of Novgorod, Sasha was actually traveling from Moscow, where he was attending the university. He was on his way to visit a friend in Pokrovskoye, and when I told him that was my home village, his eyes lit up.

"Say," he began, pensively tugging on his beard, "if you're coming from the capital and you're on the way to . . . to . . . well, I heard down below that the famous Father Grigori is on board. You wouldn't happen to be —"

"Yes, I am his eldest." I felt my cheeks flush warmly. "But like all rumors, the story you heard is not quite true. While my sister and I are on board, my father is not. He's already at home."

"Oh, that is my loss, for it has always been a keen desire of mine to meet him."

I was never eager to speak of my family — in fact, my father encouraged me not to — so I glanced at his book, and asked, "What do you study at the university, literature?"

"Exactly." Now it was Sasha's turn to blush as he bolstered his confidence and confessed, "Actually . . . actually, I'm a writer."

"Really?"

As it turned out, we were both aspiring poets, only Sasha was rather more advanced, having published not just two poems at the university but one in a national poetry magazine as well. Of course he was smart, that much I could tell by the sweet squint of his eyes, by the way he used his hands, and, naturally, by his passion for the written word.

"What do you love about literature?" I asked.

"It's so democratic. I know not everyone can read in our country — that will change — but anyone can pick up a book."

"And what writers have meant the most to you?"

Our discussion took off like a racing troika, surprisingly fast and impetuous. Of our great writers of the last century, we both cherished Pushkin most of all for the way he spoke not to the upper class but to us, the common people. Sasha enjoyed Lermontov for his emphasis on feeling, while I found magic in Gogol's strange mix of language. As to Dostoyevsky, however, we both found his stories too morose and too filled with sorrow.

"Have you heard of Tsvetayeva? She's quite young, but I really like her work — she has such passion and intensity," I said. "Plus I like how she relies on fairy tales and folk music. She will be very famous, I think."

"Perhaps. What do you think of Anna Akhmatova? You know what she said, don't you? 'I am the first to teach women how to speak.' "

The conversation went on and on, our

words tripping over one another, and I completely lost track of the time. I'd never been able to talk about these things with any boy, let alone a man, and that Sasha could be so interesting, let alone so interested in what I had to say, was nearly the most exciting thing I'd ever experienced. How could he know so much, how could he anticipate what I was going to say, how could he take my thoughts and expound upon them so easily?

Suddenly, like the crack of a thunderbolt, a grandmotherly voice shouted out my full name: "Matryona Grigorevna Rasputina!"

I jumped like a common thief, even more so when I realized that Sasha was holding my hand. Spinning around, I saw Dunya, huffing and puffing, at the top of the steep stairs.

"You are to come down at once!" she snapped.

"Yes . . . yes, of course. Just give me a minute. We were talking about poetry, and —"

"Now!"

Right in front of Dunya, Sasha lifted my left hand to his firm soft lips and kissed it. "Will I ever see you again?"

I glanced at Dunya's disapproving scowl, turned back to Sasha, and in a quick whisper said, "Meet me here at ten tonight . . . and bring some of your own poems!"

Softly, he replied, "Only if you will."

I scurried off, but as I started down the steps I turned and saw Sasha staring after me with sweet eyes and a soft smile. My cheeks suddenly bloomed with a girlish blush, and I practically flew down the stairs, along the deck, and back into our tiny cabin. And my cheeks continued to burn as I dropped on the berth next to my sister, even more so when I noticed Dunya glaring at me.

"You shouldn't talk to strangers, young lady," she admonished as she picked up her knitting. "You know very well what men want!"

I couldn't stop myself from grinning like a complete fool. "No, I don't. What do they want, Dunya?"

She shook her head in disgust. "And you most certainly shouldn't let someone kiss your hand!"

Varvara dropped her book. "Did someone kiss your hand, Maria? *Oi,* tell me! Tell me what he looked like! Was he old and ugly or was he young and . . . and —"

Almost silently, I mouthed, "Handsome!"

Her eyes grew into disks. "What happened?"

47

"Nothing," I said lightly, slapping her leg. "Nothing at all."

But as I reached for my satchel, I knew that something had indeed taken place, something different from anything else. I could feel it in the tightness of my stomach, the way I could still sense his lips on my hand, and how I kept trying to hold his image like a photograph in my imagination.

While I knew our Siberian sun would never set on that midsummer night, I feared the hours would never pass. They dragged by, and I busied myself with sorting through a few of my own poems I'd brought with me. Which would Sasha like the most? Which would win his approval? I didn't have my favorite with me — a poem I'd written just this spring about the blooming of the birches — and when I tried to write it down from memory, it came out all stupid and clumsy. Frustrated, I tore the paper to bits.

My sister fell asleep around nine, just as I had thought, but Dunya kept knitting away, more and more furiously, the sleeve of a sweater growing longer by the minute. I'd counted on her dropping off long ago, lulled by the churning of the boat and the soft waters we sailed, yet she didn't. I kept staring at our traveling clock, and when it reached ten-fifteen, I could bear it no more.

"I'm going to the toilet. I'll be right back."

Dunya scowled at me and hesitated before nodding. Clutching a folded piece of paper with several of my poems scrawled on it, I charged out. Reaching the end of the narrow corridor, I glanced briefly over my shoulder to make sure our housekeeper wasn't watching, then burst out a side door and onto the narrow deck. In seconds I was clambering up the steep stairs to the top deck, my breath coming short and quick.

Yet when I emerged above and quickly scanned the broad deck, it was just as I had feared — there was no sign of Sasha. Either he'd broken his promise and not come at all, or he'd been here at ten, waited a few minutes, and given up. Oh, no, I thought, squinting in the sharp bright evening light. I spun around, my dark dress flying wide. There was nothing, no one, only this riverboat and the huge blue sky overhead. My eyes began to well up . . . what had I expected? What sort of fool was I?

Suddenly a firm hand grabbed me by the shoulder. I gasped aloud, certain that Dunya had caught me, but when I twisted around —

"Sasha!"

Pulling me into his arms, he said nothing. It wasn't the first time I'd been kissed —

there'd been a boy who'd pecked me as crudely as a rooster — but it was the first time a kiss had burned with pleasure. I'd never felt anything like it, the rush of heat that zipped almost instantly from my lips and throughout my body, all the way down my legs. So powerful was it that I jerked away in shock.

"I . . . I —," I began, my trembling fingers reaching up and touching his soft beard. "I was afraid I'd missed you."

"But you didn't."

"I couldn't get away any sooner."

"I would have waited all night," he said, bending forward and kissing me on the cheek.

As much as every bit of me wanted him, I wanted at the same time to run away. Maybe Dunya was right. Maybe he was after just one thing.

"Listen, Sasha, I . . . I can't stay now. I have to get back," I said, quickly forming a plan. "We arrive in Pokrovskoye in the morning, but will you come visit me later? At our home?"

"Just tell me where, just tell me when."

"Anyone in the village can tell you where we live. Wait outside our gate at five. Papa always goes to the post office late in the afternoon. I'll go with him, and you can greet us when we return. I'll see that Papa invites you to join us for supper."

"That would be a great honor."

"And don't forget your poetry!" I said, as I scurried off.

"Of course."

I should have known better. I should have known his intentions were anything but honorable. Then again, how could I have guessed?

At home the following day, I rehearsed in my head how I was going to introduce Papa to Sasha and get him invited to our table. I'd never had a young man call on me. Then again, maybe the moment was lost and Sasha wouldn't keep his word a second time.

Finally, sometime after four, Papa rose to go to the post office, and I leaped at the chance to accompany him. After he had dictated his telegrams to the clerk, we returned home, my arm looped in his. Of course, by then I was nearly faint with anticipation. In fact, I couldn't believe it when Papa and I turned the corner past the spinster Petrovna's little hut and there, in a cluster of six or seven people gathered by our gate to beg Papa's blessing, stood Sasha, neatly dressed, his hair combed. Thrilled, my hand came up in a small, impulsive wave. As if in embarrassment, he glanced away.

Nearing our home, the sad group of petitioners broke into a pathetic chorus.

"Father Grigori!"

"Help me, Father!"

"Lord have mercy!"

At first I noticed no one except Sasha, of course, but then I saw one man on crutches, a woman in mourning dressed entirely in black, and, then, most terribly, a small disfigured woman, her nose ravaged and half eaten away.

"Father Grigori! Father Grigori!" she called pathetically. "Help me, please!"

Sasha, a stern look on his face, came up alongside this poor woman and helped her, pushing aside the others and nudging her to the front. When she was just steps from my father, Sasha even held back the others, keeping her approach clear and free. But rather than seeking to kiss my father's hand or falling at his knees for his blessing, this poor woman with the hideous nose reached into the folds of her dress and pulled out a long arching knife.

"Death to the Antichrist!" she screamed as she lunged forward, plunging the blade into my father's stomach.

Right before me I saw the long knife disappear completely into Papa, cutting him from navel to sternum, and I screamed so loudly that my own ears were deafened. My father, groaning like a wild animal, jerked back, and blood sprayed from him like a fountain. He stumbled away, and as I reached to grab him I saw a mound of pink entrails boil outward.

Again the attacker charged at Papa, her knife raised high, her voice a scream. "Death to the Antichrist!"

In the pandemonium, I searched for Sasha and saw him falling away as the other supplicants rushed forward to my father's defense. Before the madwoman could strike again, the small crowd of people grabbed her and threw her to the ground, whereupon they immediately began to beat her, mercilessly, their hands and fists and heels and crutches raining down on her.

But still the crazy woman screamed, "I must kill him, kill him!"

And as my father collapsed on the dirt lane, blood and more gushing from him, I caught a brief glimpse of Sasha, not coming to our aid but dashing away. Dear God, I thought, he's fleeing!

In the end, it was only the swift actions of Mama and Dunya that saved Papa's life.

Sturdy Siberian women, they rushed from our house, my mother already barking orders. Within moments she had commandeered three men to carry Papa inside, whereupon Mama and Dunya threw the dinner dishes from the long table as if they were crumbs. Papa was laid right there, where we should have been eating, and within seconds they were winding him in a wet sheet, which stemmed the flow of blood and kept his entrails from falling out. All of us, however, were convinced that Papa's end had come. Indeed, by the time a wire had been sent to the closest doctor, who was in Tyumen, and by the time that doctor had come racing into town not by steamer but by troika, a trip that took no less than eight hours on Trakt No. 4 — a horrible, bumpy road that linked us with the outer world — it was well after midnight and Papa was clinging to the last threads of life. With no other option, an emergency operation was performed right there on our dinner table under the glow of stearin candles, with my father, who refused to breathe the ether, clutching a gold cross. Fortunately for him, and for all of us as well, he fainted after the first incision.

Papa should not have survived. In fact, the doctor doubted he could. But thanks in great part to his internal strength and great physical vitality — not to mention my constant prayers — he did not pass from this world. A few days later, when he had recovered enough, we took him by *telega* — a cart without springs — ever so slowly to Tyumen, where Professor von Breden, who'd been sent by the Empress, reopened the wound and made a few things right. After that it took weeks and weeks of convalescing — during which time war broke out, much to Papa's sorrow — but in time my father was back on his feet. Never, however, did he regain his magnificent strength. In fact, from then on my father lost the look of the holy, that drawn hollow-cheeked appearance of one who observes the fasts. So plagued was he from constant pain that he took to drink as never before, which not only dulled his discomfort but undoubtedly his powers. Soon my father's appearance became bloated, even corpulent. I never spoke to anyone of Sasha, and months later I no longer cried at the thought of him and his obvious betrayal. How could he have led that crazy woman, who, it turned out, was suffering from syphilis, right to my father?

When Dunya and I finally accompanied Papa back to the capital, we found a greatly changed world. War against the Kaiser had broken out, and spy fever was raging everywhere. Our glorious city, aflame with patriotism, was no longer known by the German-sounding name of Sankt Peterburg but as Petrograd. Even the thousands of Germans settled along our Volga River were being driven from their farms. All this greatly disturbed my father, for he abhorred bloodshed of any kind, and when he made known his opposition to the war, he not only fell out of the Tsar's favor, he was labeled a traitor by many. In this way, weakened by his wound and demoralized by the defeats our brave soldiers suffered month after month, Papa fell into the greatest depression of his life.

CHAPTER 3

Even two years later, the memories of Sasha and the murder attempt, fueled by my lingering guilt, now kindled my fears as much as Papa's vision of death. Though my father was under constant police surveillance for his own protection, I knew very well that those who hated him were as clever as they were well connected. Indeed, *Gospodin Ministir* — Mr. Minister — Protopopov, who headed the Interior Department, had repeatedly warned my father of dangers lurking everywhere.

"Listen to me carefully, Father Grigori," *Gospodin Ministir* Protopopov had said. "People are openly plotting your death. Be on your guard every moment! These are very difficult times!"

As I now rushed out the door, I called to the two secret agents posted on our staircase. Coming to our aid, they each took Papa by an arm, and all of us quickly descended. Once downstairs, we stepped from the small lobby, across the courtyard, through the archway, and onto the frigid street, where a dark blue limousine was already waiting for us. It was a Delaunay-Belleville and certainly from the imperial garage, though it lacked a coat of arms and official markings. When the chauffeur jumped out to open the door for us, I could see by his khaki-colored full-dress uniform and the double-headed eagles stamped on the gold braid around his collar that he was in fact one of the Tsar's personal drivers. That an unmarked motor had been sent was no surprise, for the Tsaritsa always took great pains not to draw attention to my father's visits to the palace.

As we flew off, rushing down the street and then turning along the embankment of the Fontanka River, I leaned over and lowered Papa's window so the brisk night air might rouse him to his duties. Sitting back in the rich leather seat, I pulled my cloak over my shoulders and buried my hands in my fur muff — which the Empress had gifted me just the year before.

It was slightly past midnight, and had this been before the war and these the White Nights of summer, the streets would have been flooded with dusky sunlight, people in search of entertainment, and any number of horse cabs. In December, however, the planned boulevards and *prospekti* of the capital — all of which were big and straight and therefore so very foreign, so uncomfortably non-Russian — were dark and freezing and filled now with droves of wounded soldiers and hungry peasants, some huddled around open fires, others sleeping right out on the pavements, with a few marauders roaming about. Not long ago Papa had had a vision that the Tsar needed to bring trainload after trainload of grain into the capital. And he was right. The *liodi* — common people — needed food. Back home in our village, we had lived through many hard seasons, and my father knew very well what the Tsar did not — that a peasant without bread was a very dangerous man.

When we turned onto Nevsky Prospekt I saw only a small handful of sleighs and just one place that looked lively and warm, the Sergeeivski Palace, which had been home to Grand Duchess Elizabeth, the Tsaritsa's sister, before she'd taken to the cloth. Now it was inhabited by the young Grand Duke Dmitri, and the second-floor windows of the stunning red building were ablaze with electric lights and some sort of revelry, for of course there were not and never would be any shortages among the nobility. After that, all was depressingly quiet, the streets filled with litter and lost souls, who, I began to realize, looked increasingly less like wounded soldiers and more like deserters.

Within a short time we left the edge of the city and were speeding through the countryside. Father and I sat silent in the rear seat, he gazing out his window, I staring out mine. The moon was surprisingly bright, and as my eyes followed the snow-laden landscape, I saw flat white fields, then a strand of birch, next a cluster of small huts with smoke curling from the chimneys and a tiny church with a gold onion dome, then again dormant fields tucked under a pale blanket.

There was little doubt in my mind that by morning all good society and then some would know of tonight's events. I was sure that by sunrise the drunken princess, the half-naked countess, and the balalaika player, even the secret agents, would start spreading the word that the Empress had called Rasputin to the palace yet again — and at such an ungodly hour, no less. By teatime tomorrow afternoon, all the court would probably be gossiping about how a late-night call had been placed for the Tsaritsa, a call begging the besotted Rasputin to rush to her private rooms and soothe her desperate needs. Yes, the tongues would wag, for we Russians were the most vicious of gossips, and there were sure to be nasty rumors of the wild peasant romping in bed with the Empress Aleksandra Fyodorovna — that German bitch — and even with her devoted friend, that slut Anna Vyrubova, perhaps all three of them together. There might even be gossip of a *Khlyst* act, a "rejoicing." After all, didn't the name Rasputin come from the word *rasputa* — a debauched, depraved good-for-nothing? The counts and dukes and princes might even hold an emergency meeting at the Yacht Club, where they would smoke and drink and mutter that something had to be done about that filthy monk who was ruining the prestige of the Tsar, the peasant who was nothing but a stain on the entire House of Romanov. After all, wasn't he more than likely spying for the Germans, even quite possibly drugging the Tsar himself? *Gospodi* — good heavens — for the sake of Holy Mother Russia, shouldn't he be eliminated?

Yes, I thought with a shudder, Papa's visions of his own end were not so hard to believe.

The closer we came to Tsarskoye Selo, the more I could see that the bite of cold night air was invigorating Papa like a dip in the Gulf of Finland. Indeed, as the wintry countryside gave way to villas and small palaces tucked in parks, I was relieved to see that my father appeared in complete control of himself.

Within minutes of entering the royal village, we came to the long iron fence surrounding the vast palace grounds. Staring across a plain of snow and into the deep night, I caught a distant glimpse of the buttery-yellow walls and white columns of the home Catherine the Great had built more than a century earlier for her favorite grandson, Aleksander I. When we reached the entrance itself, the guards hurriedly swung open the gates without so much as a single question, and the limousine followed the drive up a slight hill. I couldn't hide my surprise, because for years my father hadn't been allowed to approach the home of the tsars so directly. Because of an uproar of protest from, among others, nearly the entire Romanov clan, the infamous Rasputin had been forced to sneak into the imperial home via a pretend meeting with a maid in the right wing of the palace. In fact, the outrage against him had grown so vocal recently that the only place he could meet their Imperial Highnesses was down the road at Madame Vyrubova's tiny house. All this because the chamberlain's staff listed any visitor to the palace in the *Kammerfurier* — the court log — available to many officials. Needless to say, whenever the name Rasputin appeared, it sparked another wave of protest about his dark influence on the throne.

Tonight, however, none of that apparently mattered, for the Delaunay-Belleville limousine pulled up not to the main entrance at the rotunda, or even the right wing, but directly to the left wing, which contained the private apartments of the Tsar and Tsaritsa. And there, dressed in a huge fur coat and perched on the fountain of steps, was plump Madame Vyrubova herself.

"Come this way at once, Father Grigori," she pleaded anxiously, leaning heavily on a cane.

The Empress's confidante led my father into the palace, and I, ignored, scurried after them. Madame Vyrubova limped horribly, for several years earlier she had nearly been killed in a train accident. When she'd been pulled from beneath a steam radiator and steel girder, no one thought she would live, let alone walk. Taken to the hospital, she received the last rites as the Emperor and Empress, who had been quickly summoned, wept by her side. It was then that Papa had appeared, pushing everyone aside as he rushed to the wounded woman. Taking her limp hand in his, Papa used all his forces, commanding her back to us, the living.

"Anushka! Anushka!" he called, as the Tsar and Tsaritsa watched in amazement.

She stirred and opened her eyes for the first time.

"Speak to me!"

Her lips trembled and she barely spoke. "Pray for me, Father. . . ."

"Wake up and rise!"

Her eyes opened wider but she did not move.

Father dropped her hand and stumbled in exhaustion from the room, muttering, "She will be a cripple, but she will live."

Now, wasting no time, Madame Vyrubova hobbled along, steering us through the large doors and into a reception area, forgetting the registry — where our presence was, nevertheless, duly noted by an official who had worked for this tsar's father and even the one before that. We passed some silent guards in magnificent uniforms, moved through a double door, and went down the long center corridor with its magnificent roll of carpet from the Caucasus. The Tsaritsa's private chambers were here, in the rooms on the left, and the stories to be told about tonight, I was sure, would place Rasputin there, probably in Aleksandra Fyodorovna's favorite room, her mauve boudoir. Adding to the tales of Rasputin was a national obsession; I'd just heard of a fashionable hostess who'd tacked up a sign in her salon that read NO TALK OF RASPUTIN. Mention of my father in the press was strictly forbidden, so "supposed" eyewitnesses were always cropping up, conveying "supposed" information about Papa in the time-honored Russian mode: gossip. In this way, endless nasty stories were spread, both at court and at the market and as far away as the front. Not long ago I had heard Dunya ranting in the kitchen, complaining that the stories had traveled as far as Berlin, where the Kaiser's propagandists not only expounded on them but made sure their spies returned and planted them again in Petrograd, creating yet more uproar.

"Mark my word, there are German spies doing their dirty work everywhere," Dunya had said, furiously stirring a pot. "Gossip heard once is titillating, heard twice and it's interesting, but when it's heard three times people take it as fact. And the Germans are cleverer than we are. They know the best way to topple the Tsar is to attack his consort, who of course is one of them, a German princess by birth."

When I saw no trace of stockings beneath Madame Vyrubova's thick sable coat, I could only imagine what would be going around tomorrow. Someone would claim, no doubt, that she had been waiting for Rasputin naked beneath her resplendent fur.

I heard a door open at the far end of the long corridor, and a tall elegant woman stepped through. It was the Empress Aleksandra Fyodorovna herself, one of the most beautiful women I'd ever seen, tall and thin, her face finely carved, her hair thick and long, though tonight, much to my surprise, it was let down as if for bed. Along with her ever-present strands of freshwater pearls hanging from her alabaster neck, she wore a long white silk robe, nothing more. Her eyes, usually clear blue, were swollen and red.

Upon seeing me, the Empress couldn't hide her surprise and froze, shaking her head ever so slightly. Madame Vyrubova, who maintained her coveted spot by her keen ability to read her mistress's wants, immediately stopped and caught me by the arm. Papa, however, continued on, marching right up to Her Imperial Highness. And, no, he did not fall to his knees before her, nor did he bow and seek the *bizmyen* — the opportunity to kiss his sovereign's hand. Rather, he strode up to the Empress as if he were her equal, even her superior, and kissed her Siberian style, three times on the cheek. Then, much to even my surprise, the Empress muttered something ever so quietly and swooned like a lost lover into Papa's arms.

"Come, my child," said Madame Vyrubova, spinning me around lest I see more. "The driver will take you home."

"Please may I visit Maria Nikolaevna?" I begged, referring to the Tsar's number three daughter, with whom I had become quite friendly.

"All good children are asleep at this hour, as well you should be. I don't know what I was doing, I should never have let you in. And I wouldn't have if it weren't so cold."

"But —"

With her hand firmly planted in the small of my back, Madame Vyrubova steered me quickly down the hall, through the double doors, and to the reception hall, where several guards snapped to attention.

"See that she is returned at once to the city," Anna Aleksandrovna commanded imperiously. "Make sure the driver escorts her not just to her building but right up to her apartment."

"What about —," I started to say.

But there was nothing I could do. For all intents and purposes, I was being returned to the city by imperial order. I could not protest, just as there was no question but that the orders would be obeyed.

Madame Vyrubova stepped to a side table and scooped up a handful of candies wrapped in wax paper. They were my favorite, butterscotch balls made right here in the palace confectionary. She then grabbed my muff from me, pinched one end of it shut, and stuffed the candies inside. Pressing the muff back into my hands, she whispered in my ear.

"You must not talk about tonight to anyone, no matter their position. Am I clear, my child?"

"Most certainly, Anna Aleksandrovna."

"Good," she said, kissing me on my forehead. "Now hurry off, my dear!"

One of the guards, a burly man with a dark mustache, took me gently by the arm and escorted me to the main door. Just before I stepped into the frigid night air, I turned. Rushing like a jealous lover, Madame Vyrubova had pulled up her magnificent fur coat and was hobbling as fast as she could back into the palace.

Not only were her ankles completely naked, so were her legs.

You ask when did I myself first make Rasputin's acquaintance? Well, the first time I ever laid eyes upon him was four winters ago. I had heard he was in town, and, since I was eager to see him for myself, I stopped by my friend's house, where Rasputin was apparently residing for the week. I knocked on the door, but my friend was not home. I was just about to leave when I heard screaming. Quite worried, I ran around back to the kitchen . . . and what did I find but that monster on top of a young scullery maid, ripping away her clothing. He was quite drunk even though it was still morning, and he was having his way with her, this young girl, can you imagine! I reached for a large iron pan and hit him. I hit him so hard, he fell to the floor and didn't move. When I saw the blood flowing from his mouth and nose, I feared I had killed him, but after a moment he started to stir.

Do you know how many times since then I

have wished I had hit that devil a second time or stabbed him with a knife? If only I had killed him back then! Just think how much pain I would have spared the Motherland.

CHAPTER 4

Tucked into the warm brown leather seats of the same Delaunay-Belleville limousine, I ate one butterscotch ball and then another and another. As I was whisked back into town at nearly the same speed with which we had been taken to the royal village, I consumed a total of six candies. It was approaching two in the morning, and I should have been lulled into a quick, comfortable sleep. Instead, my mind whirled faster and faster. If Papa was sure someone was plotting his death, why wasn't he doing anything to prevent it?

As we turned onto Goroxhovaya, I looked behind us and saw the looming Tsarskoye Selo train station. Staring ahead, I saw the golden spire of the Admiralty pointing into the gray-black sky. And yet there wasn't a single soul to be seen scurrying along the slippery sidewalks. The snowy street itself was completely empty of sleighs and troikas, and there was only one motorcar, a plain black one I had never noticed, parked across the street from our building. Smoke bellowed from its tailpipe, but I couldn't see who, let alone how many, were sitting inside.

When the limousine came to a stop in front of our building, the chauffeur jumped out and scurried around the side. As if I were a princess, he opened my door with great grace — so silent, so powerful, so majestic — and offered me his hand. Accepting his firm grasp, I wondered if I could ever become accustomed to such royal treatment. There were 870 noble families that dominated Russia, and we Rasputins were definitely not among them. But it was not inconceivable that we would be elevated, perhaps soon. Throughout history, the rulers of Russia — including Catherine the Great, who had a habit of turning her numerous lovers into princes and counts — always granted vast estates and titles to their favorites, and Papa was definitely Aleksandra Fyodorovna's. So as his elder daughter, would I one day soon become, say, Countess Matryona Grigorevna? Or, taking the name of our own village, would I become Baronessa Pokrovskaya?

Nyet, nyet, I thought, with a smirk on my face, as I scurried through the frigid air.

Papa would never stand for such nonsense, and he would slap me on the head for such vain thoughts. Not only was he far too proud of our Siberian heritage — her freedoms, her sense of equality, not to mention her reliance on nature and her seasons — but I was sure his religious beliefs would preclude accepting a noble rank. On the other hand, a position in the Most Holy Synod would be for him a totally different matter. Then again, that surely wouldn't happen, for the likes of Bishops Hermogen, Sergius, and Illiodor would never allow it. They were totally opposed to Papa, calling him *dyavol* — the devil incarnate.

The chauffeur escorted me through the archway, through the courtyard, and as far as the front door, which he opened for my benefit. When he began to follow me in, my countryside good sense returned, and I assured him it was not necessary to accompany me all the way up. He insisted, gently but firmly, saying he had orders to escort me to the apartment door. Quite sure of myself, I declined.

"Really, it's not necessary." Nodding to the motorcar parked on the street, I said, "As you can see yourself, we have security outside as well as inside. I'm sure there are at least two men in that motor, not to mention another two or three men posted on the staircase."

"Very well, mademoiselle," he replied, with a submissive nod of his head.

Escaping the cold, I quickly ducked inside. When I entered the dark lobby of our building, however, I found no one, neither doorman nor guard. Even the fire in the little iron stove had burned out. At first I thought nothing of it, assuming that the agents had slipped off, perhaps either to warm themselves with a glass of tea or to catch some sleep. Or could they all be warming themselves in the motorcar?

But then, in the faint light of a single sconce, I saw a dark puddle on the white marble floor. Stepping closer, I could see that the puddle was not simply dark but red, and that in fact it was not a puddle at all but a viscous pool of blood.

The words of *Gospodin Ministir* Protopopov came screaming through my mind: "Be on your guard every moment!"

Immediately, my terrified eyes scanned the lobby. I didn't see anyone waiting to club me or drag me away, but for the first time there were no security guards either. Dreadfully aware of how alone I was, I hurried back to the front door to call out for the chauffeur; his offer of an escort all the way to our apartment now seemed imperative. No sooner did I open the door, however, than the Tsar's beautiful, safe limousine sped off and disappeared around the corner.

Standing half outside, my breath billowing in short quick puffs, I glanced across the street at the dark motorcar. In one sure, steady movement, a man, big and stout, climbed out. I knew most of the security men by sight, but this one in a black leather jacket and black Persian lamb hat didn't look familiar. And when I saw the pistol gripped so firmly in his right hand, I knew my only course of action.

Darting back inside, I pulled the outer door tight. I fumbled for a key, something, anything, but there was no way to lock it. Taking one last look out a side window, I saw that the strange man in the leather coat was trotting directly toward the building.

I turned. Suddenly I wanted Papa, who was always there for me, caring, soothing, blessing. I wanted to be in our apartment, safe asleep in the bed I shared with my sister. No, I wanted to be out there with Papa, locked within the gilded walls of the Aleksander Palace and surrounded by a thousand armed guards. I wanted to be anywhere but in this dark, dank lobby.

Clutching the muff with the candies and

gathering up the length of my cloak, I turned and made for the staircase. Just as I reached the first step, however, the thin sole of my right shoe slapped into that wet and sticky spot. I skidded a tiny bit, nearly fell, and screamed. The beautiful fur muff, the only royal gift I'd ever received, nearly went flying from my hands. Instead, the candies spilled out, shooting through the air into that grotesque puddle. Horrified, I rushed on, running up the marble steps, one shoe stamping every other tread: red . . . red . . . red.

Don't panic, I told myself as I climbed. It could be blood from something else. Sugar has been rationed. Butter too. There's talk of meat next. People are getting food anywhere they can, any way they can. One of the neighbors could have made the mess. Someone could have bought a mass of fresh meat and dragged it home, perhaps a whole hindquarter. Hadn't I seen a farmer with an entire sledge of drippy meat just yesterday on Litieny Prospekt? Or maybe Ivanov, the factory manager who lived above us, had slipped off to his dacha and shot a bear, just like he did last year, and then made a horrible mess as he dragged the carcass up to his flat.

Or had something happened to one of the

agents posted for our protection?

As faint as the rustle of a leaf but as clear as the call of a crow, I heard the door open down below. And then the stranger's steps, fast and heavy, hurrying across the marble floor and through the puddle.

Radi boga — for the sake of God — I thought, as I rounded the steps upward and upward, where were the security men? They were always here, always in the way, always snooping and spying, writing things down. *Rasputin received Madame Lokhtina at 8 pm; she stayed until one in the morning. . . . Rasputin almost daily receives the Golovins. . . . Rasputin returned home carrying a bottle of Madeira. . . . Rasputin returned home at midnight with the prostitute Petrova, whom he hired on Haymarket Square. . . . At 4 pm Rasputin and his daughter Matryona departed in a horse cab hired by one of his devotees. . . . Rasputin spent the entire night carousing with the Gypsies and squandered two thousand rubles.* My father, that sloppy, humble peasant from the wilds of Siberia, was probably the most well-observed and well-documented soul in all of Russia.

So where were the security agents now? Why had they abandoned us this very night, right when I needed them the most? There was no reason, none whatsoever, for them to have abandoned us now.

Unless . . .

More afraid than ever, I realized the only reason why the security agents weren't here tonight would be if they had been ordered away or, worse yet, paid to leave us. It wasn't just the grand dukes who wanted my father dead. The many orthodox monks detested Papa too, not simply because of his infamous sensuality and his support of the Jews but, most important, because his beliefs deviated from the approved and accepted liturgy. And the powerful generals wanted him silenced; they were disgusted by his antiwar statements and convinced he was a spy, obtaining information from the Empress and at the very least leaking it to the Germans. The only ones who loved Papa were those at the very top, the Emperor and the Empress, and those at the very bottom, the impoverished millions living in pathetic huts scattered all across the vast Russian Empire.

The footsteps behind me were gaining speed, getting closer, banging harder, louder, as the stranger charged after me faster and faster. Climbing as quickly as I could, I came across another splash of blood on the marble steps. Then I saw a bloody handprint smearing the wall.

Holding my cloak and my dress up over my knees, I ran faster, higher. Following the broad, rounding sweep of stairs, I had nearly reached our floor. I wanted to cry out for Dunya, faithful, loving Dunya who had served us for so long, who was nothing less than a second mother to me. She would come. She would rush to the door. She would save me. She wouldn't have gone upstairs to her small room, not yet. No, she would never leave Varya alone in the apartment. Dunya would be there, dozing on the tiny cot in the kitchen, waiting for Papa and me to come home. I was going to bang on the door, and she was going to come to my rescue.

But when our door came into view, a wind of panic swept through me. Crumpled on the floor and leaning against the door itself was a young man. Instantly I spotted the source of all the blood: the wounded left arm, clutched so tightly to his side. When he looked up at me weakly with his dark brown eyes, nothing could have surprised me more.

"Maria . . . help me," he pleaded.

Shocked, I gasped. "Sasha!"

It had been two years since we'd met on the steamer to my village, and yet I recognized him at once, just as I recognized the fear and desperation in his eyes. Yes, Sasha, as full of terror as a wounded deer, glanced up at me and then toward the stairs. Who was the stranger after, Sasha or me?

"Please, I . . . I —," he began.

Sasha had been the first and only one to steal my heart, and for a single day he'd been the love of my life. Then he'd burned me with a kind of betrayal I'd never thought possible. But right then and there as I stared down on him, his strength and will sapped from loss of blood, I forgot all the damage he had done to my family. Without thinking, I knew the right thing to do.

I lunged over Sasha and at our apartment door, finding it, as I feared, locked. Not wasting a moment, I jumped up, snatching a hidden key from a ledge above the door. As quickly as I could, I jabbed the key in the lock, twisted, and heaved open our door. Sasha made a feeble attempt to get up but couldn't, so I grabbed him by the shoulders and half dragged him inside. Glancing out at the staircase, I saw the shadow of the burly man coming up the last steps, and I hurled our door shut and slammed the lock, bolting it tight. *Slava bogu* — thanks be to God.

Sasha crawled across the floor and collapsed again, and I stood by the door, breathing hard. Outside I heard the stranger charge the last few steps, hurling himself right against our door, which shuddered from the dull forceful thud. Standing in our reception hall in near darkness, I clasped my hand over my mouth. Who was he? What did he want?

Then everything was quiet. I could hear nothing but my own panting breath, deep and quick. The next instant I saw the doorknob itself twist ever so slowly, to the right, to the left, as the man tried yet again to force his way inside.

Backing away, all I could think was, Where is Dunya? Dear God, could something have happened to her? To Varya?

Recoiling from the door, I turned and looked down at Sasha, whose left arm was drenched with blood. My country sensibilities told me there was no time for anger, no time for questions. Throwing my muff and cloak to the floor, I hurried to him.

"Where are you hurt, just your arm?" I asked, as I bent over him.

"Yes. . . ."

"Come on. We've got to get you bandaged."

He stared up at me, his eyes glassy and faint.

Taking him by his good arm, I said, "Can

83

you stand up? I need to get you into the kitchen."

"I was . . . was attacked —"

"Yes, I can see. I want to know everything . . . I want you to tell me everything. But first we have to take care of your arm."

"I'm sorry. . . ."

"All the way up, that's it, that's good."

I had to lift him to his feet, and then, with his right arm over my shoulders and my left arm clutching him around his waist, we started slowly toward the kitchen. I just hoped he wouldn't pass out before we got there.

Whatever role Sasha had played in the attack against my father, there was nothing to fear now; he was too weak, too faint. As I led him stumbling along, I was actually relieved. Somehow I would make sense not only of this — what had happened tonight and how he'd come to our home — but also of the past events.

As we stumbled along, I glanced into the salon, half hoping to see the drunken Princess Kossikovskaya and Countess Olga dozing away. Instead the room was dark, its many chairs pushed neatly up against the walls. When we passed through the dining room, I noted that the bronze chandelier was still lit, but the pastries and nuts, the dried fruits and candies, had all been put away, as had the large brass samovar. Dunya had obviously worked hard after we left, not only seeing that the ladies departed without a problem — perhaps she had called one of their footmen to escort them — but making our apartment ready for the following day, when another horde of my father's seekers and devotees would line up outside our door and down the long stairs. So she should be still awake.

When I steered Sasha into our kitchen, however, I found it dark, the single electric bulb hanging from the ceiling extinguished. Dismayed, I led him across the room.

"Just hang on to the sink while I get a stool. Can you do that?" I asked, as I reached out with one hand and pulled the light chain.

Flinching as the light burst on, he nodded.

Leaving him at the sink, I dashed to the far corner, where I yanked aside a curtain. To my dismay, the cot tucked into the corner was empty. Grabbing a small wooden stool, I returned to Sasha and placed it right behind his knees. As he sat down, a deep, painful moan trickled from his lips.

"It's okay," I said.

But it wasn't. None of this was right,

particularly Dunya's absence. She was supposed to be with us from early morning until late at night, cooking and cleaning, until, just like all the other maids in the building, she would retire to her small chamber under the rafters of the very top floor. She shouldn't have left yet, not without either Papa or me at home. She should be in her little corner, resting and watching out for my sister. Dear Lord, was Varya all right? Could she be missing too?

"Sasha, I have to check on my sister. Are you all right for one minute? You won't faint, will you?"

He shook his head, attempted a small laugh, and said, "And I won't run from you either."

"No, I don't think you could."

I raced from the kitchen and down the hall. Papa's first child, a son, had died soon after birth. His second, Dmitri — our brother, Mitya — was sweet but mentally simple and lived and worked with Mama in Siberia. I was next and had moved to the capital seven years earlier. Last was Varya, several years younger, who had come to St. Petersburg just three years ago. She was my friend and confidante. Please, I prayed with pounding heart, let her be safe, let her be unharmed.

Dashing to our room, I threw open the door. And there she was, the dear lump, buried beneath the comforter and fast asleep, blessedly hogging most of the bed, as was her annoying habit. Despite the ruckus and my deep, heavy huffing and puffing, she did nothing more than moan and squirm. After a moment of standing there, staring at her peacefully sleeping, I shut the door.

So had nothing happened here tonight? No, I thought, as I made my way back to the kitchen, that wasn't right. Sasha, after two years, had shown up wounded, and Dunya had gone missing. Worse, some thug had chased me up the stairs — was my would-be assailant still lurking outside the door? *Gospodi,* perhaps I should place a call to the Aleksander Palace. A message could be got to my father, who would be beset with worry. And the Tsaritsa would see that someone was sent at once for our protection. I must call immediately, I thought.

Then I heard Sasha moan. No, I thought, the very first thing to do was take care of him. Returning to the kitchen, I found him still sitting on the stool but slumped against the sink. Just how bad was he?

"Sasha, let's get your coat off."

He nodded ever so slightly but didn't

move, so I reached around and undid the heavy buttons of his wool coat. Touching him, I felt the hard strength in his back, his arms, and his chest. His dark brown hair, long and curly, was tousled, and that face I had once found so sweet and inviting seemed lined and hardened under a coarse beard. It struck me that in the two years since I had last seen him he had easily aged five. I couldn't help but wonder if he had enlisted in the war effort, and, if so, if he'd served in the trenches at the front.

Once I had his coat undone, I slipped his right arm free without any problem. When I came to his left, however, he winced in pain.

"What happened?" I asked.

"Someone . . . someone stabbed me."

"Bozhe moi!" My God! "Sasha, I'm going to have to call a doctor."

"Nyet!"

"But —"

"You don't understand! I can't see a doctor, I can't!" He tried to get up. "It's too dangerous for me."

"Stop! Just sit still. Let me get your coat off and clean you up, at least. Then we'll know how bad it is."

Reaching over his shoulder with his good hand, he clasped my right, and said, "I'm sorry, Maria. So very sorry."

For coming here tonight? Was he sorry for that . . . or for using me and lying to me as we steamed up the River Tura on that beautiful summer day and then leading my father's would-be assassin right to him?

All I could manage was a pathetic "What for?"

"There's so much I need to explain. It's just so . . . so complicated. I wanted to come to your house the day after your father was attacked . . . but I couldn't. I didn't dare."

"Why?" I snapped. "Because you were afraid you would be arrested?"

"What do you mean?"

"It's obvious you were part of the conspiracy to kill him."

"What? You don't think I had anything to do with that, do you?"

"Of course I do. I told you when and where my father would be, and then you led that madwoman right to him. I asked around later, and someone even said you were both staying in the same boarding-house. And —"

"No, Maria, you don't understand!"

"No, I don't." I winced as if I myself had been stabbed. "But you can start by telling me why you came here tonight. How did you find me?"

"Everyone in Petrograd knows where the

89

Rasputins live. It's no secret."

"Tell me honestly — do you mean us harm?"

"Dear God, no!" He hesitated, then added, "Maria, trust me, please trust me, when I say I've never stopped thinking about you."

Nothing could have surprised me more. I refused, however, to show my own wound and the pain that burned even now. Instead, I turned away.

"We'll talk later, Sasha," I said sternly. "First we have to take care of your arm."

I pulled his coat from his left shoulder, slid it down his arm, and pulled it brusquely past the wound and over his hand. It hurt him, I know — he winced terribly — but I didn't care. What did he know about confusion and pain? What did he care about the suffering of others?

Although I was surprised by the amount of blood, the wound itself wasn't so horrible, a deep gash through his shirt and up his forearm. With blood still readily flowing, however, it was no wonder Sasha was weak. What had happened and who had done this? Was he a deserter; had the military police chased him down? I was no stranger to gore, having helped Mama deliver countless foals and calves. Not only that, but in the fields surrounding our village, laborers and workhorses alike were always getting injured. It struck me, staring down at Sasha's wound, that this wasn't nearly as bad as some of the things I had witnessed.

"You're lucky," I said, as I turned on the faucet and began rinsing the wound. "It looks like the knife didn't cut down to the bone."

He said nothing, only winced. I carefully ran the water up and over his arm, rinsing away blood and grime and tiny bits of his shirt. His forearm, which was thick and strong and covered with a haze of dark hair, now lay weak and limp in my hands. I knew so little about him — and doubted everything he had ever said. Whether or not he was from Novgorod, whether or not he had attended university in Moscow — things he had told me that day on the riverboat — I didn't know, and yet despite his strength it was obvious he had never worked the fields. I could tell his fingers were not those of a peasant, for they were not calloused but soft.

Once I had flushed his arm, I realized the main problem was not the gash but Sasha's loss of blood. How long ago had this happened? How much blood had he already lost?

"Sasha, you're going to have to see a doctor to get this sewn up."

"Can't you —"

"Absolutely not. The only thing I can do now is wrap it up in a bandage. If I get it tight enough, it should slow the blood. But the sooner you get to a doctor, the better. Besides, it needs to be thoroughly disinfected."

He shrugged.

I reached to the side for a clean white tea towel, which I wrapped almost as tightly as a tourniquet around his forearm. Although the towel blossomed immediately with blood, I was sure it would help. I then took his good hand and placed it on the towel.

"Press down good and hard and don't let go," I commanded. "I'll be right back."

Hurrying from the kitchen, I passed through our dining room to the darkened salon. Papa's most regular visitors were society ladies who came three or four times a week for tea and to hear Papa's religious convictions. These well-bred women had been taught the evilness of idle hands, so as they drank their tea and listened to my father, they picked up knitting needles and worked away. And since the outbreak of war, of course, they'd made only one thing: bandages from string. Scattered around our salon were no less than six wicker baskets, in each of which sat a set of fine knitting needles, a ball of string, and bandages in varying lengths of completion, all just waiting for a lady's busy hands. From one pile I snatched a bandage and its attached ball of string.

As I was turning back to the kitchen, however, I heard a faint noise, a voice or a moan coming from somewhere. There couldn't be someone else in here, could there? I listened for one more second but heard nothing. Worried, I went to the front door and pulled on it, but it was still locked.

Returning to the kitchen, I worked quickly, cutting the bandage free from the ball of string and tying the loose end. The bandage itself was good and dense and long, and with Sasha's help I wrapped it around his arm no less than three times. I then tore another towel in half and tied it around his arm to hold everything in place.

And then . . . again I thought I heard something. Standing quite still, I listened for more sounds, either from the street out front or from somewhere in our apartment. Why was I so sure it was the latter? Why was I suddenly so afraid?

I knew I should be making Sasha tea or soup. I knew I should be looking for some fish or, better yet, a jar of caviar, which was so rich and healthful. Instead, I ordered him from the stool.

"You need to lie down," I told him.

Escorting him across the kitchen, I pulled aside the curtain and led him into the nook were Dunya's cot was tucked. Gripping him tightly, I lowered him onto the edge of the bed and eased him onto his back. Finally, I slipped off his filthy, worn leather boots and lifted up his feet. As I tucked a small pillow behind the curls of his hair, he gazed up at me and offered the slightest of smiles. I couldn't help but blush.

"Just keep your arm raised," I said. "I'll be back in a minute."

Before I could escape, however, Sasha grabbed my hand and raised it to his lips. *"Spasibo."* Thank you, he said, kissing me just as tenderly as he had done two years ago. "I'm sorry. I'm very sorry."

I had believed him before. I had trusted him before. Did I dare do so again?

"Just don't move," I said, frightened of the softness in my voice.

"I don't think I can."

I stroked his brow. "I don't either."

I wanted to stay right there, on the edge of the cot, and hold his hand and talk as we had done on the boat. But I didn't dare, not on this strange night. Stepping away, I shut the curtain and started out of the kitchen. No sooner had I passed into the hall than I heard it again, a faint noise emanating, I realized, from one of the bedrooms.

CHAPTER 5

I poked my head into my room first, only to see Varya still sleeping soundly. Moving on, I approached Papa's bedroom. As I neared the partially opened door, I saw the faint light of a lamp leaking out, and for a bizarre moment everything seemed normal. It was almost as if my father were home, studying the Scriptures or on his knees, praying in the corner before his favorite icon, the *Kazanskaya,* the Virgin of Kazan. It was almost as if he were right there in that room, ever so slowly scrawling the little notes to hand out the following day to his devotees, little notes that would open doors all over the country: *My friend, see that this gets done. Grigori.* Plus the little cross, always the little cross, at the bottom. But of course Papa wasn't home, and I wasn't coming to bid him good night.

Someone, I realized, was in my father's bedroom who shouldn't be there. It could be someone harmless like Countess Olga or someone as dangerous as an assassin.

I should have rushed right then and there to the telephone. But I wasn't scared, not really, for exhaustion was taking over now, drugging my mind and body like a narcotic. Quite determined, I brazenly pushed open the door. But instead of finding someone with a gun pointed at me, or even someone rifling through Papa's belongings, there was no one carousing about. Instead my eyes traveled through warm, reddish light emanating from an oil lamp hanging before Papa's icon. And eventually my eyes fell upon a heap of unfamiliar clothes thrown on a chair. Turning to the narrow bed, I saw that someone was curled up beneath the bright patchwork quilt.

I wasn't that surprised, not really, for women were always throwing themselves at Papa. Last year I had been in my room when I heard a terrible scream coming from the salon.

"Chri-i-ist is ri-i-isen!"

When I went running in, I had found Madame Lokhtina, wearing a bizarre white dress decorated all over with little ribbons, lunging at Papa. The force of this woman, a former society lioness who had abandoned her family and become Father's most rabid devotee, was so great, her determination so devilish, that she had ripped open Papa's pants and was hanging on to his member.

"You are Christ, I am your ewe, take me!" the woman screamed. "Take me, dear Chri-i-*ist!*"

"Off, you skunk!" Papa was beating on her head, trying to fend her off, and when he saw me, he shouted, "Help me, Maria! She's demanding sin and won't leave me alone!"

Now, approaching the bed, I realized in a second that it wasn't Madame Lokhtina, some anxious devotee, or even Countess Olga lying there peacefully. So who in the name of the Lord was it? I stepped closer and saw something familiar.

Oh, my God. . . .

The body shifted like a languid lover awaiting some kind touch and tender kiss. Taking note of the short hair, I realized this was no woman. Instead it was perhaps the most beautiful and definitely the richest young man in all of Russia.

"Fedya?" I said.

For the past several months, Prince Felix Yusupov, or Fedya, as he warmly asked my sister and me to call him, had been visiting Papa nearly every day. Tall and fine-boned, with a narrow face, small mustache, and beautiful narrow eyes, the prince was particularly effeminate in both looks and manner, taking after the famed beauty of his mother, Princess Zinaida. He rolled over and smiled sweetly up at me.

"Oh, it's you, Maria. I was hoping for Father Grigori."

Speechless, I stared down at this scandalous creature now lolling in Papa's bed. Lurid stories of him abounded — everyone in the capital knew that on a number of occasions he'd dressed up in his mother's finest dresses and jewels and then visited the most expensive restaurants. There was even a story floating about that the King of England, upon spying the young prince in a diamond-studded dress in London, had made suggestive inquiries via one of his footmen. And even though Prince Yusupov, nearly thirty years of age, was now married to the Tsar's niece, Princess Irina, it was widely believed he still suffered from "grammatical errors." This, I had quietly assumed, was why the young man had become such a frequent visitor to our household: Surely Papa, who had treated a number of women for lust, was likewise treating Prince Felix.

"So do tell me, child, where is your father?" said Prince Felix, lifting his bare arms from beneath the blanket and stretching.

Good God, I realized, quickly averting my eyes, he's not only in Papa's bed, he's lying there in nothing but his undergarments. Glancing over at a chair, I saw that the clothes so casually strewn there were actually Prince Felix's military shirt and pants and that his tall leather boots stood nearby on the floor.

"Has he gone out to hear some Gypsy music?" pressed the prince.

"I don't know," I replied, my voice faint.

"Really? You don't know if he's off at the Villa Rode? The Bear? If I knew where he was, perhaps I could catch up with him."

"I said I don't know."

"Well, if he's not at some restaurant, perhaps he's off with some princess, hmm? Or who else? What is it, my dear, why the silence? Why aren't you talking to your Fedya?"

Usually, I was quite friendly with the prince. Usually, we would talk for hours. Tonight, however, I kept my silence.

"I can see you're hiding something, Maria, my sweet. What is it? Is your papa off at the Palace in Tsarskoye?" He laughed and, with a devious twinkle in those slim delicate eyes, said, "Perhaps the better question is, where have you been? That's why you're so quiet, isn't it? Have you been off on a little affair of your own? Tell me everything. Have you a lover?"

"Fedya!"

"You do, don't you! Well, is he your first? Handsome? A soldier? I promise not to tell your father!"

"Please, Fedya, that's not it at all. It's just terribly late and —" I went to the window and looked down on the street; the motorcar was gone. "Did you see any of the security agents when you came?"

"Of course not. That's why I always come up the rear staircase into the kitchen — just to avoid them. Of course, my dear, you know it's best if I'm not seen coming here."

Actually, I didn't understand, for I agreed with those of my father's followers who thought it shameful that Prince Yusupov would only sneak into our home through the back way under the cover of night. What was wrong with sunlight and the front door?

"Now don't change the subject, my sweet Maria. Tell me about yourself and where you've —"

"What about Dunya? Was she here when you came? I'm quite worried — she's not here now, and —"

"Calm down, little one. Everything's all

right. Dunya was here when I came. In fact, she was the one who let me in. But she was so tired, I sent her up to bed and told her I'd personally wait until Father Grigori returned."

"Oh."

I bowed my forehead into my palm. So everything was all right? Everyone was safe? But what about the guards — where were they? And who had chased me up the stairs?

"What is it, Maria? What's troubling you so?"

I turned around to see Prince Felix, wearing only an undershirt, underpants, and socks, climbing out of my father's bed. It was not the first time I had seen a man so scantily clothed, of course, for back home our entire family would traipse through the snow to cleanse ourselves at the *banya* — the sauna — while in summer we all bathed in the River Tura. It had all been quite natural and innocent, without the least impure thought. But somewhere I knew that Fedya's motives were anything but simple. I should have spun quickly away, but in the reddish light of the oil lamps, my eyes burned upon him. He was the first member of the nobility I had ever seen so exposed, and I was transfixed by his long thin arms, which appeared as beautiful as they did weak, not to mention his skin, which looked astonishingly smooth and pure, without a single bruise or scar.

"Nothing," I replied, turning and averting my eyes. "Nothing at all. I . . . I just need to get some sleep." Behind me I heard the rustle of clothing as he dressed. "There's not much sense in your waiting for Papa. Knowing him, he won't be home until after the sun rises."

"I don't doubt that. But are you and Varya quite all right by yourselves?"

"I assure you, we're perfectly fine."

"Very well." He came up behind me in his stocking feet and hugged me. "But someday, my sweet one, you're going to have to tell your Fedya what you've been up to! Imagine, you out so late on your very own! And without an escort! Aren't you the little devil? But not to worry, I promise I won't tell your father!"

When he gave me a little squeeze, I flinched. Prying myself out of his grasp, I excused myself and hurried from my father's bedroom. Why didn't I trust Prince Felix? Papa certainly did. Indeed, my father seemed to be genuinely fond of him. One might even say that in the past months they had become close personal friends. Had my father, perhaps, seen and seized a chance to endear himself to another branch of the Tsar's extended family? Or was he in fact helping the prince deal with certain proclivities that didn't mesh with married life?

Knowing that Prince Felix would leave our flat via the rear door, I hurried down the hall to the kitchen, where I made a quick but somewhat feeble attempt at rinsing the blood from the sink. I then took the filthy coat over to the nook where Sasha lay and dropped the garment in a corner. Sasha looked up at me from Dunya's cot, his brow wrinkled with confusion.

"Not a word from you!" I whispered, as I pulled the curtain tight, hiding him behind it.

A moment later Prince Felix did indeed come into the kitchen, pulling his great reindeer coat over his shoulders as he made his way to the door. Slipping right up next to me, he leaned over and pressed his buttery cheek against mine.

"Good night, my dear," he said, with a light but moist kiss. "I hear a *flying angel* just blew into town, so perhaps your father is out *rejoicing*."

Recognizing the code words of the *Khlysty,* I shuddered. What was Prince Felix implying? Exactly what was his business, tonight or anytime, with Papa?

"In any case," continued the prince, "be sure to tell him his Fedya stopped by."

My voice faint, I replied, "Yes. I'll be sure to tell him."

And then he opened the rear door and slipped down the dark, narrow stairs as easily as a black-capped marmot into its frosty Siberian hole.

Because the *Khlysty* were severely outlawed, their greatest oath was one of secrecy. For that reason, my father was the only person I knew who'd actually met someone who belonged to the sect. From bits and pieces of things Papa had said, I had come to understand that years upon years ago, when he had wandered the countryside on foot in search of God, he had drunk tea and eaten raisins with a small group of *Khlysty*. But while my father believed as they did in the concept of sin driving out sin — a concept that fit so neatly into our Russian soul — there had been nothing more to the encounter. My own mother had grilled him on the issue, and right to her face Papa had denied ever taking part in a *Khlyst* ritual of rejoicing, when members would whirl and twirl themselves into a frenzy, eventually collapsing onto the floor.

Whether or not Prince Felix knew that

Papa was at the palace, the very fact that he had even insinuated that Papa was out "rejoicing" scared me to the bone. My father had already been accused and investigated for being a member of the sect, but what about Prince Felix? Could he belong to a local ark, a *Khlyst* community of nobles devoted to group sinning? Had a flying angel — one of their mysterious couriers who moved from ark to ark, keeping them all in secret contact — really just come to town?

I had heard many such rumors, that an ark of the highest-born personages gathered in the depths of some palace right here in the capital, some said even within the shadow of the Winter Palace. Others whispered that a certain Prince O'ksandr headed an ark that gathered beneath one of the Kremlin cathedrals. I had no idea what was true, but was Prince Yusupov, like Madame Lokhtina, who had been clutching my father's member and screaming that he was Christ and she was his ewe, seeking the penetration of my father as a way to sin, repent, and cleanse himself of his "grammatical errors"? I shuddered at the thought.

And yet . . .

I had witnessed how the Holy Spirit had come down upon Papa. Not only did he have the greatest of Christian gifts, the gift of healing hands, and not only did he possess second sight, but many women claimed he was also able to treat the sin of lust. Was this the key to Papa's suddenly intense relationship with Prince Yusupov? Was he performing treatments upon the prince just as he would upon one of his female devotees? Was he trying to restore the purity of love between Prince Felix and Princess Irina, the Tsar's own niece?

I knew Papa would never speak of any of this, any more than I could ever bring myself to ask. But the prince, gossipy and open, would certainly tell me. And I could certainly broach the subject with him. In this night of extremes, I was determined to find out, and so I dashed over to the nook and peered around the curtain. Immediately, Sasha started to get up.

"No!" I whispered harshly. "Just stay there. I'll be right back!"

I hurried to the kitchen door, which I threw open. Without a cloak or even a shawl, I moved through the hall and to the top of the steep rear stairs.

"Fedya!" I called in a loud whisper. "Fedya, stop!"

Though I could hear his steps quickly descending, he apparently could not hear my voice. I charged downward. Why was Prince Felix — sole heir to an enormous fortune that included Rembrandts, Tiepolos, jewels like Marie Antoinette's, dozens of estates, and some 125 miles of the Caspian coast — so interested in a dirty peasant with a dirty reputation? What could someone so high and noble want from someone so low and uneducated? Had he found the same kind of love for my father that Empress Aleksandra Fyodorovna had?

Or did he mean to harm him?

After all, it was no secret that Prince Felix's mother, Princess Zinaida, was one of Rasputin's greatest enemies. She — the stunningly beautiful matriarch of Russia's richest family who was once one of the Empress's close friends — had essentially been banished from the palace because of her hatred for my father. Was Prince Felix keeping his visits to our apartment secret in order to deceive his mother, or, God forbid, were his visits perhaps under her shadowy auspices and part of a greater plot? Rejected by the Empress, Princess Zinaida had become, I'd heard, especially close to several of the Tsar's uncles, the very grand dukes who despised Rasputin and saw in him the ruination of the Romanov dynasty.

I flew down the dark narrow rear steps

even more quickly than I had so recently come up the front staircase. No matter my haste, however, I couldn't catch the young prince. By the time I had descended from our third floor, the back door of the building was shut tight. Wiping the frosty ice from a window, I peered out. From the back I saw Prince Felix, wrapped in his heavy coat, moving quickly through an arched passage, and the next instant he disappeared.

I was so tired and confused I didn't hesitate. Would Fedya really tell me all I wanted to know? I was just so close, I had to try. When I saw a loose brick on the floor, I grabbed it, used it to hold the rear door open for my return, and charged out. A small but very real part of my mind was sure that if I didn't find out tonight, I never would, and I hurried into the bitter night. My shoes crunched in the snow, my dress swung from side to side, and as I scurried through the rear archway and into the courtyard of another building, I saw him, his fur hat pulled snugly over his head.

"Fedya!"

But my voice disappeared, caught and blown away by a snowy wind. Prince Felix didn't stop, so I chased after him as he ducked to the left, following a small discreet alley.

We were never, ever allowed to go out with our heads uncovered, and my mother would have been furious had she seen me rushing hatless and cloakless through the terrible cold. But I paid no heed, felt nothing, not even when my feet slipped on the icy cobbles and I nearly tumbled into a snowbank. Hardly anyone knew this back way to and from our apartment, which was why the rear steps weren't guarded and why Prince Felix used it almost exclusively. I assumed he had parked his car or had a chauffeur waiting for him in some discreet location. And indeed, I caught another glimpse of his narrow figure as he made a final turn through a low passage that led onto the small side street. Ducking, he moved on, reached the snow-covered sidewalk, and turned right.

"Fedya, stop! Stop!"

Running as fast as I could, I struggled to catch up with him. But just as he disappeared from sight, a long motorcar eased past the end of the archway. My heart immediately tensed. Wasn't that the very same touring car I had seen earlier, parked on our street?

Flushed once again with fear, I slowed, easing my way through the passage. Stopping, I clasped the ice-cold stone walls and peered around the edge of the building. Yes, it was the same one, and it now pulled alongside Prince Felix and came to a stop. Sure that the man with the gun was about to leap out, I nearly screamed for Fedya to run. But the prince appeared not in the least bit apprehensive. Rather, it was as if he had been expecting the car. And he not only seemed to know the vehicle but also its occupant — not the man with the gun but someone altogether different, a tall handsome young man who climbed out of the rear seat. I couldn't believe what I was witnessing, for I knew him too. It was none other than the Tsar's twenty-five-year-old cousin, Grand Duke Dmitri Pavlovich, also clad in a military hat and greatcoat. An Olympic athlete and lover of fine automobiles, he was known about Petrograd as something of a rake and better known as the Tsar's favorite. The Empress had once loved him dearly as well but had come to feel otherwise, for she'd heard rumors of the young grand duke's drinking, of his late-night activities during wartime — and of his inappropriate affection for Prince Felix.

Of course, there had been great gossip about town of the relationship between these two young men who belonged to the very top tier of nobility. At first and for one simple reason, the Tsar and Tsaritsa tried to ignore what they were hearing: Dmitri had become engaged to their eldest daughter, Olga Nikolaevna. When the sordid stories of Dmitri started cropping up, however, Aleksandra was so upset that she had forbidden the young grand duke from seeing Felix, even setting the secret police upon the two. Nevertheless, reports came back that her orders were being ignored. People had seen them together, tongues were wagging more than ever, and the Empress heard it all, both whisper and report of Dmitri and Felix drinking until morning, dancing, and inviting male ballet dancers into the private dining rooms of the Hotel Europe. Worse yet, when Dmitri moved into his own apartments in the Sergeeivski Palace, Felix not only helped him lavishly decorate his rooms but moved in with him for a while as well.

One night during those days I had accompanied Papa to the Aleksander Palace, where we dined with the royal family en famille. Afterward, over tea in the Maple Room, I had sat on a pillow at the feet of the Tsaritsa herself, and while she kindly stroked my tresses, I listened as she told Papa of the reports being circulated about the two young men. Upset by the dishonesty that would certainly be apparent in a marriage between Grand Duke Dmitri and Olga Nikolaevna, Papa minced no words — he strongly condemned the union. And the very next day Empress Aleksandra Fyodorovna quashed the royal engagement. Ever since, needless to say, Grand Duke Dmitri had viewed Rasputin as his archenemy.

Knowing this, I wasn't at all shocked when I spied Dmitri kissing Felix, not even Siberian style, three times on the cheeks, but kissing him quite fully on the lips. In the next moment, the grand duke took the prince by his gloved hand and pulled him into the dark backseat of his motorcar, and off they sped, either for a night of revelry among the Gypsies or perhaps a night of seduction.

Or was I all wrong? Just a few hours earlier, when Papa and I had been whisked off to Tsarskoye Selo, I had taken note of the grand duke's gorgeous red palace on the Fontanka. The huge windows had been ablaze with, I had assumed, a kind of inappropriate party, a gathering of nobility flaunting their fine wines and rich meats while the rest of the city suffered shortages of simple bread. Prince Felix could have been there at the time. But what if I was mistaken? What if the palace was full not of drinkers and dancers and Gypsy musicians but of a party of plotters?

Trembling with terrible fright and cold, I turned and scurried home through the blustery night. This much I had learned: In my father's life it was as impossible to tell who was a friend as who was a lover, let alone who was an enemy.

Even worse, that truth seemed paramount for me as well, for when I returned to our apartment and checked the nook, Sasha was not resting on the cot. He had disappeared.

No one of good society talked of anything else but Rasputin and the need to do away with him. And yet no one took any action, not even the senior grand dukes! That was when and how we came up with the plan. We — a small group of young titled men — were dining in the Winter Garden at the Astoria Hotel, and suddenly Grand Duke Dmitri Pavlovich — the Tsar's own cousin — blurted it out: It was up to us to do the deed and save the dynasty.

Of course, everyone looked immediately to me, not only because of my connections but because they knew I was the only one who could successfully infiltrate Rasputin's home.

CHAPTER 6

Ya spala kak ubeetaya — I slept like the dead.

Partly out of depression, partly because I was exhausted, I didn't rise until noon. And when I finally did get up, the first thing that came to mind was a question I couldn't ask a soul, let alone answer: Why had Sasha fled yet a second time? Immediately, a better question came to my mind: Why had I allowed him into our apartment in the first place?

Making my way to the kitchen, I found Dunya distraught about the blood smeared against our front door as well as around the sink. Obviously, I had not cleaned up well enough to deceive her thorough eyes.

Lying to Dunya for the first time ever, I said, "When I got home last night, one of Papa's petitioners was huddled against the door. He was bleeding badly, and the best I could do was wash him up and send him on his way."

"*Oi,*" muttered Dunya, with a shake of her head. "Will people never leave your father alone? The poor man, he didn't return home until after ten this morning. I just hope he sleeps all the way until suppertime . . . or tomorrow!"

Oh, Papa, I thought as I turned away. I took several steps toward the dining room, then stopped. I hated these days of rumor and innuendo, spy-mongering, war and death. How would it all end: in victory, defeat, or, as so many were whispering, revolution? I stood there shaking. One day the war would be over, but then what for me? Marriage — to whom? Children — how many? And what of Sasha? Would I ever see him again? Would I ever understand his secrets?

Suddenly I felt the arms of a woman, soft and gentle, encircling me.

"Why, child, what's the matter?" asked Dunya. "You're crying."

I spun around and clung to Dunya, burying my face in her deep, soft chest. If only I could have told her about Sasha.

"I'm afraid," I sobbed. "I'm afraid for us all."

"Shh, child," she said, kissing my forehead. "These are such difficult times, such dark days."

"But —" What, I wondered, did she know of broken hearts?

"Don't worry. Everything will get back to normal once the war is over. Right now, everything's just a little crazy and there are so many problems — there's not enough food, and this winter has been so horribly cold! Once God has granted us victory over the Germans, all will be well, you'll see. Trust me, you have many wonderful days and years ahead."

"Me?"

"Yes, you. Why, just the other day your father confided that he'd had a vision of you — he said you would live a long and healthy life, and you would give him grand-children, and you would accomplish many interesting things. Isn't that wonderful?"

"Really?" I replied, wondering if that meant I would marry for love and one day publish a book of poetry.

"Yes. He even said you would travel and live abroad."

"Live abroad? In another country?" I said with a bitter laugh as I wiped my eyes. "That's impossible. I don't ever want to leave Russia."

Dunya took me and held me and hugged me as warmly as the large oven that heated the core of our village home. But then out of nowhere our doorbell rang, making us jump apart.

"Gospodi!" gasped Dunya. "I told the security agents your father would receive no one today — and not to let anyone even into the building. Evidently, it must be something important."

There might be agents posted in and around the building for our security, but no one ever passed through our door without Dunya's permission, and today was to be no exception. Wiping her hands on a towel, she smoothed back some loose hair and headed straight to the front hall.

Who could it be? Who had got by the agents stationed in the lobby, let alone those posted on the stairs? As soon as I thought that, it struck me: Were the agents even here? What if they had abandoned their posts, just as they had done last night? *Bozhe moi,* I hadn't told Dunya that we'd been left unguarded. If the agents were gone again, who could that be outside our door, one of father's ordinary petitioners, some important personage — or assassins sent by my father's grand ducal enemies?

Wasting no time, I charged after Dunya, out of the kitchen, through the dining room, and down the hall. I feared a squadron of muscular men in black leather jackets, who, brandishing guns and brass knuckle-dusters, would tear through the rooms, gun down Papa, and beat him into a bloody pulp.

"Dunya, wait!" I shouted. "Don't open the —"

But it was too late. Dunya was already pulling open the heavy door. Standing there was neither a small herd of men nor a grand duke or prince, or even a prime minister, but a lone woman, perhaps in her late twenties. As I studied her plain black cape flowing from her shoulders and noted her hands buried deep in the folds of a tired muff, my panic subsided only slightly. After all, if a small woman whose nose had been eaten away by syphilis could nearly kill my father with one lunge of a knife, what damage could an attractive healthy-looking woman like this one do?

"What is it you wish?" asked Dunya of our visitor.

"Please, I'm seeking Father Grigori," said the seemingly gentle woman, her eyes misty with tears. "My name is Olga Petrovna Sablinskaya, and I am in terrible need of help."

"I'm sorry, my child, but you should not have been admitted into the building. Father Grigori is receiving no one today."

"He must see me! Please, I beg you!" she

121

exclaimed, pulling one hand from her muff and wiping her eyes. "I need Father Grigori's aid on behalf of my husband, who is an ensign. He was gravely wounded and now lies in Princess Kleinmichel's hospital. Tomorrow, however, they'll move him out of the city to a terrible sanatorium, and I fear for his life. Can't Father Grigori do something for a young man who has taken a bullet for the sake of the Motherland?"

Dunya started to press shut the door. "I'm sorry, my dear, but you will have to come back tomorrow. Father Grigori is totally spent and assisting no one."

"You don't understand, you —"

From the back of the apartment came my father's voice, sleepy but booming. "Dunya, who calls on us? If it's a woman visitor and she's pretty, by all means let her in!"

Dunya studied the young woman, who was actually quite attractive, her skin pale and pure, her face sweet with a small mouth and nice blue eyes. And our housekeeper, who never could disobey my father, knew she had no choice.

"God has heard your plea . . . and so will Father Grigori," Dunya said, swinging open the door. "Please, come in."

Slava bogu," said Olga Petrovna. "I'm so afraid that my husband will die if they move him, and —"

"Please, child, save your words for Father Grigori's ears. I myself can do nothing."

This stranger seemed genuine. Hospitals had been set up in palace ballrooms all across town, and her husband could very well be lying in one of them. But as she stepped across our threshold and into our home, I flushed with fear. Did she have a gun hidden in her clothing, perhaps a little pistol cradled in her muff?

From down the hall, I ordered, "Dunya, take her cape and her muff at once!"

Surprised by my imperious command, Dunya turned and glared at me. Nevertheless, she complied, taking the woman's worn garments in hand. But there was nothing strange, no hidden dagger or gun. Relieved that at least this woman carried no weapons, I turned and hurried back down the hall, skirting the salon and hurrying around to Papa's study. I still didn't understand how she had gotten into the building, let alone all the way up. Why hadn't the security agents stopped her? Had she somehow bribed her way, either with a fistful of rubles or an open dress?

Afraid that there was only one explanation, I dashed into Papa's little study, raced past his desk, and went up to the window.

Gazing down into the courtyard, I saw nothing and no one. Were the security agents simply hiding in the shadows, or had they left us — Rasputin, his two daughters, and their housekeeper — to our own pathetic defenses?

Good Lord. . . .

In Papa's perfect world, there existed little more than love and freedom, absolute faith, spiritual study, and a world devoid of material belongings. These were the things he sought for his own life, the frame of mind he chose to inhabit, and the very utopia he so dearly sought for his followers. So how had everything become so twisted; what had he done to make so many connive against him? Worse, even though Papa knew how dangerous things had become, he was just like most Russians, accepting fate as nothing less than God's will. But not I. Like most everyone these days, I feared the future but I refused to see myself as a lamb predestined for slaughter. Always, always, would I struggle to shape my own path, no matter the heavenly will. And, yes, in this way I differed radically from my naïve father, whose world was one of blacks and whites with no shades of gray in between.

Leaning against the chilly panes of glass, I peered out, checking every nook and corner in the courtyard. As far as I could tell there was no one. Should I ring the palace at once? Should I call the Empress herself and report our vulnerability? Yes, absolutely. I couldn't risk the alternative. What if this seemingly innocent visitor was instead a beautiful bee with a deadly sting? True, she wasn't carrying any noticeable weapons, but what if she had a vial of poison tucked up her sleeve? Or what if someone else sneaked into our home on this, one of the darkest days of the year?

Turning away from the window of Papa's study, I gathered up my skirt, determined to telephone the palace. I had never interceded in my father's world before, but now I had no choice. While my father was infinitely wiser than I, I was beginning to realize I was more worldly.

No sooner had I started for the door, however, when I heard my father's large voice coming down the hall. "Come with me and tell me all your troubles, my sweet young kitten."

"Yes, Father Grigori. And thank you, Father Grigori. Thank you for seeing and hearing me."

"It is not I who will hear you but the Lord God."

"Yes, of course, Father Grigori," replied

Olga Petrovna meekly.

I did it not because I meant to spy on him. I did it not because I wanted to witness how he handled these things. I did it only because I was beginning to understand that my father had no idea how evil this world really was. Papa was always so eager to help people, always so eager to give away money or use his connections, that he rarely thought of the consequences. If he couldn't protect himself, I would. So, ducking into the small shallow closet on one side of Papa's study, I pulled the door nearly shut behind me. Hidden in cool darkness, I peered out a crack only a finger wide, realizing that for the first time I was about to witness how my father treated those in need.

From my hiding spot, I watched as my father escorted our unexpected guest into his private room and shut the door securely behind him. As always, the first thing Papa did was turn to the icon in the "beautiful" corner, bow slightly, and cross himself with three fingers — forehead, stomach, right shoulder, left. Then, his clothing and hair more a mess than ever, he half stumbled to the chair by his small wooden desk. Dropping himself into the narrow chair, he reached out and took Olga Petrovna by her small hand and pulled her close to him.

"Come closer, my beautiful one," he said, peering up at the young beauty standing before him. "What is it you need from me on this cold afternoon?"

"I need your help, Father Grigori. Your intervention. My husband was severely wounded and he needs the best medical care. Unfortunately, they plan to move him from the city, and it scares me. I'm afraid his care will suffer, and I won't be able to visit him more than once or twice a month during his recovery, and without my presence I don't think he'll recover so quickly. And, Father Grigori, I . . . I —"

Radi boga, I thought, what a groveler. How I hated the way she tiptoed, just like everyone else, around our ugly-sounding last name. People, particularly here in the city, went oddly out of their way to avoid using it, particularly in my father's presence, for fear of offending the powerful peasant with access to the throne. Didn't they know that the name Rasputin was not derived from the word *rasputnik* — a debauched, dissolute, immoral person — but from *rasputiye* — an intersection of roads? No matter what these learned city people said about the way Russian names were derived, that was where my family name came from. And not only ours, but half the village's, for little Pokrovskoye was located at the intersection of two major roads, one leading to Tyumen, the other off into the never-ending Siberian wilds.

As the woman rambled through her story, Papa barely paid her any attention. Instead he ran his hand through his hair, tugged at his thatched beard, and started scratching, first his chest and then his lanky thigh. I was wondering if he was even paying any attention to her when he cut her off, waving his hand brusquely through the air.

"Take off your clothes!" he commanded.

"What?"

"Off with them!"

"But . . . but I have money. I have . . ."

Papa mumbled something incomprehensible, and then shouted out, "God will not hear your prayers until you humble yourself! Do you hear me? You must humble yourself before the eyes of God! Do as I say, child: Take off your clothes!"

I nearly leaped out of the closet right then and there, but my shame captured me, paralyzing me right where I huddled. No. Please, not this way. Clenching my fist to my mouth lest I cry aloud, I bit my knuckles. Papa was all strictness and propriety with us, his children. He knew where we were and what we were doing every hour of the day. So what was going on here? What in the name of the devil was he doing? This couldn't be the way he treated all his visitors behind the closed door of his study, could it? Dear God, as my imagined truth collided with the real one now unfolding before me, it was more than I could bear. Peering from the darkness into the light, I stood as still as a rock frozen to the ground.

"Yes, Father Grigori, as you wish." She pulled her hand free from my father and started unbuttoning the back of her dress. "You see . . . you see, all I need is a slip of paper, some kind of word from you. People say that you give out such things, a little note with your signature. I would be happy to pay generously for it, one of those pieces of paper."

"Ach, money! People are always throwing money at me, but what good does it do? Nothing, I tell you! Money is worth nothing!"

"Yes, but" — as she began to strip, the pretty woman struggled to fight back tears — "I'll do anything . . . anything for my husband, if only you'll intervene. What . . . what is it you'd like from me?"

"Ach, what do I need but love? That's all. I can have anything, I tell you, anything at all! And yet what do any of us have need of but sweet love?"

And so she went on. Her hands trembling, her voice shaking, young Olga Petrovna began to shed her clothes, piece by piece. She did not stop talking, not for a moment, nor did she stop undressing. Staring blankly at a wall, she unbuttoned the top of her dress, and the bottom, and dropped it to the floor. When she stood in nothing but her plain cotton camisole and tattered petticoat, she stopped. As if she were about to be devoured by a lion, she stood there trembling.

"Why do you hesitate, child? Take it off, all of it!" demanded my father. "Do you think God does not see your doubt? Of course He does! And do you know what doubt signifies to the Lord Almighty? A lack of faith! A lack of belief! That's what He sees in doubt! Let me warn you, divine acts cannot take place in the presence of doubt!"

As if she were somewhere else, she continued staring at the wall, prattling on and on, her voice quite flat as she mumbled. "My husband is a very fine man. He has beautiful brown eyes, he's very strong, and he loves his country and his tsar very much. Yes, and he's anxious to get well so he can return to the army and be of further help. . . ."

Continuing, she pulled off her camisole and then dropped her poor petticoat at the feet of the all-powerful Rasputin. Within moments the last of her garments fell from her body, and she stood there, pale and trembling, totally naked except for long tattered stockings that came up over her knees. Spying her perfect, slightly upturned breasts and full, shapely hips, I realized that whereas her tears failed her, mine did not. My face was awash.

"Oh, what a pretty one you are," mumbled Papa, as he reached up with one of his big gnarled hands and plucked at one breast, then the other. "I think I like you, my little Olga Petrovna. Kiss me!"

Papa hadn't moved from his little chair, and as she bent over, he reached up and cupped both her breasts that swung, like pendulums, forward. First he cupped those breasts in both his hands, coddling them like a naughty boy, then giving them a firm squeeze. Next he pawed at her stomach, massaging that buttery skin as if it were a fine piece of meat. And finally he splayed the calloused fingers of his right hand and reached at the patch between her legs, poking there once, twice. Our guest flinched and whimpered, but not with joy, only painful sublimations.

"Just a note, that's all I need," Olga Petrovna begged, pulling back slightly from my father. "Something from you saying they must keep my husband here in Petrograd until he's well. That's all I . . . all I need, really. And that's all I'm asking for, a short note."

"I have a whole stack of such notes right here on my desk. *Make it so!* — that's what they say! Now stop your talking. Just kiss me, little one, and I will give you this note! Yes, I love you, I do!"

She bent over again, her small lips pressing through my father's greasy hair and planting a hesitant, horrible kiss on the top of his forehead, right above that little bump that was reminiscent of a budding horn.

"Yuri, that's my husband, is a very loyal man," she continued, chattering nervously. "You would like him, Father Grigori. He comes from a respected family, too. Very hard-working. And —"

"Ach!" roared Papa, suddenly angry, pushing her back onto the pathetic leather sofa.

"What? What did I do wrong?"

"Enough with this talk! Get your clothes, be gone! You make me angry!"

"But, Father Grigori —"

"Leave me!"

"But my husband! The note!"

My father slumped to the side and closed his eyes. "Come back tomorrow morning, and we will see!"

Now Olga Petrovna finally cried. She could stand it no more. And as she reached to the floor for her clothing, a pathetic sob erupted from her throat. In a flash of a second, her entire pale body blushed a shameful crimson.

"God help me!" she cried. "Please, Father Grigori, I beg you! Please help me!"

"*Oi!*" shouted my father, clasping his hands over his ears as he leaped from his chair. "I thought you were a cute little kitten, but you're nothing but an awful cat! Such noise! Such gabble and crying! I can't stand it!"

And with that Papa stumbled for the door and charged out of the room. Olga Petrovna, hysterical and more desperate than before, couldn't stand it, couldn't bear to see her only hope flee from her grasp. Scrambling, she scooped up her bits of clothing and raced naked after him.

"Wait, Father Grigori! Please, wait!"

"You're the devil! Nothing but a squealing devil! Be gone, I tell you!"

Hurrying after him, she disappeared out the door, crying, "I promise I'll be quiet! I promise I won't say a thing! Help me,

Father Grigori! For the sake of God, please help me!"

They vanished from sight, but I could hear them. I could hear my father's bellowing and Olga Petrovna's screaming as she charged naked after him, the two of them hurrying this way and that through our entire apartment. Within moments I could hear Dunya yelling too, first locking my sister in her bedroom so she wouldn't see, then chasing the woman who was chasing my father. From my dark spot I could hear them all, three mad people tearing through our rooms, one holy man, one naked petitioner, and one furious housekeeper. Despite her shrill pitch, Dunya's was the only voice of sanity, the only one who could shout at my father and herd him into his bedroom, the only one who could admonish our pathetic visitor to get dressed and leave.

And during it all I stayed right where I was, hidden in the closet of my father's study, crumpled on the floor of that tiny space, sobbing because I had never before known I could hate my own father.

CHAPTER 7

Oddly, as I sat there crouched in revulsion, I was flooded with memories of better times. Just last winter a great honor had been bestowed upon me: I had been invited to join Papa for tea at the palace. Dunya, overwhelmed with pride and joy, had spent an entire day shopping for a new frock for me, finally selecting a blue dress with a white collar, tied neatly at the waist. The morning of the tea, Dunya spent nearly two hours reviewing my curtsy and how I held a teacup, explaining how I should address the Empress and coaching me on interesting points of conversation. Toward one o'clock, Papa came out of his room wearing black velvet pants, boots that were freshly polished, and a lilac silk *kosovorotka* with a sash embroidered by the Empress herself. When it finally came time to go, it seemed the entire building came to see Papa and me off. We even took a horse cab to the Tsarskoye Selo train station, though it was only a few blocks away, just to keep my dress clean.

But of course before tea there was play-time with the children. Once I had curtsied to the Empress and been allowed to kiss her hand, and once the Empress, the ever-present Madame Vyrubova, and Papa retired to the Maple Room for conversation, an equerry in a red cape and a hat feathered with ostrich plumes led me to the rear door. My young hosts, it seemed, were waiting for me outside, and no sooner had I stepped into the cold than I was pelted by a handful of powdery snowballs.

"Surprise!" shouted Anastasiya Niko-laevna, the youngest of the grand duchesses, who was so covered in snow she looked as if she'd been rolled in confectioners' sugar.

For the briefest of moments I wanted to burst into tears — I had never been dressed in finer clothes. But then, of course, my young sensibilities took hold, and I dashed into the fray, joining the younger sisters — Anastasiya Nikolaevna and Maria Nikolae-vna, who was my age — and their young brother, the heir, Aleksei Nikolaevich, in a brawl of winter fun that was just like those back home. The only difference was that the snowballs were formed and handed to me.

"Here, my child," said Nagorny, the *dyadka* — bodyguard — to the Heir Tsarevich, as he handed me a feather-light ball of snow, "you may throw only those that I give to you."

I didn't understand until much later, but of course I did exactly as I was told. And after a half hour of merriment in what had to be the softest snow, we were led inside. As the daughters dressed in fresh white frocks with blue sashes and the Heir Tsarevich in a sailor suit, a maid took me into a private room and combed my hair and straightened my clothing. Finally, I was led to a large set of doors guarded by a pair of huge Ethiopians, the blackest men I'd ever seen, dressed in gold jackets, scarlet trousers, and white turbans. Entering the Maple Room, I found the Empress, Madame Vyrubova, and Papa.

"I see it all, understand it all," said my father, his voice booming and his eyes wide. "Papa must give the order as I see it: Whole trains must be given up to food."

The imperial children — all five of them, including the older pair, Olga Nikolaevna and Tatyana Nikolaevna — joined us minutes later. As the Heir Tsarevich, Anastasiya, and Maria settled on the floor with great picture books, the likes of which I had never seen, the older daughters, fashioning themselves as young women, sat down in chairs and picked up embroidery. As for myself, having neither book nor needle, I listened to my father rant on.

"Each wagon of the train must be filled with flour and butter and sugar. All the passenger trains should be halted for three days — three days! — and this food should be allowed to pass to the capital! It's even more important than ammunition or meat! People must have bread! People will grow angry without bread!"

"But what about all the passengers?" asked Madame Vyrubova. "Don't you think people will scream?"

"Let them scream! I saw all this in the night like a vision! Mama, you must tell Papa. I beg you, you must tell him! You must write to him at once of this."

"Yes, of course. I see your point quite clearly," said Aleksandra Fyodorovna, nodding pensively as she gently twiddled with her long necklace of large pearls.

"Three days — no other trains except those carrying flour, butter, and sugar," my father repeated. "Otherwise there will be great unhappiness. And into this unhappiness will rush a flood of problems. It's quite necessary!"

"Yes, essential." The Empress nodded. "I will tell my husband, and he will make it so. It is his will, and he is master."

Papa puffed out his lower lip and bobbed his head in agreement and approval.

Vyrubova spoke up. "Now, what of the new minister? The position of Minister of Internal Affairs is quite —"

"I know, I know!" Papa rubbed his hands together. "Now . . . well, the Old Chap came to see me, this Boris Stürmer, but I had an interesting vision of this other fellow, Proto-popov!"

"Really?" said the Tsaritsa in amazement.

"Yes, a vision from on high!"

Precisely at four, right on cue, the doors opened and the Empress and her small cabinet of advisers ceased conversation. As we watched, a bevy of liveried footmen with snow-white garters swept in and spread a tablecloth over two small tables, then set out glasses in silver holders and plates of hot bread and English biscuits. Had the Tsar not been at the front, where he had taken personal command of the troops, he would certainly have joined us.

"We shall continue these discussions later," commanded the Empress, rising from her chair. "First let us refresh ourselves."

Aleksandra Fyodorovna paid Papa and me a great honor by pouring our tea with her own hand. Accepting my glass, I carefully eyed the bread and biscuits.

With a wry smile, the Empress said warmly, "I'm sure, my child, you've been to many more interesting teas than this one. Others, I know, serve different cakes and sweetmeats, but, alas, I am unable to change the menu here at the Palace. All runs on tradition and is the same since our great Catherine."

But it was an interesting tea. Amazingly so, I thought, as I carefully took a biscuit and found my seat. Just imagine, my father giving so much help and advice, so many of his visions, to Empress Aleksandra Fyodorovna, who would pass it all on to the Tsar. Just imagine Papa emerging from the depths of Siberia and coming to the aid of the Motherland. Incredible, I thought, beaming with pride at my father, as he slurped his tea and munched on a biscuit and the crumbs flew.

CHAPTER 8

So what was I now to do with those memories of my father the hero? Burn them, stomp them, rip them to shreds?

Tormented by confusion, I fled the closet and ran to my room, where I leaped into bed and fell into a black hole. When my sister wanted to know what on earth was wrong, I shouted at her to get out, and then my tears came so quickly, so heavily, that by the time I finally stopped crying my eyes were practically swollen shut. I just lay there, hidden and huddled under the down comforter, my arms and hands clasped around my knees. But I could find no comfort, no matter how hard I hugged myself. I simply cried and cried.

Many in the highest society, including the Tsar and Tsaritsa themselves, clung to the myth of the Russian peasant, believing that only in the huts of the poorest of the poor lived the true spirit of Christ. And yet now I knew what even the Tsar did not, that in my peasant father there dwelled both the spirit of Christ and also, at the very least, the spirit of a fool — not a holy fool but a simple one. We should leave the capital. For his own protection, not to mention ours, I should force Papa out of the city. He should abandon any pretense of holiness and simply melt away into Siberia and her endless forests. A life of fasts and visions and ragged clothing — that was what was meant for my father.

My head buried beneath my pillow, my body protected by the billowing feathers of the comforter, I lay curled up for hours, drifting in and out of misery and sleep. Finally, toward six, I heard Dunya beckoning us all to the table, for like all Russian women, she believed in the sanctity of coming together around food. Rising, I made a feeble attempt at brushing my hair and went to the dining room.

Dunya and Varya had obviously been busy. Our brass samovar, polished until it glowed like gold and boiling with water, sat by the window, and our heavy oak dinner table, the kind so popular among the city bourgeoisie, was covered with plates of cold *zakuski:* pickles, sour cream, salted herring garnished with onions, grated carrots mixed with mayonnaise and garlic, salted tomatoes, pickled mushrooms, smoked fish, stuffed eggs, and Papa's favorite appetizer, jellied fish heads. Tonight, it was obvious we would feast not on fancy city things but real food.

"Girls, please take your places while I fetch your father," Dunya said.

As she scurried off, the two of us stood behind our chairs, and my sister looked up at me, asking softly, "Are you all right, Maria? Why were you so upset?"

"Nothing," I mumbled.

I stared at Varya, who was so proud of studying at middle school here in the capital that even now she wore the black-and-white frock of the *gymnasia*. She had my father's blunt chin, his dark hair, his large full lips, and short black bangs, which she kept flipping back. She worshiped Papa, and to her, it wasn't unusual at all that our humble father should be telephoned once or twice a day by the Empress herself, let alone summoned at any hour to the palace.

"What happened this afternoon?" she asked, not particularly concerned as she scooped up some carrot salad with her finger. "I heard a woman screaming."

I shrugged. "You know how people are always after Papa for things."

For the first time ever I was dreading a

family meal. What was I going to say to my father? How would I even be able to look at him? But when he came in a few moments later it was not with his booming voice and quick step. Rather it was with a shuffle, for he was walking only with the aid of Dunya, who held him by the left arm.

"Papa, what's the matter?" gasped Varya, rushing to his side.

He looked awful, as if he'd just aged twenty years, and for a brief moment I felt a pang of worry. His hair fell every which way like a field of wheat after a summer storm, his face was pallid, and his eyes were red. He was dressed terribly too, wearing a dirty pair of baggy pants and an unbelted tunic of coarse cotton.

"I had another dream . . . another vision. . . ."

"Please, Father Grigori," coaxed Dunya. "Just tea and a little food. Then you'll feel better, I promise."

They led Papa along, Dunya on one side and Varya on the other. Back home there was a bent old man who lived in a falling-down hut, and we taunted him mercilessly, calling him a *starii xhren* — an old piece of horseradish. Right here and now, that was my father. Had he fallen into a pool of remorse? Had he begged God's forgiveness for the way he'd treated that woman? I could only hope so.

I stood motionless behind my chair as Dunya poured some tea concentrate from the small pot atop the shiny samovar, to which she added hot water from the spigot. As if it were nothing but cool water from a stream back home, he downed the glass in one gulp. Dunya then poured him another, which he likewise drank to the bottom. And another. Papa sometimes drank as many as fifty glasses of tea in a day, but never like this, as eagerly as a sunburned man just in from the desert. Finally, with his fourth glass in hand, he sat down. Only then did the three of us take our seats.

"What is it, Papa? What did you see?" begged Varya, her smooth young brow wrinkled with concern.

"Blood. I have seen the entire River Neva running with blood."

Her eyes suddenly beading with tears, Varya pressed, "Whose blood, Papa?"

"The blood of the grand dukes."

"Oh," Varya said, not without a bit of relief.

Dunya spoke up softly. "Please, Father Grigori, you mustn't say such things. Talk like that will only scare the girls, it will only —"

"I'm not scared," I interjected defiantly.

"Let us pray!" intoned Papa, reaching out.

Beneath the heavy bronze chandelier, with Papa at one end of the table and Dunya at the other, we clasped hands and bowed our heads.

"Dear Heavenly Father, I beseech you to come to the aid of us, your miserablest children who seek Thine forgiveness. We will sin no more. I pray unto you, Thou, to grant us salvation, to drive away our enemies, both those within our borders and beyond. O God, O Wondrous Lord, how can one fail to believe?! The street is crooked, but ahead layest only one destination, and we struggle there on foot. We believe heartily, Thine Lord, and woe unto those who does not! The waves of calumny can only be stilled by good deeds, but it is true, there is far more sickness on land than in your great sea. So in you, Thee, O Lord, O God, help us rejoice, so that in your miracles of forgiveness we find everlasting peace. *Ahmeen.*"

"*Ahmeen,*" chimed Dunya and Varya in chorus.

When I failed to speak, Dunya glared at me, and I reluctantly muttered, *"Ahmeen."*

As a child I never understood my father's prayers. Nor did I this evening. What was

146

different about tonight, however, was that I no longer felt awed by my father's words or his supposed wisdom. I only felt something . . . something sad, even pathetic.

Papa took a piece of bread in his hand, put a single large pickle on it, and stuffed it into his mouth. It was gone in two bites.

"Wine!" Papa commanded.

"Yes, Father Grigori," replied Dunya, pushing back her chair and getting up from the table.

Disappearing into the kitchen, Dunya quickly returned, not with a mere glass of wine but with a full bottle. As she poured Papa a glass, however, I could tell it was not with pleasure. Of course Dunya understood that Papa's physical pain was as great as his mental anguish, but I knew it hurt her terribly to see Papa drink as many as twelve bottles of Madeira in a night, as he had done a number of times in the last month alone. How, I thought for the first time, could my father consume so much and still stand? Indeed, how could he claim to be so blessed and have so many gifts and yet be blind to his gross mistakes, which even I could now see so clearly?

Papa grabbed another piece of bread and piled it with salted herring, an entire stuffed egg, and a ring of onion, all of which he gobbled down like a wild animal. Next, still with his bare hand, he reached into the bowl of jellied fish heads, pulled out a whole cod head, and swallowed it.

"The other day I greatly offended a woman because I ate with my hands and didn't use a napkin. She even gasped out loud when I wiped my mouth with my beard like this." Papa chuckled as he pulled up the bristly ends of his beard and cleaned his mouth. "Tell me, girls, does it bother either of you?"

Varya, who was eating a salted pickle dipped in sour cream, grinned and shook her head.

I, on the other hand, blurted out, "Of course it does. It's awful and . . . and embarrassing. Why haven't you ever learned how to eat like a normal civilized person?"

"Maria!" gasped Dunya, horrified. "You mustn't speak to your father like that!"

Papa only laughed. By court standards, let alone the etiquette of good society, his manners were atrocious, no better than a dog's. He knew it, exulted in it, and flaunted it, particularly in the presence of the proper titled folk of Petrograd. Any number of times I had watched him wipe his filthy hands on the fine silk dresses, fur coats, or ties of his guests. Any number of times I had watched him order a princess to lick his filthy fingers clean. After a while his devotees understood and even begged for such treatment. Yes, they pleaded for Papa to do such rude things to them. Like washing the feet of Christ, it was all about meekness, submission, and mortification of the flesh.

"No, no, it's quite all right," Papa insisted. "My little Marochka speaks the truth of her heart, as she must. As must every Rasputin. And indeed as must every person. And it's true: I never learned how to eat with the weapons of the court, those forks and knives!"

This, actually, was why Papa always came home from the palace of the Tsar ravenous. After *zakuski* he could never manage anything but soup. All the rest he could barely take a stab at, literally.

"But do you know why I have never learned, Marochka, my sweet one? Do you know why it's important to eat with your hands?"

Of course I did. He'd told us not once or twice but a million times. And yet I said nothing.

Finally my little sister blurted it out. "I know! Because *Xhristos* and the Apostles did."

"Absolutely correct, Varichka. It's a rule of the Apostles to use your hands, and that's why I never cut bread but break it, just as they did. And also why I eat fish and never meat."

"I've never seen you eat a single piece of meat, Papa. Not ever," said Varya.

"That's right — never! Meat blackens one's soul, whereas fish brings clarity and light. I learned this when I was a boy — even before my vision of the Virgin of Kazan. It started one summer night when one of my grandfather's best horses injured himself and fell lame. This beautiful horse could do nothing but hobble, so I took hold of his bad leg. I clung to the leg, but my grandfather kept telling me it was hopeless, there was nothing to do, and he went to get a gun to shoot the poor thing."

"No!" gasped Varya.

"Oh, yes. But I took hold of that bad leg and held it in my strong young hands. And do you know what I did, girls? I threw back my head and closed my eyes and I prayed with all my being! I prayed to *Xhristos* for healing, for compassion, for blessing. And I took the pain from the horse's bad leg and sucked it into my body and out the top of my head . . . and then I said to the horse, 'There is no pain — walk!' And by the time

150

my grandfather returned with his gun, the horse was just fine, even trotting around a little. Yes, my grandfather's favorite horse lived for ten more years, never limping again."

"It's true," said Dunya, her voice just above a whisper as she chewed on a piece of bread. "Six people witnessed the healing, and they still talk of it today!"

Yes, I thought as I sat there in silence. People in our village still talked of my father's first healing, but . . . but . . .

"Mind you, I am not *Xhristos*. I can heal no one, I only do His work. It was the Lord God who healed that beautiful creature, and I only served as His vehicle. But right then and there I understood that all beasts are our brothers," Papa continued, "and I've never eaten meat again, not once. And every day since, my powers have grown. Such is the rule of the Apostles and the powers of fish."

"Is that why you don't eat pastries or sweets?" asked Varya.

"Scum! Nothing but scum! I never eat sweet things and you shouldn't either, little girl! In fact, Dunya, we must not allow it anymore! We must tell all those who come to leave their tortes and their sweet pies at the door! We mustn't let such foul things as

151

sweets into this house ever again!"

"As you wish, Father Grigori."

I watched in disgust as my father swiped one of his greasy hands through his coarse beard, leaving bits of food here and there. He poured himself another full glass of wine, which he drank down in one enormous swig.

"Dunya, fetch us soup while I talk to the girls."

"Yes, Father Grigori."

Dunya, who was simply glad to have my father walk the floors she mopped, was only too happy to get up and clear the table of *zakuski.* As she did so, Papa reached out and clasped my hand in his right and Varya's hand in his left. I tried to pull free, but my father's meaty, calloused grasp only tightened.

"Great is the peasant in the eyes of God!" declared my father, uttering his favorite phrase yet again. "I have brought you, my precious daughters, here to the capital city, but I see trouble ahead. When things erupt, when this trouble flows through the streets, you must retreat from this decadent capital. You must flee to the place we have come from — our village. There, with your mother in the bosom of your family, you will find safety."

"Papa," begged Varya, "I don't understand. Where will you be? You'll come too, won't you?"

"My work is nearly at an end, my child. There will soon come a time when I am gone, and then so will the court be gone and all the riches that you see here in the Tsar's city. Into this void dangerous waters will flood, drowning those who refuse to repent. And when this happens, you must repent with all your heart and flee that very moment."

I looked at my sister and saw fear ripple across her face, but I felt nothing. Didn't everyone see the dark waters swirling at his feet?

"Simply believe in the Divine power of love, my daughters, my beautiful girls," he said, in his rich, deep voice. "Believe in that, and you will find safety of heart and peace of mind in Thine God, O Lord." Papa tossed down another glass of wine. "One day you will marry. And in that marriage, you must find truth and honesty. Never forget, my children, that though there are a man and a woman in marriage, the success of that union depends on one thing — that it beats not with two hearts but with one. Do you understand, my little ones?"

Averting my eyes, I managed to say,

"Yes, Papa."

"Keep your hearts simple and your minds clear, and you will find God. Eat kasha for breakfast, for it is the caviar of the people. Bake it in the oven until it's hot and firm, never mushy."

As timid as a mouse, Varya ventured, "I'll always serve it with crispy onions and mushrooms, just as you like it, Papa."

"Yes, good! Very good!" Papa caught sight of Dunya carrying two large wide-rimmed bowls of soup. "And don't forget that every meal must have soup! Without soup, your family and your guests will be poor both in spirit and in health!"

"Yes, Father Grigori, soup feeds the soul, does it not?" said Dunya, proudly setting down a steaming bowl in front of him.

"Absolutely. And there is nothing better for the soul than fish soup! Fish soup all the time!"

"Fish soup!" cheered Varya.

Which is exactly what it was: cod soup. Papa loved cod above all other fish, and we ate it once, if not twice, each and every day, either jellied as a *zakuska,* boiled as a soup, or fried as a main course. Sometimes Dunya made cod soup merely from the juices left over from jellied fish heads, adding cream and a bit of chopped root of ginger

— Papa claimed this was his magical soup, the one that would guarantee a strong, long life — but tonight whole pieces of cod floated in the thick creamy mixture.

By the time Dunya brought out the other bowls, Papa was well into his dish, slurping and gobbling down whole pieces of fish. He clutched the large spoon like the peasant he was, in his fist. I remembered the first time Papa had taken me to the palace, how the Tsar and his family had sat across from Papa and me, how the finely behaved imperial children had stared at Papa as he crudely gobbled down a bowl of Villager's Soup chock full of whitefish and salmon, shrimp and pickles. I was sure their mother, the Empress, would have banished them to a far wing of the palace for eating like that, but the four girls and the heir were not watching Papa in disgust. No, he was Father Grigori to them, the most mystical of people, a man of Siberia and of course a man of God, and they were as fascinated and transfixed by him as I was by *their* father, God's Own Anointed, the Tsar Nikolai II. More important, the royal children never saw, let alone talked with, anyone but courtiers, so my father, with his loud laughter, warm kisses, and endless stories of Siberian tigers and bears, was something incredible to them. He was both surreal and yet more real than anyone they had ever before seen or experienced in their sheltered lives.

Glancing at my sister, I noted that she held the spoon just as we'd been taught and ate her soup politely — not in big slurps and gulps but slowly, quietly, properly. Yes, we had been taught well at our school for daughters of good families. How odd, I thought, for the first time. While Papa had always fiercely clung to his Siberian manners and traditions, he had arranged for them slowly to be washed from both of us, his cherished daughters.

Papa poured the last of the Madeira into his glass, took a large drink, and said, "I eat only fish not as part of a diet to prove my faith. No, my sweet children, my thoughts are more sincere than that. Fish is part of a path, a path illuminated by the Apostles, who showed us that by eating fish their bodies were never darkened. People who eat meat have dark bodies, you see, but the Apostles didn't, not at all. Instead, they found light, they found the Divine way."

"How did they find that?" asked Varya.

"How? I'll tell you how! The Apostles ate so much fish, morning, noon, and night, that light started coming from their bodies.

Beams of light. At first no one could see it, but then it began to grow until this sweet light glowed around their heads. Yes, they had halos right above their very own heads. And this light, which came from fish, showed them the way, the Divine path."

Never before tonight had I questioned my father. Never before this evening had I doubted him. But staring at this man with the beastly hair on his head and that thicket on his cheeks, this crude man with bits of food hanging from his mouth and from his filthy, greasy fingers, how could I not? How could he have mistreated that woman, and how could he now drink so much? How could he dress so terribly, and how could he not care for money and the things we, his family, needed? And these words he spoke: Where did they come from? What did they mean? I stared at my father, wondered how many women he'd groped in his study — hundreds? — and understood for the first time why so many people hated him. Was he nothing more than an insane peasant from the distant forests, as his enemies claimed?

"But Papa," I challenged, "you eat so much fish, why isn't there a halo over your head too? You claim to be a man of God, so why should the Apostles have halos and not you?"

My father dropped his spoon into his bowl, chipping an edge of the cheap china, and turned and glared at me with those deep icy-blue eyes. But the eyes were not steady; they searched my body, my face, my thoughts. My heart started pounding. Everyone claimed to be frightened of my father's penetrating eyes, of his hands that never seemed to stop moving. But before me I saw not the man whose name was on the lips of every person in the country, not Father Grigori or Rasputin or Grishka. No, I saw my very own father, and I refused to be intimidated. After all, who was he, this man who insisted that everyone speak the truth? Nothing but a fraud? A charlatan? So I glared back at him, my eyes not as deep as his, or as blue, but every bit as radiant, I was sure. In response, this deep, guttural sound emerged from my father's throat, an angry sound like a tiger ready to pounce.

Not intimidated, I couldn't stop myself from pressing the point, as I asked, "So why can't I see your halo?"

Her own voice trembling, our dear Dunya muttered, "But, child, it's right there."

Not taking my eyes off my father, I demanded, "Right where?"

"Why, there above his head. Can't you see

the faint glow?"

I couldn't, so I turned to Dunya and in her face saw nothing but confidence, nothing but total belief. She saw something, of course she did, but what? Glancing at my sister, I found her staring right at me, and I spied in her young face nothing but fear and disbelief. No, total shock, that was it. How did I dare question our larger-than-life father? And yet as I gazed at him, I saw nothing. I stared and checked, even squinted, but above that crazy mass of hair was . . . a void.

I was not going to lie, particularly not today when I'd witnessed what had gone on in my father's study. Full of certainty, my head moved, shaking slowly from side to side. Who was I if I did not practice what Papa had taught me all these years? Who was I if I did not espouse the heavenly beliefs he had instilled in my heart? Better yet, who was he?

It was still there, that blank space above Papa's head, and I stared at the invisible place, and said, "I don't see a thing."

All of a sudden, like an eagle grabbing its prey from a river, Papa jabbed his fingers into his bowl of soup and scooped up not one, not two, but three large pieces of milky cod. He threw his catch into his bearded mouth and down his gullet, consuming it all in nearly one swallow.

As spidery traces of creamy soup swirled on his hairy chin, my father shouted to Dunya, "The lights!"

Her eyes aflame with conviction, Dunya threw back her chair, nearly tipping it over. As quickly as she could muster, she hurried to the wall, where with a slap of her hand she pushed the light button. In one single snap, the heavy bronze chandelier went dark. At first the room was black and then slowly, every so faintly, red — in the "beautiful" corner of the room an oil lamp burned before an icon of the Virgin Mary.

"Bow your heads, my children, and pray! Pray, I tell you!" roared my father in the blood-red darkness. "Pray as if your lives were about to end!"

As if he were smashing a mouse with his bare fist, my father's paw came whooshing downward, trapping my hand beneath his. I tried to pull away but could not. On the other side, Dunya came clambering back to the table, her hand feeling all about for mine, finally finding my fingers and clinging to them.

"O God! O Lord!" shouted Papa. "Woe unto us that have waxed faith into pride! Magnificent is the brilliance of Thoust

160

power! But woe unto the Devil! Woe unto Satan, who tries through his darkness to trap us all! Only for the light of God do we find Thine path!"

I found myself starting to shake, horribly so. Not just my hands, not just my shoulders, but every limb, every muscle. I bit my lip but could not control it, could not stem the deep sob that erupted from within me and exploded into the blackness of our dining room. Never until that moment had I feared my father. Never until this day had I seen in him anything but kindness and love. And yet all I knew right then was terror, so I bowed my head, squeezed my eyes tight, and buried my soul in humble prayer, pleading for forgiveness. By transgressing the word of my very own father I had sinned, had I not? But no more. No, I was ready to repent, and deep inside my being I begged, even chanted: Lord, O Lord, take pity upon my miserable soul and gather me unto Thy feet!

Out of nowhere Varya's small voice bloomed like a tiny flower as she gasped, "Maria, look! Look!"

I was so afraid that at first I dared not. When I finally opened my eyes, I saw nothing but a reddish fog of darkness. I gazed across the table, searched the spot where my sister was sitting, but could barely see her. I turned to the right and could only discern the vague outline of Dunya, whose hand I was clasping so hard. When I slowly focused on my left, however, everything was different and — yes — even miraculous. Immediately I was aware of something, some kind of glowing light, which gently filled that end of the room and even my soul. And when I slowly raised my eyes, I saw it and started weeping quietly. A wave of awe and glory surged through my body, for there, right above Papa's head, hovering just above his messy thatch of hair, glowed something that seemed quite like an arc of light.

CHAPTER 9

When we finally finished eating our fish, I volunteered to do the dishes.

Awash with remorse and twisted in confusion, I lingered at the sink over each glass, each plate. For good or ill, I had to recognize what I had always known, that Papa did have a kind of power. But did that mean I should support him, no matter what?

I had just finished washing and drying everything right down to the last spoon when the doorbell rang a second time that day. At first I couldn't imagine who it could be. Then it struck me: Olga Petrovna had returned. Had that poor woman come back, perhaps on her hands and knees, pathetically determined to service my father in any way possible, just in exchange for one of his notes? Oh, God, I thought, bolting out of the kitchen. I had to protect her from the very thing she so desperately sought: my father's so-called help.

Determined to reach the front door before Dunya, I raced from the kitchen, through the dining room, and into the salon. But there was no sign of our housekeeper, let alone my father or sister. Had Dunya retreated to her room upstairs and Papa gone back to bed? Was Varya reading in our room? I didn't know, didn't care. Simply relieved that no one else was around, I made a beeline for Papa's study, knowing exactly what I needed and where to find it.

Like most of our countrymen, Papa could barely read, let alone write. For that reason he would write out his notes ahead of time, sign them in his bearish scrawl, and keep a stack of them ready to hand out to petitioners who pleased him. Wasting no time, I went directly to his desk and snatched one from the pile:

Dear Friend,
I beseech you to have pity on this poor, suffering creature and do as requested. My blessings upon you.

Father Grigori †

These few lines were, I knew, more than enough to open any door and almost enough to accomplish any task in all of Russia. This, I thought as I quickly started out

164

of the room, would do her fine. This would be more than enough to keep Olga Petrovna's husband in Petrograd.

Determined to get to the front door before Dunya, I raced down the hall and through the salon. When I reached the front hall and the foyer, however, I still saw no sign of our housekeeper or anyone else. Though I should have been worried, and though I should have called out to see who was actually ringing, neither occurred to me. Both ashamed of my father and worried about what he would demand of Olga Petrovna, I clutched the note in one hand and with the other threw open the door — to find not a small woman in a cape standing there, but a man in an enormous fur coat.

"*Gospodin Ministir* Protopopov!" I gasped, immediately recognizing him by his thick pointed nose.

For the past few months he'd been coming to our house often, no doubt because his career had been advanced only due to Papa's influence. When he'd been plucked from the Duma — our parliament — and named Minister of Internal Affairs, none had been more shocked, more outraged, than the famed monarchist Vladimir Purishkevich, whose hatred of my father was known across the land. But Papa thought

Protopopov a good man who would prove to be a good link between the throne and the Duma, and he had insisted on the appointment to the Empress. In turn, the Empress, believing in my father's heavenly visions, had insisted on it to the Emperor.

"Good evening, young one," said the minister, politely removing his puffy fur hat from his greasy head. "Is your father at home?"

Glancing down the hall into our salon, I still saw no one and heard nothing. I had no idea whether or not Papa was asleep or passed out from drink, but I wanted no one else in our home tonight. What should I say?

"Papa's asleep and asked not to be disturbed."

"Well, then, perhaps you can tell me. I received a report that a young terrorist was in the area last night. Apparently some of the agents chased him into your courtyard."

"What?" I asked in disbelief.

"Yes, and the bastard was bleeding quite badly. One of the agents thought he disappeared into your building."

Dear God, I thought. He couldn't be talking about Sasha, could he? Suddenly my face was burning, and I clasped a hand over my mouth.

"This would have been quite late. You

didn't hear or see anything, did you?"

All I could manage was a terse shake of my head.

"Better yet, I trust you weren't disturbed?"

My voice barely above a whisper, I said, "No."

"Very well. However, please tell your father I stopped by." Handing me an envelope, he said, "And please give him this letter. My agents intercepted it, and while we don't know who wrote it, I have my suspicions. In any case, I believe the threat is real. Please ask him to read it very, very carefully, yes?"

"Of course, *Gospodin Ministir.*"

"And remind him not to be going out late at night. Things are much too dangerous for him to be traipsing about in the dark hours."

"Of course." Taking the envelope in hand, I realized that our security was ultimately the responsibility of this minister, and I asked, "Did you see any of the security agents downstairs? They were gone last night, and they might be gone again tonight."

"Ah, well, I suppose I didn't see any of them," he replied, without any great surprise. "I'll check on that right away. Good night, my child. I wish you a peaceful sleep."

He bowed his head again, slipped his hat

back on his slick head, and disappeared like a big bear rumbling down the steps, grunting as he went. I had no idea why Papa cared for this man, for I certainly didn't, and neither did most of the country, from what little I'd read in the papers.

As I shut and locked the door, I started trembling. There'd been only one person bleeding in our house yesterday, of course, and that had been Sasha. But what did that mean? What had happened and what was he involved in? Terrorism? Revolutionary activities? It couldn't be. I couldn't have misread him so horribly, could I? And yet . . . he'd been hurt and on the run, obviously scared and definitely unwilling to explain what had happened.

It suddenly occurred to me why Protopopov wasn't surprised there were no guards: He knew there weren't. In fact, he'd probably ordered them away, because even though he needed Papa's blessing to keep his position, he didn't want to be seen coming here. If there were no guards, there were no written reports. And if there were no written reports, his regular visits to Rasputin would not be revealed.

Oh, Lord, was the adult world I was just entering really so dirty, let alone so conniving?

Envelope in hand, I hurried back through the salon to the window in Papa's study. Peering down, I saw a large, fancy vehicle. It had to be the minister's car, and of course it was, for seconds later Protopopov emerged from our building and scurried into the rear seat. As the vehicle quickly disappeared, all I had to do was wait.

And as I waited, of course, I started fiddling with the envelope. *Gospodin Ministir* Protopov wanted Papa to read the anonymous letter, but that would be difficult if not impossible because my father was only semiliterate. Ultimately, I knew, it would probably be me who read him the letter anyway, so within seconds I was tearing it open.

Grigori,
Our Fatherland is in danger, both from beyond our borders and within. The fact that you receive telegrams from high places in cipher proves that you have great influence. Hence we, the chosen ones, ask you to arrange matters so that all ministers should be appointed by the Duma. Do this by the end of the year so that our country may be saved from ruin. If you do not comply and if you do not stop meddling in affairs of govern-

ment, we shall kill you. We will show no mercy. Our hand will not fail as did the hand of the syphilitic woman. Wherever you are, death will follow you. The die has been cast; the lot has fallen on us ten chosen men.

So, I thought, my heart shuddering, Papa's second sight of his own death was not really so difficult to envision. It was, instead, little more than common sense, given how many enemies he had. In fact, could we even trust Protopopov, whom many called nothing more than an excitable seal? *Bozhe moi,* could he in fact be one of the "ten chosen men"?

I heard a noise on the street and looked back out the window. Without any urgency, a black automobile emerged on the edge of the street. A few long moments later, several men got out and made for our building. So. I was right. Now that Protopopov was gone, the guards were back.

In disgust, I turned away from the window and threw the envelope on my father's desk. The truths of the world were being laid down before me like cards, each one trumping the last, and I was deeply pained. And yet the truth I most wanted — that of Sasha — was unseen, the most illusive card. If only

I could talk to him and ask what in the name of God he was involved in. Would another two years go by before I saw him again, or this time had he vanished forever?

Making my way out of Papa's study, I stepped to the edge of our empty salon and glanced around. I saw a simple room lined with many chairs, the walls hung with a few plain etchings. How many fine women had sat here, women with fancy feather boas and diamonds of the first water, women who were lost in their meaningless lives and wanted nothing more than to kiss my father's hand or at least the hem of his filthy blouse. How many poor souls had come here as well, for who else was willing to listen and help them, the downtrodden of my country, except one of their own who had by fate risen to the very top? Everyone in Russia, it seemed, was desperate for a miracle, and many people were turning to Papa in search of it. Oddly, if he were to survive these dark days of rumor and innuendo, no one required that very miracle more than my own father.

With still no sight or sound of either Papa or Dunya, I moved on. As I passed his bedroom, I saw that the door was shut. I wanted to knock but dared not, for I heard his deep, muttering voice from within. Was he on his knees lost in prayer? Was he begging for forgiveness? I certainly hoped so.

Actually, it wasn't hard at all to gain entry to Rasputin's home and family. In fact, I was quite eagerly received. After all, they were just simple peasants and that is the peasant way, to open heart and home.

I never met his son, the simple one. And I never really got to know the younger daughter. It was the older one, Maria, with whom I became friendly. I remember how surprised I was the first time I met her. She looked so much like him. Not just the hair. Not the small chin, either. No, it was her eyes. She had his eyes, so piercing, so intense. The resemblance actually frightened me.

But, no, I feel no remorse for what I have done, none at all. We did what we did because we had to, because we had no choice. Rasputin was destroying the prestige of the monarch and tearing the nation apart.

The only mistake we made was in not acting sooner.

CHAPTER 10

If I'd learned anything at all from the titled ladies who visited us, it was this: The single most valuable commodity in Russia had never been serfs or land, money or jewels. Rather, it was — and probably always would be — information, which was so tightly controlled by the government, from the censors on down. From eavesdropping on these women as they waited for my father's blessings, I'd come to understand that it wasn't through good deeds or integrity that one was elevated. Rather, it was with the right tidbit of knowledge, real or, better yet, fabricated. Whom you knew. Who knew what. Who knew when. If you possessed any or all of these, you were covered in luck, for that was how titles were given, lands awarded, even how one secured a simple clerical position or, if you were lucky enough to read, a spot in a good school. As these fancy women knew all too well, one didn't achieve, one connived.

Not long ago I'd brought a cup of tea to a princess, who was laughingly saying to an old baronessa, "Everyone knows that gossip and *vranye* — our beloved art of creative lying — are the only two things that keep our huge, ignorant country rolling ahead like some giant steamroller, wouldn't you say, *ma chérie?*"

"*Oui, bien sûr,*" chuckled her aged friend, who, like so many of her class, only spoke the tongue of her native land to her lowly servants.

So when I woke the next morning I knew exactly what to do. I needed information, and I knew precisely where to get it.

By the time I had finished my breakfast of steaming kasha and tea, Papa was already receiving his first visitors of the day in the salon. There was a little man from Moscow who, from what I'd overheard, had come because he wanted to supply the army with large-sized military undergarments and needed my father's help to moisten the deal. Another, a mother of six in dire financial need, had come in search of a prophecy: Would her husband come back from the front alive, or should she start giving up her children for adoption? Papa, as far as I could tell, declined the first, and in regard to the second, the mother, he opened a drawer and tossed her a stack of 2,000 rubles that someone had left as a bribe the day before. As I drank the last of my tea, I heard the woman fall sobbing on the floor to kiss his dirty boots in gratitude.

There was already a line outside our door, and one by one they were let in, humbling themselves before Father Grigori and begging to press their lips to his filthy hand. Sometimes Papa would see scores of petitioners in a single day, sometimes only a few. There was simply no telling how many he would receive this morning; when he'd had enough, he would just turn away and tell Dunya to send the rest packing.

While Papa was busy humbling several fashionable ladies by kissing them directly on the lips, and Dunya was occupied with a tiny nun who was quietly asking for one of Father Grigori's dirty under linens — "But, please, give me one with sweat" — I ducked into his study. Going directly to my father's desk, I took two things that were sure to lubricate the lips of any Russian, a small stack of rubles plus, most important, a handful of Papa's already signed notes. Less than five minutes later I was sneaking out the back door of our apartment, disappearing down the service stairs completely unnoticed.

With my cloak bundled over my shoulders and my hood thrown over my head, I emerged from the courtyard of our building and through the front arch without being recognized. A damp, freezing wind whipped all around me, and I turned right on Goroxhavaya. As I walked toward the River Fontanka, just a block away, a flurry of horse cabs and a motorcar passed me, all hurrying in the opposite direction, I was sure, for the train station. It was ten in the morning and the sun, nearly at its weakest point in the year, was barely rising. Glancing at the low, steely-gray clouds blowing in from the Baltic, I realized we would have little more than five hours of light today, and by four this afternoon it would be dark.

Like all the canals and waterways in Petrograd, the River Fontanka had been captured and tamed several centuries earlier by the work of thousands upon thousands of serfs. Essentially transformed into a broad granite-lined canal, the river had once marked the very edge of the city but was now an elegant waterway lined with five- and six-story apartment buildings, none taller than the dome of the Winter Palace's cathedral, as was the imperial decree throughout the entire city. Where our street,

Goroxhavaya, crossed the dark waters, many wealthier merchants lived in expansive flats, while up and around Nevsky Prospekt, many palaces, including the Anichkov Palace, the home of the Dowager Empress herself, could be found.

Reaching the river, I turned right again, heading directly into a freezing wind that came whooshing down the frozen river and bit at me like a wolf. Clutching my cloak as tightly as I could, I trekked on.

Some ten minutes later I was within a block or two of Nevsky when I felt someone tugging at the back of my cloak. Spinning around, I saw a filthy young boy dressed in ragged homespun, probably a war orphan who made his living stealing from people's pockets and bags.

"Get away from me!" I shouted.

The boy, no more than ten, didn't flinch. Instead, as the freezing wind whipped around us, he lunged toward me. I jumped back and was ready to scream when I saw that he was pressing a piece of paper at me.

"What is it? What do you want?"

He touched his throat and then his mouth and shook his head, and I realized the child couldn't speak. He was obviously not only dirt poor but mute. And staring into this child's narrow blue eyes and noticing his bright cheeks, I thought of the rubles I had taken. Of course I could give him some. Before I could, however, he grabbed my hand and shoved the bit of paper into it. I assumed, of course, it was simply a note begging for help — written by someone else, for surely this destitute urchin was illiterate — but when I unfolded it I saw a few lines of verse scrawled in fine handwriting.

Love tyrannizes all the ages
But youthful, virgin hearts drive
A blessing from its blasts and rages,
Like fields in spring when storms arrive.

Recognizing a few lines from Pushkin's prose poem *Evgeni Onegin,* my heart suddenly started pounding.

"Where is he?" I demanded.

The boy grinned a sloppy smile — half his teeth were missing — and waved me to follow. It didn't even occur to me to hesitate, and I quickly followed him across the wide road. As we headed down a narrow side street, the child grabbed my hand and clutched it in his, squeezing my fingers tightly.

Within a half block he steered me through an arched passage and into the cobbled courtyard of a four- or five-story building.

There he stopped immediately. Holding up just one of his fingers to me, I understood.

"Sure, I'll wait right here," I said.

The boy nodded, dashed back to the edge of the passage, and peered around, obviously checking the street to see if we had been followed. Satisfied that we were alone, he scurried back with a grin, snatched my hand again in his, and led me to a far corner of the courtyard. Descending three steps, we entered a decrepit *chai'naya* — teahouse — with a low ceiling, hardly any light, and a handful of heavy wooden tables. Behind a counter stood two plump *starushki,* their heads bound in kerchiefs, one tending a large nickel samovar, the other making blini on a black iron skillet.

"Greetings, Boriska," said one of the old women to the boy. "Can we get you a glass of tea today?"

His grin as big as ever, he shook his head and continued pulling me along. At least, I thought, the child has somewhere warm to go.

Following Boriska, I passed through a beaded curtain and into a room with just two tables. Boriska pointed to me and then to a stool.

"Of course," I said, sitting down.

Nodding with pleasure that he'd done his

job, the child then raised a hand in farewell.

"Wait," I said, grabbing him by the hand. "Where are your parents?"

He smiled sadly and shrugged.

"Where do you live? Do you have anywhere to go at night?"

He scratched his neck and shrugged again, squinting his eyes in obvious embarrassment.

"I'm going to give you two things, Boriska," I said, reaching into my pocket and pulling out the roll of money. "Here's two hundred rubles — that's a lot of money."

His eyes widened and his head bobbed up and down. Whoever had given my father this stack of bills, this child could certainly use it as much or more than anyone else.

"And here's something even more valuable," I said, handing him one of my father's little notes. "Can you read?"

He shook his head.

"It's from a man known as Father Grigori Rasputin — he's my father."

The child's eyes widened and he stepped back, biting his bottom lip.

"Don't worry, the note just asks that your request be granted. For example, if you want to stay at a children's home, all you have to do is present this paper and they will take you in. Do you understand, Boriska?"

He nodded, pushed the money and the note into his pocket, and leaned forward and kissed me on the cheek. In a flash, he turned and darted off, charging through the beaded curtain.

I was sitting in a small room with yellowed pine paneling and a low ceiling that sagged in places. Running my hand over the rough tabletop, I noted that it was clunky and heavy, made out of crude pieces of wood. I doubted if anyone but locals ever came here, either to warm up with a cup of tea during work or to sober up before going home. My eyes turned to the beaded curtain. Would he really come through there, pushing aside the clattering wooden beads?

Instead, Sasha came quietly from behind, saying softly, "That was terribly kind of you."

Rising quickly to my feet, I spun around to see him emerging from a small doorway. "What was?"

"Helping that boy."

"I didn't know you were watching." Glancing at Sasha's left arm, I saw that it was wrapped in a fresh white bandage. "How's your —"

Before I could finish he wrapped his good

right arm around me, pulled me into his embrace, and kissed me firmly on the lips. In the first instant, every bit of confusion seemed to flee my body. In the second instant, I knew this was wrong.

"Sasha, no," I said, pulling away. "I can't."

"But —"

"We need to talk." I stepped back, but only slightly. "Did you get a doctor to look at your arm?"

"Yes. The wound's been cleaned, disinfected, and stitched up. I'll be fine."

"Good."

He raised his right hand, pressing the back of his fingers against my cheek. It was as if we were old lovers who'd said it all and had no need to say more. But of course nothing could have been further from the truth.

Like a soldier bidding farewell, he said, "I can only stay a moment, Maria — I have to leave town in a day or two — but . . . but —"

"Sasha, someone came to our door last night, a very important person: a minister, actually. And he told me there'd been a disturbance the night before, something about a fugitive."

He cast his dark brown eyes downward but didn't say anything.

"That was you, wasn't it, Sasha. They were

chasing you, right?"

He nodded. "I was at a meeting . . . it was secret, you see. But somebody informed on us and we were raided. Half the people were beaten and arrested. I got away, but not before someone lunged at me with a knife. I jumped out a window and started running." He turned away from me and shook his head. "I know I shouldn't have come to your house; it put you in danger as well. But I'd been running and bleeding and . . . and I didn't know where else to go, I really don't know anyone here in the capital. The day before, I'd already walked by your house five or six times, just hoping to see you. . . . I'm sorry."

"Sasha, what's going on? What are you involved in?"

"I can't tell you."

"That's not good enough."

He turned, looked me straight in the eyes, started to say one thing, and then said another. "Of course not."

"I thought you were someone special, Sasha — a man who loved poetry and words. I assumed you were someone terribly open and honest — a man who wasn't afraid of his own heart. And yet I find no complete truth in your words, not a scrap of honesty, not a —"

"My grandfather was a serf," he began, in a plain matter-of-fact voice, "who, after he was liberated, started building barrels, cutting and sawing and hammering them one at a time. They were wonderful barrels, the best. My father — Igor Pavlovich is his name; I wish you could meet him — eventually took over the business. Today it's a real factory, the largest barrel factory in Novgorod. Actually, our barrels are used for shipping almost all the soap flakes in our province.

"As for my mother, Olga, she is the daughter of a priest. She's nice, she can read. I have one younger sister. And I had a young brother, Anton, but . . . but he was killed."

When he ventured no details, I asked, "How? In the war?"

Sasha shook his head. "Anton was twelve, I was fifteen . . . we were playing on a frozen creek. There was open water up ahead, and he told me to come back. But I wanted to look into the water and see if there were any fish. Just then I saw this huge one, a sturgeon, which used to be plentiful but by then were very rare. I couldn't help but step forward. And that's when the ice broke. I fell in and sank like a rock. I would have gone right to the bottom if Anton hadn't jumped in and pulled me up. Do you understand? He was my baby brother, and . . . and he saved me! He pushed me up on the ice, but when I reached over to grab him his hand slipped and he was washed away by the current. The water . . . it was so clear, so cold . . . the last I saw of him were the bottoms of his felt boots. . . ."

"I'm sorry," I said, reaching out and touching him on the arm.

"What can I say?" He let out a deep enormous breath. "It broke my father's heart. My world changed after that from one of simplicity to, quite frankly, one of torment. It was all my fault, of course. I was the older one, the big brother, the one who was supposed to look after him."

"And that's why you write, to ease you conscience?"

He shrugged. "I've been looking for answers ever since."

"So tell me, Sasha, you're not a terrorist or a revolutionary, are you?"

His brow furrowed and he turned away. "I can't talk about it."

"Are you a deserter?"

"Maria, please . . . I've taken an oath." He turned back to me and took my hand in his. "There's only one thing you have to know — that I want you to know: I never betrayed anything you said to the woman who tried to kill your father, I never spoke to her or even laid eyes on her before those moments. Please, you have to believe me when I say I've never done anything to hurt your family, and I never would. I can't leave with you thinking otherwise."

"Then —"

Suddenly a herd of deep voices emerged from the other room, and Sasha immediately stiffened. Had I been followed after all?

"Maybe one day I can explain, Maria," he whispered, as he pulled away. "Maybe one day you'll understand. I hope so. I don't know if we'll ever see each other again, but —"

"Don't say that!" Determined not to lose him again, I said, "We have to talk more. There's an alley that comes to the rear of our building. Meet me there at the back door in two hours."

"But —"

"Don't worry, that door isn't guarded, no one will see you. I'll come down and we'll go somewhere and talk. You can't keep running in and out of my life like this. Meet me there, agreed?"

He nodded quickly, glancing toward the noise coming from the other room.

"Two hours!" I reiterated. "And if you're

not there, if you don't show up, don't ever dare try to see me again."

"I'll be there, I promise."

Now came the sounds of heavy boots pouring into the little teahouse. In a panic, Sasha pecked me on the cheek, turned — and disappeared.

CHAPTER 11

I sat there for a few minutes, wiping my eyes on the sleeve of my cloak. When I returned to the front of the *chai'naya,* I saw not a group of military police or secret police. Rather, they were factory workers, come in for a glass of tea and some hot blini to warm their bones. But Sasha was already gone.

Would he really come to our house in two hours' time? I had to believe he would, for the thought that he wouldn't was almost too painful to bear. I knew, of course, that if he didn't show up, I would have to end it all, whatever hopes and dreams I had. But at least he'd told me what my heart needed to know — he hadn't, after all, betrayed me. I believed him. Even more, I believed that he cared every bit as much for me as I did for him.

Shaking my head, I hurried from the teahouse and into the chilly air. Within minutes I was making my way once again along the Fontanka. As I stared across the frozen waters, I knew something had been rekindled, something I had thought long extinguished. I knew that what I felt was going to burn a good long while, if not forever. And it was going to hurt, of that I was sure.

But I had a task to do, did I not? Although I was tempted to return home and wallow in self-pity, I continued toward Nevsky Prospekt, my pace slower than before, my thoughts far sadder. In the harshest way, I had come to understand that Papa was a lover of a great many, something I knew for certain I could never be. Indeed, I was beginning to realize my heart had been stolen by one person and I doubted if I would ever recover it — even if I never saw Sasha again.

As I approached 46 Fontanka, the palace of the very noble Galitzine family, I glanced up and saw the elegant figure of Countess Carlowa herself staring anxiously, it seemed, from the center box bay window on the second floor. She'd been pointed out to me before, so I knew it was her, and there she now stood in a long blue silk dress with a strand of pearls draped from her neck. She turned and glanced down at me on the sidewalk, and our eyes met for the briefest of moments. I knew of the sadness over-whelming me, but what of her? Why did she appear so anxious? Who knew what lay ahead for either one of us — for her, married into a branch of the Romanov family, and for me, daughter of an infamous peasant — but right then I couldn't help but sense that she too felt as if we were treading a quagmire. Was Peter the Great's beloved city, built by thousands of pathetically downtrodden serfs on nothing but swampland, about to open up and swallow the entire Empire? Perhaps. Rumor had it that even the Dowager Empress had fled the capital.

Glancing ahead, I spotted the massive bronze horses of the Anichkov Bridge, poised so elegantly at each corner, and, beneath them, seemingly in miniature, a sleek black horse pulling a fanciful sleigh across the Fontanka. Rather than proceeding as far as Nevsky, however, I stopped at the rear of the corner building, the huge red Sergeeivski Palace, which the Tsaritsa's sister had all but abandoned after her husband was assassinated. Leaving her glittering position, the Grand Duchess Elizavyeta Fyodorovna had founded a monastery outside of Moscow, and now this most impressive palace was inhabited by her nephew and onetime ward, the young and dashing Grand Duke Dmitri Pavlovich.

I ducked through a narrow rear gate and into a dark alley that ran directly behind the palace, whereupon I immediately encountered a line of some thirty or forty destitute and freezing souls. Nearly half of them were soldiers, some missing both legs, some only one, while the rest were impoverished women and *babushki,* the entire shivering lot awaiting the grand duke's mercy and maybe a tin cup of hot soup and a slice of black bread. Even in my simple cloak I was better dressed than any of them — indeed, some of the soldiers weren't even wearing coats but stood there with filthy blankets over their shoulders. As soon as they spotted me weaving in and around them, a small charge rippled through the group, and any number of filthy, begging hands were thrust into my face. While these pour souls stood nearly freezing to death down here, I wondered what the young grand duke's French chef was preparing for him upstairs on the *belle étage.* Caviar and veal, accompanied by a pleasant Baron de Rothschild wine? Crab and goose paté, served with an elegant French champagne?

Papa had strictly warned me to avoid such indigent groups, which, as the war dragged on, were cropping up all over the city. And he was absolutely right. I shouldn't be back here mingling with them, not because they might attack me but because the threat of typhus and typhoid was growing day by day. From the moaning and hoarse coughs I heard, there was no doubt these people were either covered with lice or had drunk infected waters. Or both. For fear of being recognized, however, I knew I couldn't go to the main entrance, so I pressed the folds of my cloak over my nose and mouth and tried to avoid brushing up against anyone. I didn't waste a moment before proceeding to a large, rather dilapidated wooden door on which I quickly pounded.

"It's no use," said a worn voice behind me.

I turned and looked down at a sickly woman, bent and shivering on the frozen granite cobblestones. Her face was splotchy, her nose swollen and drippy, and her eyes weeping with yellow mucus. Though half her teeth were missing, she couldn't have been more than forty. I supposed she would be dead within a week or two. Perhaps sooner.

"If the Grand Duchess Elizavyeta Fyodorovna were here, she wouldn't leave us to freeze out outside like dogs," the ill woman muttered, as spittle dripped in a long stream from her mouth. "But she's off in Moscow at her monastery. They say she's as beautiful as ever, though instead of gowns and jewels she now wears a gray habit. A pity for us, because" — and she swiped goo from her lips — "because now all we have is the young grand duke."

"And he doesn't care about the *narod*," the masses, complained the scratchy voice of a man in line. "Two days ago he sent down a bit of soup, but that was all."

"For the sake of God," countered the woman, "let's hope he does at least that again today."

I kept pounding, harder and faster, and finally I heard a heavy bolt being worked and pulled aside. A long moment later, the door was cracked open, revealing a skinny old man with a huge forehead and narrow chin. His eyes were milky white and he leaned toward me, squinting like a mole.

"How many times do I have to tell you — *sevodnya soopa nyetoo!*" he shouted, like a prison guard.

"Please," I said, "I'm not here today asking for soup."

He looked me up and down but was obviously unable to see much. "Then who are you and what do you want?"

"I'm here to see Elena Borisovna."

"And why should I admit you?"

I reached quickly into my pocket and pulled out a hundred-ruble note. When he failed to see the money, I took his hand and stuffed the bill into it.

"Here's one hundred rubles for your trouble. Please, tell her that the daughter of Our Friend is here."

He shrugged, massaged the note between his fingertips, and then pushed the door open. "Come in."

Leaving the line of destitute women and soldiers in the cold, I stepped through the short doorway into a long dark corridor with a low arched brick ceiling. As soon as I was across the threshold, the old man slammed the thick door shut and slid a long iron bolt in place.

"Follow me," he commanded.

"I would prefer to wait here," I countered, handing him another hundred-ruble note.

He lifted the note close to his eyes and smiled. *"Konyechno."* Of course.

Surely this old man had worked at the palace his entire life, perhaps as the cloakroom attendant, where he would have handled princely capes and furs until his vision deteriorated. In any case, palace intrigues were nothing new to him, and he tottered off, using one hand to feel his way along the heavy stone wall. My eyes did not leave him as he made his way to the far end of the corridor and disappeared to the left.

I found a short wooden stool and sat down. Elena Borisovna, whom I sought, had been the *lectrice* who'd taught Russian to Grand Duchess Elizavyeta Fyodorovna when she'd first arrived in this country from Germany. And it was none other than my very own father who had received Elena one dark and rainy night just two years ago. Her eyes flooded with tears, the older woman had burst into our apartment and fallen on her knees. Her ten-year-old grandson, Pasha, had been hit by a carriage and was dying, she sobbed. The doctors said there was no hope. Couldn't Father Grigori do something? Anything? Papa didn't hesitate, not one moment, even though Elena was part of Grand Duchess Elizavyeta Fyodorovna's court, which was well known for its hatred of my father. Rushing off with Elena to a secret location, Papa spent the entire night laying hands on the child and praying. And that night Father proved yet again to be a funnel for *Xhristos,* pouring divine benevolence from the heavens through his own body and into the boy's crushed limbs. Miraculously, not only did the boy live through the night, he was back up and running around within a mere two months, just as my father had predicted.

Nearly ten minutes later I finally heard some feet slowly shuffling toward me. The old man emerged around the corner and beckoned me with a brusque wave of his arm.

"This way."

I got up and hurried after him, following him through a maze of brick passageways, each one smaller than the last. At last he opened a door framed with cobwebs and showed me into a small chamber. My eyes darting about, I saw that the only light came from a small barred window set in a wall that was as thick as the bastions of a fortress.

"Wait here," he said, his breath like steam in the cold room.

He disappeared, shutting the door behind him. It was near freezing, and when I touched the white tile stove in the corner, I found it as cold as a cobblestone. Looking around, I saw ancient blue-and-gold wallpaper peeling in great sheets from the walls, a brown horsehair couch covered with thick dust, a crooked table on which stood a terribly dented samovar, and an ash bucket overflowing with gray grit.

Minutes passed again before I heard

another set of steps. Finally the door creaked open and Elena entered, her gray hair covered by a scarf, which she carefully removed and folded. Slightly heavy, with a round, sweet face, she wore a pale yellow dress that dragged on the ground behind her.

"Hello, my child," she said in a hushed voice, as she extended her hand. "I'm so sorry to receive you in such a horrid manner."

I understood. Of course I did. If her mistress the grand duchess found out that she had contact with us, the Rasputins, Elena would more than likely lose her courtesy room in the palace. This was why we were meeting back here in this lost chamber and why she had covered her head with a scarf: she didn't want anyone to notice her back here, she didn't want any tongues to start fluttering. It was also why I hadn't gone to the main entrance on Nevsky. There might be only a single young grand duke in residence, but palaces such as this were nothing less than small hotels, housing upwards of several hundred courtiers and servants. Naturally, the fewer who saw us the better.

"How is your grandson, Elena Borisovna?" I began.

"Spasibo, xhorosho." Thank you, well.

"I'm happy to say he's fully recovered. My gratitude a thousand times over to your father."

"He was only doing his duty." I reached into my pocket, pulled out one of my father's small notes, and held it toward her. "I need some help."

"Please, child, I don't know what you have there, but it's not necessary," she said, folding my fingers around the note and pressing it back. "I am forever indebted to your father. What can I do for you?"

"I'm afraid I've come here because I have every reason to believe my father's life is in great danger."

Elena stepped closer and wrapped both her hands around mine. She looked at me tenderly, softly, her eyes moist with sympathy.

"My child, your father's life has been in danger for years."

"Yes, but last night an anonymous letter was delivered to Papa, threatening his life. It was sent by a group of men, ten of them, and — and I was wondering if you might —"

"I'm sorry. I know nothing about any such letter." With a sad smile, she added, "But you're right, it's worse now. I know." The older woman sighed and shook her head, then stepped away and peered out the window. "Everyone's talking about him — everyone in the salons of fashionable homes, everyone in the stores, almost everyone on the street."

"He's that widely" — I could barely say it — "he's that widely hated?"

"Yes. I'm sorry to say that, among proper society, most definitely."

My eyes welled up, and for a moment I was speechless.

Elena Borisovna, unable to look at me, continued staring out the small barred window. "You should be aware that people in the highest society talk openly of the need to do away with your father. They speak not only openly but also of how it should be done. And soon."

"Do you mean the grand dukes?"

"Yes, exactly. They consider your father a great stain on the House of Romanov, a stain that must be forcefully and quickly removed. They believe your father has not only ruined the prestige of the Sovereign Emperor himself but of all of them as well."

"Does this include Grand Duke Dmitri Pavlovich?"

She turned slowly yet purposefully toward the door. Could someone be on the other side? Not daring to risk it, Elena Borisovna simply looked right at me and nodded.

"I see," I replied.

"Even worse, there's gossip that German spies have infiltrated your home and surround your father."

"I've heard that too, but it's nothing but lies!"

"I know, but such is the talk."

Gathering my courage, I broached a subject two women were never supposed to address. "Can you tell me, please, what is the true relationship between the grand duke and Prince Felix?"

The old woman's face blanched at the question; then she returned to me, gently taking my hands again in her grasp, and in almost a whisper, said, "The grand duke, of course, is a lover of many women, and the prince, of course, is married to the Tsar's own niece, but . . ." She paused, drinking in her own breath as if afraid of speaking the words. "But under this very roof I have seen the passion the two men have for each other. There is frequent touching and mutual kissing, that much all servants in the palace have seen with their own eyes. I believe, however, that the real nature of their relationship is darker, even . . . lascivious."

So now it was confirmed by an eyewitness: The prince and the grand duke were lovers. But how did that make them dangerous to my father? Or were they not? Wasn't there something far more worrisome — the plot by the elder Romanov uncles seeking to dispose of the peasant who had penetrated their family? Of course, the danger posed by the young grand duke could be of a far more carnal nature. Yes, most definitely. As horrible as it sounded, Grand Duke Dmitri could be seeking to destroy Papa for reasons of the flesh. He could see my father as some sort of competition for the object of his own affection, Prince Felix. Or were things even more twisted than I could fathom? Could the grand duke and Prince Felix be working in conjunction, not to kill my father but perhaps to bed him? I knew of many women who fawned over my father, who begged to be taken by him. Then again, it could be something altogether different. Perhaps it was really true, perhaps the much-rumored *Khlyst* ark of nobles, headed by the fabled Prince O'ksandr, did exist, meeting secretly beneath some palace, and these two young men belonged to that clandestine group. But even in these dark, desperate days of war, could these young nobles really be trying to draw my father into their mysterious world? Quite possibly. And yet . . . though I could see the three points — my father, Prince Felix, and Grand Duke Dmitri — I couldn't connect them in a triangle, at least not one that made any sense.

"But, Elena Borisovna, is this simply all a game for Grand Duke Dmitri and Prince Felix? Are they merely playing with an innocent peasant, seeing what they can make him do or what they can get out of him?"

"Absolutely not," she said, quite sternly. "Please, the dangers are very real. Everyone knows the country is about to boil over. There's talk of nothing else, and I have no reason to doubt it. In more than one salon, I've heard that the grand dukes have formed a cabal intent not only on killing your father, but . . . but on kidnapping the Empress and banishing her to a monastery in Siberia."

"Bozhe moi," I said, quickly crossing myself.

"There's worse." She hesitated, clearly afraid of the treasonous words that were about to pass her lips. "They talk of deposing the Emperor himself and crowning the little Heir Tsarevich, with one of the grand dukes as regent."

I couldn't imagine such treachery and deception in any family, let alone our royal one, and I quickly crossed myself yet again and again and again. Was this how low Russia had fallen, that to preserve its power the House of Romanov felt it necessary to obliterate a mere peasant?

"Please, child, I beg you, pass these words to your father and see that he passes them to the very highest personages," continued Elena Borisovna, obviously referring to the Tsar and Tsaritsa. "And remember: Once an angry tiger is released from its cage and tastes fresh blood, it's almost impossible to recapture it. Instead, the beast prefers a knife to its heart."

She took my hand in hers and kissed it, then spread her scarf over her head and headed out the door. Just before she disappeared, she turned back with a sorrowful smile.

"God bless you and yours, child, for I doubt we shall meet again."

I stood there barely able to move. The Empress locked away in some distant monastery? The Emperor dethroned and perhaps — dare I even think it — executed? It was too hard to imagine such heinous events in such modern days. After all, this was not a drama of Shakespeare and we were not living in ancient Muscovia, where tsars killed their own sons and disdained wives were thrown to the wolves.

However, if all this came to pass, if the frail Heir Tsarevich were placed on the throne, who would rule as regent, one of the Tsar's uncles, those towering, aged men now in their sixties and seventies? No, in these days of turmoil and war, the common people wouldn't accept that. An ancient Romanov, one of the brothers of Aleksander III, would mean a complete return to autocracy and authoritarianism. If that were to happen, there was no doubt in my mind that a regent like that, one of the "dread uncles," as they were commonly known, would ignite revolution.

Another possibility might be the Tsar's younger brother, Grand Duke Mikhail. And yet while he might be acceptable to the people, he wouldn't be to the Romanov clan, because he had married morganatically — breaking strict family laws, he'd not taken a bride from another royal house. Worse still, he'd not even wed a woman of title but rather a mere commoner, the divorced wife of a cavalry captain.

So who would be an acceptable regent? It would have to be someone young, someone who could offer hope to the Russian people and symbolized a promising, progressive future. But who was that? Who could the powerful Romanov uncles control and dominate, even manipulate?

Of course: none other than the young and dashing Grand Duke Dmitri Pavlovich, who suffered from such horrible "grammatical errors."

Which one of us, I thought standing in that freezing room, was a greater fool, my father or me? Just last month, a treacherous speech had been made at the Duma, and my father had not only brushed it away like an annoying hornet, he had persuaded me to do so as well.

"There's no need for me to hear it!" Papa had insisted.

"But, Papa, listen!"

"The only thing to the right of Purishkevich is the wall!"

Copies of this speech made by the notorious monarchist Vladimir Purishkevich were already all over town, and it came as no surprise that one had been slipped beneath our door. My voice trembling as much as my hands, I stood in my father's study, reading aloud.

" 'The disorganization of the rear is without doubt being manipulated by the enemy, and it is being accomplished by a strong, relentless hand. I take here the freedom to say that this evil springs from the Dark Forces, from those who push into high places people who are not worthy or capable of filling them. And these influences are headed by Grishka Rasputin!' "

"Lies!" shouted my father, pounding on the table. "Nothing but lies!"
I continued reading.

" 'These last nights I could find no sleep, I tell you in honesty. I lay in bed with eyes wide open and saw a series of telegrams and notes which this illiterate peasant writes, first to one minister, next another, and finally, frequently, to Aleksander Protopopov, demanding that his actions be fulfilled.' "

"Evil dogs!" snapped my father. "Black evil dogs! No more reading, daughter of mine. That's it. Enough! I will hear no more!"
"But, Papa, listen!" I begged as my eyes flew to the last lines. "Listen to this:

'The Tsar's ministers have been turned into marionettes, marionettes whose strings have been taken confidently in hand by Rasputin, whose house and home have been infiltrated with German spies and by the Empress Aleksandra Fyodor-ovna — the evil genius of Russia and her Tsar — who remains a German on the throne, foreign to country and people!' "

"Enough, I tell you!" shouted my father, grabbing the speech from my hand and ripping it to pieces. "It's nothing but lies! No one will pay attention to this . . . this Pur-ishkevich! How dare he speak of the Tsaritsa like that! In fact, it's treason. No doubt about it, he will be in jail by tomorrow! Now forget it!"

I took a deep breath. Was Papa right? Were these just the rantings of a fanatic? They had to be because the speech was just that: unequivocally treasonous.

"Everyone knows how terrible this Pur-ishkevich is," continued my father. "Why . . . why, he's part of the Black Hundreds, and just look at what they did to the Jews! The pogroms!"

"I'm so worried, Papa —"

"Nonsense. Just hornets, mettlesome hornets! If you aren't used to it, even kasha is bitter. Now take a piece of paper and write this down. I want to send a telegram to the Tsar at the front."

My hands still shaking, I snatched a piece of paper and pencil.

"19 NOVEMBER 1916," dictated Papa. "GOD GIVES YOU STRENGTH. YOURS IS VICTORY AND YOURS IS THE SHIP. NO ONE ELSE HAS AUTHORITY TO BOARD IT. Do you have that down, Maria, just as I've told you?"

"Absolutely."

"Good. Now go and see that it is sent. And then forget it. Forget all about that stupid little man's stupid little speech."

Now, waiting for the old man with the milky eyes to escort me out of the Sergeeivski Palace, I started shuddering violently. At the time, Papa had persuaded me to dismiss the speech, but I no longer could do so. All too easily I could imagine the entire scene: the fury of Purishkevich's rhetoric, and the cries of *Bravo!, A disgrace!,* and *How true!* that were said to have erupted from the other Duma members.

CHAPTER 12

Fearful of spending any more time in the grand duke's palace, I finally opened the door and stepped into the dark corridor. But which way should I go, right or left? Better yet, I thought, as my eyes searched the low vaulted passage, which was the quickest way out?

I turned right and immediately felt a fine silky veil over my face and entire head. I cried out and grabbed the strands of a spiderweb from my cheeks and hair. Feeling a creature crawl up my neck, I nervously swiped at something, and a spider, large and black, fell to the floor. Wasting no time, I ceremoniously stomped on it with my leather boot.

I wanted nothing more than to be out of here, out of these lost rooms of a ducal palace and back in our simple apartment. I wanted nothing more than to be not in my father's massive arms but pounding on his large chest, screaming and demanding to know what in the name of the Lord he was doing. How had he wandered into this minefield? What was he doing to all of us, his entire family and everyone else in the nation? Didn't he see that the Motherland was one huge tinderbox and he, sitting upon it like a *kroogli durak* — a round idiot — was the perfect fuse, which he himself had already lit? Was Papa really so naïve as not to know that everything could blow at any moment? There was only one way to save Holy Mother Russia and our Tsar: Papa had to be removed.

With this realization, I practically broke into tears, for I had arrived at the same conclusion as the powerful grand dukes. Yes, Papa had to be got rid of. The very noble relatives of the Tsar, who had disposed of countless serfs over the centuries, were probably discussing it this very moment at the Yacht Club, that hotbed of aristocratic dissent. The thought horrified me. Would they do it the way our masters always disposed of problem serfs — run him over with a troika? Or would they tie a rock to him and toss him in the river? Before they acted, I had to make Papa do what everyone wanted and no one had succeeded in doing: make him go back whence he had come, the unimaginably deep and the untouchably distant forests of Siberia.

But how?

The pleading of a youthful daughter would not be enough. Could I hire some *banditi* to drag him away? Could I slip him *narkotiki,* bundle him off, and lock him up in a monastery until the political winds shifted? No, neither would work. There was no way I was strong enough to overpower Papa's sheer physical strength, let alone the will of the mightiest and the most powerful person in the entire country, the Empress herself. Sadly, I had to recognize the truth: There was no way Aleksandra Fyodorovna would let Papa out of her desperate and hysterical grasp. By all but imperial decree, she required that he be no farther from her than a short phone call. To remove Papa from Petrograd, I would have to battle not only him but also the strong will of the powerful Empress.

As I stopped and brushed away the last of the cobwebs, I knew that, no matter my determination, there was little I could actually do. I was just going to have to be clever. Perhaps I could get my mother to send an urgent telegram, saying Dmitri had been seriously injured and, because of his mental limitations, needed his father at once.

Maybe I could convince my mother to write that she herself was just days away from death and begged for her husband's presence. No, I realized as I slumped against the stone wall. None of that would work, for, just as my father was unable to tell a lie, so was my dear innocent mother.

From somewhere I heard a set of footsteps. At first I thought it was the old man, finally come to lead me out of this tangled mass of passages. But no, these were not the shuffling steps of a half-blind fellow feeling his way along. They were much too quick for that. In fact, they were even hurried. And when I listened carefully I could tell they were the footsteps of not just one person but two.

Knowing I dared not be found down here, let alone questioned, I scanned the corridor, spotting a dark archway just a few *arzhini* ahead. Picking up the folds of my cloak and skirt in both hands, I hurried to the opening, finding not a chamber but a steep set of stairs that curled down into darkness. Within seconds it was I who was feeling the walls for direction, and I moved downward with my right hand groping the ancient, crumbling brick walls. Beneath me, my feet sensed the smooth worn stone steps, one after the other. Wasting no time, I continued until I curled around a corner into a curtain of darkness. Below me I could see virtually nothing. Turning, I gazed upward at the last of the light leaking toward me.

The footsteps were drawing ever louder, ever heavier, ever faster. Finally they slowed, and I heard the squeal of a door as it was thrown open.

"She's not in here!" shouted a man, his voice deep and coarse.

"We'll be thrown in the fire for this," groused another, his accent none too refined. "We've got to find her."

"You go that way, I'll go down here. Hurry!"

So it was indeed me they were after. But how did they know I was here? Had the old man betrayed me, or Elena Borisovna herself — or had someone else spied me?

Suddenly I heard footsteps echoing from every direction, one set from above, another somehow emerging from the darkness below, yet another ricocheting from . . . I couldn't tell where. The opposite direction? Down another set of stairs? *Gospodi,* just how many men were hunting me? Panicking, I sank back against the wall, pulling the shadows over me like an invisible cloak. How was I going to escape from this place?

I heard it then, the rough, fatty breathing

215

of a slothful soul. It was coming from up above. Yes, one of the men was right there at the top of the staircase. I closed my eyes and willed myself not to move, not even to inhale. If he descended just ten steps, I would be found. Indeed, were he a wild dog, I would already have been sniffed out and torn to pieces.

The next instant something screamed into my left ear like a high-pitched aeroplane. Then it dove into my cheek, bit me, and took hold: a mosquito. Lord, here we were on Peter's swamp, the waters of which leaked into the cellars of every building. Never mind that it was December and the air outside was well below frost, mosquitoes bred and lived year round in the subterranean territories of nearly every structure in the city. I nearly slapped it but didn't dare. A mere rustle of my clothing would give me away, for the man, whoever he was and whoever had sent him, was still right up there, lingering, listening, shuffling, snorting. Though I had no physical image of him, it was almost as if I could sense the wheels in his thick head turning, wondering what kind of fool would have gone down these lost stairs.

Then the next moment he dashed off, big feet, heavy body, hard breath. As soon as I heard his steps charging away, I slapped the mosquito and felt a splatter of blood on my cheek.

My pursuer was gone from the top of the steps but still up there charging around with another man. I could still clearly hear their running, and they were quite correct in their assumption: I had not escaped, I was still somewhere in the rotting bowels of the palace. Sooner or later, when they couldn't find me in any of the passages up there, they would return to this staircase — and this time they would come down. Turning and looking into the depths of nothing, I knew it was my only option.

I thought my eyes would adjust. And to a degree, they did. But there was simply no light with which to see. Though I could practically sense my eyes widening, there was nothing for them to drink in. And so I moved more slowly than ever, one foot after the other, feeling my way down the sloping well-worn steps, my hand dragging along the decaying brick wall like a claw. A few moments later I stepped off the last stair and sank immediately into the cradle of the mosquitoes: a *vershok* of water. Of course I couldn't see it, I only felt it, as cool murky water flooded through my leather soles and reached almost to my ankles.

I picked one foot entirely out of the water, set it back down again, and heard something rather like an echo. Of course. This was one large room down here. When the palace had been built several hundred years earlier, this very chamber had probably been dry and used as a vast storeroom. Whatever it was that had made its feudal lord so rich — grain, rare stone, lumber — had probably been pulled up the River Fontanka by barge and dragged in here. But time had caused the floors and walls to leak, and now it was flooded with a layer of water and left empty. Or was it? As I stood in the cool black water beneath this Romanov palace, I heard something: a slight wet flutter of movement. *Gospodi,* I was not alone down here.

I took a soggy half step back to the staircase. My choices were horrible. If I scurried back up the stone steps, I would undoubtedly be apprehended. If I remained down here, God only knew the result.

As desperately as if I were drinking water in a desert, my eyes gulped in a mere glimmer of light. Moving slightly to the side, I peered around a heavy column, and there, far in the distance, was what seemed like another set of steps. I started quickly wading through the shallow waters. Another staircase would lead to another part of the palace, and another part of the palace would certainly lead to another way out.

Within a few steps the water deepened, now rising up over my ankles, now lapping at the bottom of my dress. And as I waded along, I heard it again, a flutter of noise, something scurrying through the water. As if it were a beacon, I kept focused on the faint light up ahead. But then I saw them. Rats. Off to the side I saw an entire gathering of fat rodents, some the size of squirrels, half wading, half swimming, their long tails slithering behind them like snakes on the water's surface. Pressing onward, I told myself that I had seen any number of such creatures back home, and forced myself to take faint comfort in knowing that they were as afraid of me as I was of them.

What terrified me more, however, was a large sloshing noise off to my left. I came to a thick treelike stone column and stopped. I heard it again, the heavy sound of something moving through the water. That was no rodent; by the noise I knew it to be much larger. Was it a wild dog, perhaps a rabid one? What could be alive and lost and living down in this dark chamber? Then I turned the other way, saw its sheer size . . . and screamed into my hand.

This was no animal, most definitely not.

It was a man, hunched over and scurrying, his arms low and outstretched, legs tromping, hair flying. This clearly wasn't one of the grand duke's guards hunting me down, this was some demented soul living down here. I wanted to cry out for the men upstairs to come down and rescue me. Instead I bolted forward, the dark waters flying as I charged past another column, then another. The second staircase was only fifteen or twenty *arzhini* ahead, and bit by bit the light increased. If only I were quick enough, I might make it. A horrible thought struck me: My family didn't know where I was. If I was overtaken, if that crazed person tackled me and did me mortal harm, I would simply disappear. No one would even know where to begin looking for me.

Suddenly, just as I passed another of the stone columns, something leaped out. It was another man, strong and able, who grabbed me in both arms as easily as a huge bear snatching a fish from a rushing river. Before I could open my mouth to scream, his filthy calloused paw slapped over my mouth. I kicked, bit at him, and threw myself from side to side, but I was caught, hopelessly and completely, that much I immediately understood.

The next moment I felt the cool sharp

blade of a knife at my throat. "Be quiet or I'll kill you!"

I twisted to the side, but when I felt his arms and hands tighten in readiness, I forced myself to fall as still as a hare. It took every bit of my concentration to do as he instructed, and a second later the blade was lifted from my throat. The foul hand, however, was not removed from my mouth, and soon I could barely breathe.

There was a quick scratching noise and a nearby burst of light. My terrified eyes darted to it, and there I saw the first man, equally as filthy, lighting the stump of a candle with a simple match. In but a moment, the entire underground space blossomed with murky yellow light. And then I saw a third and a fourth fellow, all of them covered with unbelievable grime, all stepping out of the darkness, swarming through the water toward me like confident crocodiles circling a kill. By their haggard bearded faces and from their torn khaki clothing I recognized who they were: not mere soldiers but deserters. And not wounded men who had hobbled from the front but healthy ones who had run for their lives from the trenches, only to flee to the capital city and be forced to hide beneath its festering surface. There was no question that if such

221

young, strong, seemingly healthy men as these were discovered, their punishment would be quick and definitive: They would be shot. So here they were, somehow existing in the last place anyone would ever look for a deserter, the dank cellar of the Tsaritsa's own sister.

"Who are you, princess?" said one of them, square-jawed and eager, it seemed, to devour me. "Or maybe you're a countess?"

I shook my head furiously. God only knew how they would manhandle me, but I was sure they would, for I could see not only lusty hunger in his eyes but furious, burning anger. They'd been forced to fight in a war not of their making or for their benefit, a war of and against kings.

"Are you one of them?" he said, pointing upward.

A tall lanky one stepped forward, his feet stirring through the water and a sly grin spreading on his face. "She's not so bad. Looks like we've caught ourselves a nice little morsel!"

"A tasty one too!" said the fourth, who was completely bald.

I felt it then, a crude calloused hand pawing at my neck, pushing aside my cloak, tearing at my dress. But of course there was nothing hanging there, neither pearls nor diamonds. I struggled, then froze as the arms wrapped more tightly around me. The next moment I felt a hand squeezing my breast, then groping downward and plunging into the pocket of my cloak. Like a bear cub who'd discovered honey, he pulled out his treasure with glee.

"Money!" he proclaimed.

There was a whoop of hushed excitement as they examined the stack of rubles, a veritable fortune to them. Then, as one held me from behind, the other three were upon me, crudely exploring, poking through the folds of my garb and over my body, hands plunging over breasts, earlobes, and privates. I twisted and kicked, all to no avail, as they checked my clothing over and over, pulling out a bit more money and then, of course, grabbing something strange to them. The little stack of notes.

"What's that?" the lanky one asked, leaning forward. "It's something written . . . what's it say?"

The bit of candle was lifted higher, and while one man held me from behind, the other three peered at the notes. I watched as they focused on the scraps of paper, as they examined the writing and tried to tell what it was. One of them scratched his head. Another moved his lips. These deserters were like ninety percent of our pathetic, worn army: simple uneducated, illiterate peasants, who wanted nothing more than to go home to their huts, their families, and their tiny plots of land.

The shortest of them all, a round fellow, studied the papers closely, and said, "I think they're little letters."

"But what do they say?" asked the bald man.

"It's all from the same hand, that much I can tell. And . . . and look down here. I think they all have the same signature."

"Sure, but. . . ."

The round one began to sound: "Fa . . . Fath . . . Father. . . ." So shocked was he that he stopped and stared right at me. "Father Grigori!"

A collective groan of amazement erupted from them all. The three in front simply stared, while the man who held me tightened his grasp from behind. Just who did these soldiers think I was? Some member of the nobility drawn into a plot? A messenger of the Tsaritsa? A German spy?

The square-jawed one gazed at me as if he meant to rip out my throat. "Who are you? And why do you have these notes?"

When the hand loosened only slightly from my mouth, I gasped, and said, "My name is Matryona Grigorevna." I took in a gulp of air. "I am the elder daughter of Grigori Effimovich Rasputin."

"What?" gasped the square-jawed thug, crossing himself fervently. "You mean to tell us you're Father Grigori's child?"

I nodded.

"Where are you from?"

"The village Pokrovskoye."

"Who was your grandfather?"

"Effim. Effim Yakovlevich."

The tall one muttered, "That's right. Effim Yakovlevich, that's Rasputin's father. That's who my own father used to trade wheat with, the very one."

What was this all about? My eyes ran from one filthy face to the next. Was I not about to be raped and murdered?

Suddenly the man behind me loosened his grip. Indeed, he quickly released me, and when he stepped aside I saw that he was lean and hard. To my complete astonishment, he bowed his head to me and crossed himself. The other three did so as well. In a blink of an instant they were all beating their foreheads and chests and bowing to me as if I were some kind of saint. One of them even reached out, took my cold trembling hand, and kissed it.

The round one pointed to the tall one.

"Me and him are from Tobolsk. These other two are from Tyumen."

I nearly collapsed. In a faint of relief, I nearly dropped right into the shallow waters. These were my people, my neighbors, my fellow Siberians. All of them were from towns within a few *versts* of my own. And instead of seeing me as someone from the upper ruling class, instead of branding me an enemy, they knew I was one of their own. Only more, for I was his. Right then and there I knew there was a God, for he had seen the dangers upstairs and led me down to them, these poor filthy *muzhiki,* my islands of safety.

"But what are you doing down here?" said the tall one. "You shouldn't be here. It's far too dangerous for a young woman such as you."

"My father's life is being threatened, and I came here seeking information," I explained. "But someone's after me now. Some men are looking for me upstairs. I don't know who and I don't know why they want me, but I've got to get out of here — out of the palace. And I don't know how."

Long fearful of the master's whip, my countrymen had learned centuries ago not to speak their minds, at least not outside their own huts. Instead they had perfected the art of communication by discreet glance — a downward gaze, a raised eyebrow, a narrowed eye. An entire silent conversation could be carried on in this manner, as it was just then, right before me.

The lean hard man who'd first captured me said, "Pasha and me will stay here and make sure no one follows."

The short round one nodded. "Right, and Volodya and I will get you out."

They all started scrambling to their jobs, but then the lanky one said, "We got to give back the money."

"No," I said quickly. "Keep the rubles. Go buy yourselves some food and clothes. And use the notes — they'll open doors everywhere. Use them for permission to board a train and get back home to your families."

As if they were His Majesty's Own Hussars and I a princess of the royal blood, they all kissed my hand, one by one. And then Volodya, the lanky soldier, took the lone candle, and the round one, whom he called Ivan, took me by the arm, and together they led me from the large wet storeroom through a rotted oak door and down a tunnel that led beneath the street to the River Fontanka. We scrambled along this dank underground passage that had once been used to carry goods directly to and from the river, and within a matter of three or four minutes a miracle did occur. Volodya and Ivan heaved open an ancient door, the one they used to get in and out of the palace, and which I now stepped through. Emerging like a squinting mole onto the edge of the icy River Fontanka, I found myself standing on a thick wooden platform tucked directly beneath the dark stones of the Anichkov Bridge.

Volodya bowed to me, and said, "It's nothing less than a miracle that one of us, a real *muzhik,* finally has the ear of God's Own Anointed."

"Absolutely," said Ivan, with a shy smile. "It finally seems that God has heard our prayers, for as long as Father Grigori dines with the tsars, then maybe, just maybe, there is hope."

With tears in my eyes, I turned and hurried off, my wet feet quickly turning numb and my damp skirt icing over.

You have no idea what fear shot through us when Maria Rasputina was spotted sneaking into the Sergeeivski Palace. Grand Duke Dmitri Pavlovich was home at the time, just upstairs, and he flew into an absolute panic. He sent some of his guards to find her, but they searched everywhere without success. Somehow, Rasputin's daughter had got in and out completely undetected. Can you imagine?

Almost immediately the grand duke called us all to his palace. I was sure that our plot had been found out and the Tsar or the Tsaritsa would imprison us all before we could act. I remember we gathered in the corner drawing room, the one overlooking the Fontanka and Nevsky. All afternoon we just sat there, drinking shot after shot of vodka and waiting for arrest. But nothing happened. Nothing.

Finally Dmitri Pavlovich, who had definitely drunk too much, got up and started shouting,

"That little whore is on to something, I tell you. She knows what we're up to, so now we have to kill her too! We have to kill that monster and his daughter as well!"

It was decided then and there that we had to move the whole thing up by five days. We chose the palace on the Moika Kanal because, of course, of the chamber in the basement. The walls were so thick that we were sure no one would hear the screams.

CHAPTER 13

When I finally returned home, my body trembling, my shoes frozen solid, Dunya, like all women of Siberia, was appropriately horrified.

"Have you lost your mind, child?" she screamed, for like any villager she'd seen death start with a sniffle that roared into death. "Look at you, you're soaked and your teeth are chattering like a monkey's! What did you do, jump in the river? Or did someone push you? Is that what happened, did someone attack you simply because of your name? *Ai,* what horrible days these are when a daughter of Rasputin cannot safely walk the streets!"

"Papa," I mumbled, not fully aware of how much I was shivering. "I have to speak with Papa!"

"Well, not now you're not! Not until you get out of those wet clothes and into a hot bath! What are you trying to do, catch death by the tail? *Bozhe moi,* we've got to drive the cold out of you right away. Remember what happened to your uncle, the uncle you never knew because he got wet and died?"

"But where's —"

"Your father's gone out," she said, unbuttoning my cloak as quickly as an army medic treating a mortally wounded soldier.

"Is he visiting someone?" I asked desperately. "He hasn't gone out . . . alone, has he?"

"Yes, he just slipped out by himself. Right out the door like a determined tomcat. You know him and his ways."

"I have to find him," I moaned.

I needed my father. I needed to scream at him, cling to him, and sob on his shoulder. How could he be out there wandering the dangerous streets when I needed him more than ever? When he needed me the most? *Bozhe moi,* what if I was too late? What if he didn't come back? What if it happened now, this afternoon? What if those plotting grand dukes and conniving grand duchesses snatched him away and stabbed him in the heart or hung him from a lamppost?

"I'm going back out!" I said, crazy with fear and pushing away from Dunya. "I have to find him! I have to find him right now!"

"You'll do no such thing, child!" our

housekeeper shouted back, catching me like a thief by the collar.

"But I have to warn him!"

"Just look at you, you've caught death's chill! Look at how you're shaking! And your lips . . . they're absolutely blue!"

It was only then, as Dunya stripped me and I began to thaw, that I started to comprehend the fear in her words. As my frozen shoes were ripped from my feet, my toes began to throb with pain. Next, my cloak and dress were pulled off and thrown aside, and I began to shake and shiver all the more. Warmth burned away cold, and my head began to throb, and I felt suddenly, oddly, weak, even sick to my stomach. Where had I been? How had I gotten home?

Suddenly I realized I was standing there in nothing but my underlinens. All around me were little piles of soggy clothing, and Dunya was pressing something burning hot into my hands. It was a tall thin glass nestled in a metal standard. Steam was billowing into my face and burning my nostrils. I stared at the glass — where had it come from? — then up at her.

"Drink it down, my little one," coaxed Dunya. "Drink it all the way down. It's good black tea from the Caucasus. Lots of sugar, too, and a big slice of *leemoan*. It's nice and healthy and will warm you from the inside out. Drink this down while I heat you some milk. That's what you need next, hot milk to ward off a chill. *Da, da, da,* a cup of fresh hot milk loaded with rich dark honey. I've been hiding a jar of birch-forest honey from back home just for something like this. Now drink up, drink to the bottom!"

But I was not only swaying, I was trembling so much I could barely hold the glass.

"Here, *dorogaya maya,*" my dear, cooed Dunya, holding the glass to my lips, "let me help you."

I took in a bit of hot tea, fresh from the samovar, and it burned like liquid hell all the way down. *"Oi!"*

"Good, that's good, Maria. Just drink it down. Oh, if only we were home, I'd throw you in a hot *banya* this very second!" she said. "I'd throw you in and then march right after you and thrash you with a bundle of fresh birch branches — that would draw the cold right out of you, for sure! So what am I going to do here in the city? Hmm. . . . Perhaps I'll get out my cups. Yes, that would work. We've got to get the chill out of you right away."

"Nyet," I pleaded, almost in tears.

I hated being cupped. I hated lying naked on my stomach, perfectly still, as Dunya heated her thin glass cups and placed them one by one in a thoughtful pattern up and down my spine and across my shoulders. The big purplish welts they left were horrible. Even having my back massaged with sweet butter afterward did little to help the discomfort. Whether it either prevented or cured bronchitis and pneumonia, I didn't know. But both Mama and Dunya were convinced it was the only way to draw cold and congestion out of one's body, the only sure way to get the blood properly flowing in the lungs.

"Please, just a hot bath, that's all I want. Please, you don't understand — I can't waste any time. I have to find Papa!"

"You're not going anywhere, child!" she commanded, as sternly as a wardeness at the Fortress of Peter and Paul.

"But —"

"Be quiet and drink your tea!"

I sipped as fast as I could, but it burned my tongue.

And then Dunya was screaming, calling out to my sister. "Varya! Varya, draw your sister a bath! Now! At once! And make it good and hot! I want clouds of steam, do you hear? Big, huge clouds like in a real *banya*, yes? Clouds and clouds of steam for her to breathe in and melt away the chill!"

Off in the distance I heard my sister's lazy steps, hesitant, even reticent. A few moments later she poked her curious head around the corner.

"*Oi!*" she gasped upon seeing me, her eyes opening as large as fifty-kopeck pieces.

I must have looked awful, half naked, shivering and dripping.

"Go on, Varya, do it!" shrieked Dunya. "A hot bath for your elder sister — now!"

Varya disappeared as fast as a terrified mouse, Dunya wrapped her large warm body around me like a living blanket and started rubbing my back in firm, quick strokes, and I took several more sips.

"That's it, *dorogaya maya*. Drink up, Maria. I'm going to get you in a hot bath, and then I'm going to heat you some sweet fresh milk with forest honey gathered not too far from your very own home, just past the fields where your brother and mother work. You know the place — yes? — where the birch trees are so thick and the bees so busy? Now, don't you worry, child, everything's going to be all right."

No, it wasn't. No, it wouldn't be. She couldn't see what I saw, all the terrible possibilities. They could be killing Papa at this very moment. They could be turning him inside out or dragging him behind one of their fancy motorcars.

"Dunya, you don't understand —"

"I understand everything."

"No, you don't. I have to find Papa right away. I have to warn him. He's in terrible danger."

"*Oi,* such dark days we're living through."

"But —"

"My child, you're not going anywhere until you've sat for an hour in hot water, do you understand? One full hour, am I clear? And after that you should go to bed for the rest of the day. Yes, that's the best plan, bed and soup. Lots of hot fresh cod soup. And rest. Don't worry, I'll bring you your favorite poetry books, and you can lie in bed and read. If we follow that course, I'm sure you'll be fine tomorrow and the day after, and then you'll be in an open field."

I should never have come home, I realized. I was practically shackled, trapped here for at least a day, if not two. The greatest of storms was about to roll across Mother Russia, and it would strike only one place to do any real damage: my father. He was the lightning rod, and I saw that as never before, that that was his role in the events of our country. Those who wanted revolution not only knew it but wanted the lightning to strike him so everything would explode.

Others, such as the Romanovs, upon whose House my father was so wildly dancing, were terrified that this lightning would in fact strike him. Perhaps I'd finally eaten enough fish to see what Papa did, for the storm roiling on the horizon was all too clear. I also saw the River Neva rushing with blood. I saw the bodies floating in its turgid waters — my father's, I feared, among the many. But was I not wiser than he was? Shouldn't all of us, Papa included, leave before these things actually transpired? Might not the storm then whoosh harmlessly past?

Leaving a sloppy wet trail of spilt tea behind, I was trundled down the hall to the washroom. Dunya and Varya peeled away the last of my underlinens and forced me, baptismal-like, into the burning water and right under its placid steaming skin. With all their force they held me like that, beneath its surface, until finally I screamed a mass of bubbles. As limp as a piece of soiled clothing beaten against the rocks in our river, I was finally yanked back up.

"I'm going to heat some milk," snapped Dunya to my sister. "Don't let her move from that tub!"

When our housekeeper was gone, I glanced up at my younger sister, who leaned against the wall, her arms folded tightly, her bottom lip pinched in her teeth. I'd always been the stronger one, and I wanted to shout at her to stop staring at my pale, watery body, to leave me alone, better yet, to help me escape. But when I looked up at her, all I could do was burst into one long painful sob.

Whenever the bath water began to cool even slightly, Dunya made it scalding again. Even worse, she made me drink not one but two hot cups of painfully sweet milk, thickened with so much dark forest honey that it was nearly the color of the fancy bonbons made in the palace confectionary.

An hour later I was, as promised, finally liberated. Whereas before I was faint because of the cold, now I was light-headed because of the heat. As Dunya wrapped me tightly in towels, I leaned on my sister for support.

As our housekeeper fashioned a towel around my head, she said reassuringly, "That's it, child. Everything's going to be fine. I'm sure we've driven out most of the danger. Now, Varya, you help your big sister to bed. And make sure she's covered and nice and warm, agreed?"

Varya, relishing the opportunity to lord over me, nodded her head eagerly.

"Konyechno."

"And Maria, you'll stay there in bed, won't you, while I run down the block for some more fish? Promise me, yes?"

Defeated, I could do nothing more than nod.

"You don't need yesterday's soup with yesterday's fish. You must have something fresh and cooked only once. You see, the fish will be stronger, and that in turn will make you stronger too. Now put on your *tapochki,*" she said, handing me my slippers. "We can't have your feet getting cold again. I'll be back as soon as I can. Hopefully, there won't be any lines like last week. Can you imagine, there wasn't even any cod! Oh, this war!"

Even as she quit the tiny washroom where all of us were still gathered, Dunya rattled on about this and that. I paid no attention, and as soon as she was gone I unwound the towel wrapped around my head and used it to blot and dry my thick dark hair.

"Help me, Varya," I said in a faint voice as I bent toward her.

She grabbed part of the towel, started rubbing my head, and then, for the first time, asked, "What happened to you? Did you fall down or something? I mean, how did you get so wet?"

Should I tell her? Could I? Last night Papa's visions had reduced her to tears; what would my own do today? Suddenly I felt much older than Varya, as if my youth had run away with the wind, never to return. Whereas only a few days ago my head had been aflutter with pretty frocks and fine shoes, handsome young soldiers and the glances they tossed me, now I saw only intrigue and threat, poverty and desperation. And imminent danger to my family.

"Someone chased me through the market," I said, careful not to look her in the eye. "And that's right, I fell down in a big puddle."

"Why were they chasing you? Was someone trying to steal something?"

"I suppose."

Her questions would have gone on and on, I knew, but the hard metal bell of the phone broke our conversation. Instantly Varya started out of the washroom.

"I'll get it," she said, in her carefree manner.

Had it been only yesterday, that would have been all right, I would have been happy to indulge her in one of her favorite treats, answering the telephone. But yesterday was ages ago. Without even thinking, I spun and went after her, grabbing her by the white lace on her gray dress.

"Nyet!" I screamed.

My sudden ferocity scared her, and she moved to the side. In an instant, still wrapped like a mummy in towels, I managed to lunge past her. Information, that was what I needed, and instinctively, protectively — or perhaps simply because I was a Rasputin and had my own powers of foresight — I knew it was I who was destined to answer this call.

Reaching for the phone mounted on the wall, I lifted the earpiece on the third ring and practically shouted into the mouthpiece. *"Ya Vas slushaiyoo!"*

The palace operator had undoubtedly been chosen for her voice, the tone always pleasant, elegant, and rich. Although she was surely not highborn, her accent was refined and educated, her manners cultivated to the highest. After all, this was the woman who completed the telephone connections between Emperor and grand duke, Emperor and minister, and, of course, between Empress and her beloved friend, my father. But this time there was no ease and no sophistication, let alone any formality.

The woman on the line snapped, "This is

the Palace — hold!"

Immediately my heart began to charge as fast as a young mare running from a Siberian tiger. Something was horribly wrong, and it took no gift of insight to understand that. Had something happened to Papa?

There was a distinct click as the operator pulled cords and made the connection, and the next instant a hysterical voice came on the line. It was a woman, that much I could tell, and though she tried to speak, her words were flooded by tears. Nevertheless, I recognized the otherwise beautiful voice as that of Her Imperial Highness, the Empress of Russia. I clutched the towels covering my heart and clenched my eyes, preparing myself for the worst possible news of my father.

When the Tsaritsa, so overcome with emotion, failed to speak, I gathered my courage and lunged into the void, saying, "Your Highness, it's me . . . Maria Grigorevna."

"Oh, my child!" she gasped. "I need your father! Please, he must come at once! Aleksei Nikolaevich . . . my son . . . he's dying!"

CHAPTER 14

Knowing what had to be done, I hung up the earpiece but just stood there, trembling and trying to collect my thoughts.

"What is it? What happened?" demanded Varya, for she could see the terror and the fresh tears in my eyes.

I reached out for her and she ran to me. Clutching her hand, I blurted it out.

"The Heir Tsarevich . . . Aleksei Nikolaevich . . . he got out of bed and tripped over one of his toys, and now he's bleeding inside his knee. He already lost so much blood the other day that now he's unconscious. The Empress fears his end is just around the corner. The Tsar is racing back from the front, but she's not even sure his train will carry him home in time."

As would any Russian of any age or social standing, Varya immediately understood the potential catastrophe. If the Heir Tsarevich were lost from this world, it would not be simply a tragedy for the House of Romanov, it would be a major national event that would alter the political landscape. Indeed, it could change the course of the war itself. The Empress, who had struggled for years to give birth to a male heir, knew this all too well, just as she knew there was only one way to save her son.

"We've got to find Papa," I said, turning and dashing toward our bedroom. "I've got to get dressed, and we have to go out and find him. It's the only way, he's the only one who can save him!"

Of course I was right, and Varya knew it, just as she knew that Dunya's orders for me to go to bed and stay there were now irrelevant. Instead, my younger sister acted as my dresser, helping me to pull on underlinens and socks, a warm blouse, and a heavy dress. We both worked briefly on my hair, rubbing it furiously with a towel, but it was to no avail. My hair was still most definitely damp even as we rushed to the front door, laced our shoes, threw on our cloaks, and grabbed our gloves and knit hats.

Minutes later, as the two of us bolted from our flat and down the stairs, I wondered if it was hopeless. The Empress had already sent her fastest motorcar, and it would be here in perhaps fifteen or twenty minutes.

Was there any hope that I could find Papa by then? Might we have to go driving about the city, from restaurant to restaurant and from one notorious flat to the next, in order to find him? Dear Lord, if luck were with us, it could still take hours, and even then we might find Papa in a drunken stupor. If so, would I again be able to rouse him to sobriety? And what if we didn't find him at all? What if Prince Felix and Grand Duke Dmitri had lured him away, either to a hidden *Khlyst*-type orgy of nobles or into a grand-ducal plot? As we raced down the stairs, past the security men posted on each of the floors, that worst-case possibility rolled right over me. If the grand dukes had today, right now, put an end to my father, they had not taken steps to protect their House but instead to extinguish it, for I knew what they chose not to believe: Without Papa there was no hope for the Heir.

It all seemed utterly hopeless when Varya and I hurried past the guard and the doorman downstairs, past the little iron stove, out the door, and into the frigid air. We rushed onto the front sidewalk and came to a skidding halt. I glanced down toward the Fontanka, turned, and looked up the street toward the train station. Which way? Through which alley? Into which home?

Panic surged through me as I realized I had no idea where even to begin. Papa could be a few blocks away, and just as easily he could be on the other side of the city.

Wait . . .

Given that my father's doings were more reported than even the Tsar's, he'd probably been tailed by a squadron of agents. On the other hand, if he'd gotten away without being followed, it was for a purpose, and no one knew more of my father's intimate doings than our housekeeper.

"Varya, go up to the market and find Dunya. Tell her what's happened, tell her we need to find Papa, tell her everything," I commanded, worried that, if I went, Dunya would simply drag me back to the apartment and throw me in bed. "I'm going to talk to the security agents. Either Dunya or the agents must know something."

"Right," replied my sister, turning and running off at full speed.

I glanced back at our apartment building. Should I go up and speak with the agent who'd been discreetly hidden outside our door? Should I see what the agent downstairs had noted in his little black book? No, I thought, glancing at the motorcar parked across the street, its engine idling, its windows iced over. If you needed to know what a snake was doing and where it was going, you went to its head, for everything else couldn't help but follow.

So I did just that. I crossed the snowy cobbles and went up to the back window, knocking firmly on it. Immediately something inside shifted — there were two men in there, I realized — and then the next moment the window was lowered by its leather strap. A heavyset man with a Ukrainian face stared out at me, his skin pale, his cheeks wide, his forehead large, and his mustache as big as a walrus's. Of course there was no need for introductions. I'd never seen this man before, didn't know his name, but I knew what he was doing here, just as he surely knew everything about me, right down to what I had worn yesterday.

"I have to find my father!" I pleaded.

The man stared suspiciously back at me. Only his fiery left eyebrow moved, and barely so at that.

"It's an emergency. Do you or your men have any idea where he is?"

The long hairs on his upper lip quivered ever so slightly.

Under grave threat my father had ordered us never to discuss his religious activities, never to speak of our royal connections, and never, ever, to mention his visits to the palace. And he was right to be so cautious, especially after the attempt on his life, for which I still blamed myself. Now, however, I ignored all that.

"The Empress telephoned!" I declared. "There's an emergency, and she's sending a car for him. Please — I must find him!"

Either out of duty or fear, the agent leaped from the motor, for he most certainly knew that the Empress, with nothing more than a cold shrug, could have him banished to the hinterlands. A second man, a tiny fellow with gold-rimmed glasses, remained tucked in the warmth of the vehicle.

"This way," said the agent with great authority as he twisted one end of his big mustache.

"Where is he? How far?"

"Just a few buildings away."

Slava bogu. So Papa wasn't lost, so he hadn't been dragged away. My initial panic subsided, but only slightly. I still had to get him and return as quickly as possible. With any luck we might even make it back before the imperial motor arrived.

Unlike the great cities of Europe, the capital of unruly Russia was, ironically, a planned metropolis, conceived of and built by Peter the Great according to his strict vision. Not only had the swamps been drained and the rivers contained, our roads were straight and methodical, lined with brick buildings covered with decorative, colorful stucco. Behind the endless, orderly façades, however, it was a different matter. Archways led to alleys, alleys split into passages, and passages dissolved into nooks and crannies, the lost corners that the lost characters of Dostoyevsky loved to inhabit and wallow in, festering in a dirty stew of anxiety and poverty. And it was through just such a filthy maze that I now followed the agent. We hadn't lived on Goroxhavaya Street long enough for me to have ever been this way.

Wasting no time, we crossed into the courtyard of the building opposite ours, out its back, into the rear of another, down a narrow passageway, and into an opening behind yet another building. The agent led the way boldly, without any hesitation, as if he'd been down this path many times, and I couldn't help but wonder what in the name of the devil my father was doing back here. How many times had he been tailed to this seemingly secret location? Was it a tiny bar where alcohol was sold despite the wartime ban? A little café where he could escape his throng of daily visitors?

"Wait here," commanded the agent, pointing to the snowy ground with a sharp gloved finger. "I'll bring him right out."

I obeyed like an obedient mutt, coming to a quick halt. And like a pathetic dog, my eyes trailed after the agent, watching sadly as he continued down to the end of the building and disappeared around the corner. Why, I wondered, could I go no farther? Was there something I shouldn't see? I gazed up at the back of the innocuous building and noted a handful of plain windows and two large round drainpipes half clinging to the structure. What business did my father have in there?

Out of nowhere I heard Papa's unmistakable voice, deep and resonant. Immediately I spun around. Had it come from the building behind me? No, I realized, looking at a huge blank wall painted a tired apple green. Papa's voice had merely bounced off that. Turning back, I scanned the alley, the wall, and heard it again. Not just his voice but the laughing, seductive voice of a woman. I looked everywhere — nook, doorway, rooftop — and then spied it, a *fortochka* — a small transom window — that was cracked open because, of course, we Russians were addicted to fresh air summer and winter. Yes, I realized, instinctively moving toward it. Papa was in a ground-floor room right over there, the one with the burning lightbulb dangling from the ceiling.

I could have done nothing. I could simply have waited for the security agent to rouse my father and hurry him out. But that was not my nature. And these were not passive times. Besides, I wanted information, bits and scraps that I could glue together to create a realistic image of my mysterious father.

And so, without really thinking, only knowing that I must, I hurried forward. From the side of the building, I grabbed an abandoned wooden crate and dragged it beneath the window, which stood several *arzhini* from the ground. As I clambered atop the crate, I heard again the deep tones of my father's voice, which leaked from the window above and flowed over me like a bizarre draft. Strange words spilled over me, things I didn't quite understand . . . and yet did, for they were akin to the deep, lustful words that Sasha had once whispered into the tender corner of my ear. My heart clenched, my pulse kicked like a horse. I shouldn't be doing this, but I certainly couldn't stop either.

Clenching the edge of the broad metal windowsill, I pulled myself up. Common things came into view: a plain lightbulb hanging from the ceiling, peeling brown wallpaper, a mirror, a torn curtain, a framed print on the wall. This was no luxurious apartment. It was only a single room, tattered, worn, and poor. Then I saw it, or rather him — the back of Papa's head, his wild hair moving and jerking about. Sitting in his coat, he was facing the other way, and when I peered over and around him, I saw a single woman standing there. With the exception of a pair of stockings that climbed up to her thighs, she was completely naked. Her hair was thick and blond — a mass of curly ringlets — and her lips were painted an unusually bright red. Slowly swaying and dancing before my father, the woman was cupping her enormous breasts in her hands, pushing them up and forward, offering them to my father in much the same way that a luscious, exotic, and terribly juicy pineapple had been presented to me the very first time. She then ground her broad voluptuous hips from side to side, opened her legs a bit, and ever so slowly thrust forward her delicate patch of mounding hair.

Suddenly my father's right hand came out of nowhere, slapping himself in the head with a loud thwack. Almost immediately his left hand batted at his very own cheek and gave it what appeared to be a painful pinch. Then, with both hands, he started tugging and yanking at his collar, wrestling furiously with himself. Startled, I swayed to the side and nearly fell, and the harlot spied me spying her and screamed. I screamed. And my father, who'd been sitting there, burst to his feet. Before Papa could see me, I leaped sideways off the crate and tumbled to the snowy ground. Shocked, I lay there in the frost. What was going on in there? What had I just witnessed? Papa wasn't having sexual relations with this woman — at least not yet — for, I realized, she was naked but he was not. Was it an audition of some sort? Could he be treating her for what he frequently called the most tenacious of womanly problems, lewdness?

A pair of hands came from behind, lifting me up, and I half screamed. *"Oi!"*

Turning around, I expected to see one of the security agents. Instead, whom did I see but Sasha.

"Maria, are you all right?" he asked, gently helping me to my feet.

"What are you doing here? How do you keep popping up?"

He looked at me with a funny grin. "You asked me to come to your house, you asked me to wait by the back door. And I was there, waiting, when I heard your voice and saw you coming out the front. So I followed you. I thought maybe you were leading the way to a café or someplace where we could talk."

"Oh. Of course."

"So what's happened? What are you doing back in this . . . this alley?"

I wanted to stand there and wallow in confusion, even self-pity. I wanted Sasha to wrap his arms around me. I wanted simply to saunter off with him. But of course I couldn't.

"I came to get my father."

"And where is he?"

I motioned up to the window. "Up there."

"Doing what?"

"I'm not sure, but I have to get him to" — I shouldn't have said anything, but I just blurted it out — "to the Palace."

"Really? What's — ?"

We both heard it then, a voice loudly muttering and cursing.

"Sasha, I think that's one of the security agents. Maybe you'd better not be here now."

"Right," he nodded, already slipping away.

No sooner had Sasha melted into the shadows of a doorway than the voice grew into shouting. Turning, I saw not one of the agents coming around the corner of the building, but my very own father. He wasn't wearing his thousand-ruble fur coat. No, he had on his real coat, the peasant sort, made of wool and long and tight at the waist. And he hadn't come out to yell at me. Rather, he didn't even know I was there and was instead just stumbling along, yelling, beating himself with his fists, pulling his hair, even kicking himself.

"You fool! You idiot!" he shouted, cursing no one but himself.

It emerged softly, rolling innocently across my full lips. "Papa?"

He gave himself one last forceful punch in the chest, turned, and saw me. Shocked, he stopped his flaying and stared.

"*Dochenka maya,*" he said tenderly, "what are you doing here?"

"I . . . I . . ."

I had no idea what to say, even where to begin. Instead my hand simply started to rise, and I found myself pointing up to the room with the lightbulb. Amazingly enough, the naked woman with the blond ringlets and the shockingly bright red lips was standing there in the window, a tattered quilt now thrown around her shoulders and her eyes opened wide in shock.

"Oh, her?" My father laughed. "That's Anisia, the *prostitutka.* Have you not met before?" Seeing my face twisted by the enigma of his world, Papa said quite innocently, "Yes, sure, I hire Anisia from time to time. She's very helpful. I use her, you see, to tempt me, to unearth the lust hidden deep in my soul. She brings my terrible thoughts, the very worst ones, right to the surface of my skin. She draws them out of me like sweat in a *banya,* these lascivious thoughts I don't even know I'm carrying. And when she draws them to the surface of my consciousness — well, then I can deal with them. Then I can beat them away."

As if I'd swallowed my tongue, I stared at him, unable to speak.

"Don't look so shocked, my dear Maria. It's all very deliberate. Even the saints used to do this, stare at naked harlots in order to find purity of soul. This is the path I struggle so hard to follow as well, not the path of simple Believers but that of a real Christ. How else am I supposed to make my spirit strong unless I continually battle the flesh?" Looking right at me, he hit himself in the face with his own fist. "Besides, I find self-abasement very effective. It keeps me humble and on the right path."

The joy of suffering. The eternal need to drive Satan out of one's own body. The never-ending search for self-purification. Beating away sin with sin. All in the glorious quest of repentance and holy forgiveness. What could be more pagan? More Orthodox? And who, I sobbed within, could be more Russian than my very own father, Rasputin?

As I took Papa by the arm, I stole a glance over my shoulder and waved a quick farewell to Sasha, who was only just stepping out of the shadows.

CHAPTER 15

By the time we returned home, Dunya and my sister were already waiting out front for us. Taking him by his arms, we rushed Papa upstairs and changed him into a fresh *kosovorotka*.

"You are coming with me, Marochka," my father said, as we pulled the shirt over his head. "I'm so exhausted there's no doubt I'll need your help."

Knowing that my father's commands were every bit as absolute as the Empress's, I obeyed silently, following him down the stairs and into the back of the royal limousine, which had just arrived. All at once we were racing toward Tsarskoye Selo, the vortex of Russian politics, gossip, scandal . . . and tragedy. But as we sat there in the rich leather seats, I didn't speak or even look at my father for fear of the anger and confusion that would burst forth. Besides, the most important thing was for him to gather his strength for his duties ahead. And so I gazed out the window in thought.

The greatest attack on Papa had come three or four years earlier, when his former friend and ally in Christianity, the monk Illiodor, turned so rabidly against him. Whether or not Papa had in fact raped a nun, as was proclaimed, Illiodor began shouting everywhere that Papa was a holy devil set on destroying the very foundation of Holy Mother Russia — the monarchy — and that he was pandering to the Yids as well as aiding the new capitalists, who, the fanatic monk claimed, were hell bent on debasing the Russian soul.

To launch his famous attack, Illiodor released a letter that he had stolen from our home in Pokrovskoye, a letter tucked in my father's little wooden desk and written by none other than Her Majesty the Empress, to my father:

My beloved, unforgettable teacher, redeemer, and mentor! How tiresome it is without you! My soul is quiet and I relax only when you, my teacher, are seated beside me. I kiss your hands and lean my head on your blessed shoulder. Oh, how light, how light do I feel then. I only wish one thing: to fall asleep, to fall asleep . . . forever on your shoulders and in your arms. What happiness to feel your presence near me. Where are you? Where have you gone? Oh, I am so sad and my heart is longing. . . . Will you be soon again close to me? Come quickly, I am waiting for you and I am tormenting myself for you. I am asking for your holy blessing and I am kissing your blessed hands. I love you forever.

Yours, Mama

Not even the censors could stop the wide publication of this letter, and it caused a scandal of the greatest magnitude. People of every level of society were aghast at the thought of their Empress kissing the foul hands of that dirty peasant, and the worst rumors started running everywhere, even supposed eyewitness accounts of *Khlyst* activities in the cellars of the Aleksander Palace itself. Soon thereafter an even worse story started circulating as quickly as a hot fire in a parched forest — that Rasputin had molested the Tsar's second daughter, Tatyana.

People didn't understand. Or what they did surmise was wrong. I myself had received a note from the Empress written in such a florid manner, for that was her style. She was all emotion, all soul, and she gave herself completely to those she cared for. Those *were* the exact words the Empress wrote to my father — her Father Grigori — but no one understood where the words came from or what they truly meant for one simple reason: No one knew her secret, a secret that affected everything in our country, right down to the soft snowballs formed and handed to me that winter afternoon at the Aleksander Palace.

In fact, hardly anyone realized there was one, a state secret of such magnitude that it was carefully guarded even from many princes and princesses of the royal blood. I was one of the very few privy to it, and only then because I knew of my father's activities. Unbeknownst to almost everyone in the nation, there was an explanation for the imperial family's withdrawal from the whirling social world of the capital, there was logic behind their decision to retreat to the Aleksander Palace in Tsarskoye Selo and live there in near isolation, and there was most definitely a reason for the Empress's lack of laughter and perpetually sad appearance.

It was that the Heir Tsarevich Aleksei Nikolaevich suffered from the English disease.

He was a bleeder. And the Tsar and Tsaritsa, and even their most trusted advisers, had decided that no one should know that the future of the nation was in peril not just from the Germans but from a simple bruise or bump, any number of which most little boys encountered on any given day. It all came down to blood — royal blood, to be specific — that had been passed from Queen Victoria to her favorite granddaughter, a minor German princess who became our Empress Aleksandra Fyodorovna, and who in turn passed the condition to her first-born boy, Heir to the Imperial Throne of All the Russias.

The only time I ever heard Papa speak against the monarchy was when he had groused that we simple people took better care in breeding our pigs back home — where everyone knew you needed fresh stock from other villages to keep the herd strong and healthy — than these fancy nobles did in breeding themselves. But it was in this, the inability of the Heir's blood to clot, that lay the true nature of my father's extraordinary bond with our Empress.

Less than an hour later a pair of heavy black iron gates opened before us and the royal limousine carried us once again to the very steps of the Aleksander Palace. I thought of the boy's pain, of the Empress's misery . . . and of the terrible things constantly said about her. Even her own mother-in-law, the Dowager Empress Maria Fyodorovna, had called her a traitor, first because she had given birth to four daughters in a row and then because she had birthed such a sickly boy. To make it all worse, the court of the Dowager Empress was filled with evil gossips, highborn personages who spread the most wicked stories to all the courts of all the grand dukes and beyond. There was even tittle-tattle that Aleksandra Fyodorovna had a secret telegraph cable stretching from the mauve boudoir all the way to her native Germany and the offices of her cousin, Russia's sworn enemy, Kaiser Wilhelm, with whom we had been at war for so long. Every time I heard that I shuddered, for I couldn't help but think of the poor Marie Antoinette, daughter of the Austrian monarch, whom the French had labeled the *Austrichienne,* the Austrian dog.

But none of the incendiary stories they told about the Empress was true. Not one. And yet virtually every Russian believed them because the stories had been told and retold, heard and heard again so often, that eventually no one doubted their authenticity. There were supposed eyewitnesses everywhere.

Russia had long been an aria in search of a tragedy, and as Papa and I clambered out of the deep seats of the Delaunay-Belleville limousine and up the steps, I wondered if my father would be able to forestall the finale of the doomed opera. Or were we too late? I couldn't tell, not by the tears rolling down the big round cheeks of Madame Vyrubova, who greeted us once again at the top of the steps. Forgetting the frost, today she simply stood there, wearing a gray dress and leaning heavily on crutches.

"Thank you for coming, Father Grigori," she said, profusely kissing Papa's hand. "The boy, he . . . he —"

"Yes, I know," said Father, with a godly authority. "He's still with us."

"And —"

"This I know as well. *Batushka,*" the Dear Father, meaning the Tsar, "has returned home."

"Not more than ten minutes ago."

"*Eto xhorosho.*" Good.

How my father knew these things, I didn't know, yet I knew he was right, for with each step an aura seemed to grow more clearly around him. Was it the cod? Had the endless amounts of fish he consumed made his soul so clear, his body so pure, that he had indeed become a heavenly vehicle? Or had he been purified by his session with the prostitute Anisia?

When we reached the top of the steps, Madame Vyrubova glanced nervously at me and said to my father, "Father Grigori, I think it's better if the child is returned home. You know how the Empress doesn't —"

"I'm still exhausted from the other night," said Papa firmly. "This afternoon and evening will be long and hard . . . my daughter stays. She will attend to me."

"Of course, Father," the most powerful courtier in the nation replied, submissively bowing her head. "It is as you wish."

"It is as is needed."

Minutes before we'd pulled up to the gates, Papa had clasped my hand and told me the details of the other night when we'd come so late and I had been turned away. Aleksei had come down with a chill and sneezed. Such, of course, was the nature of any cold, only the boy had started to bleed profusely from the nose. Compresses had been applied, to no avail. The doctors had been called in and the boy's nose was cauterized, which hadn't done anything but elicit screams of pain from Aleksei Nikolaevich, who was never given the likes of morphine. As always, the best and finest doctors of all Europe hadn't been able to do a thing, so finally Papa had been summoned. And only many hours of Papa's prayers beside the Heir's bed had slowed and finally stopped the bleeding.

"I can see the boy's suffering is worse than it was the other day," Papa muttered, as we entered the palace. "I do not know what I can do for him, for of course it is up to the will of God, but I shall try my best."

Once again we hurriedly followed Madame Vyrubova through the large doors, past the guards and the reception desk, and into the private apartments of the royal family. Rather than proceed down the long central hall with its roll of Oriental carpet, Madame Vyrubova, hobbling on her crutches and with her gray dress trailing on the floor, took us into the small wooden elevator on the left. In silence we rode up to the second floor, the children's floor, where we were taken down a long empty corridor. I noted that the doors on the right were all shut tight, for these were the rooms of the Tsaritsa's personal maids, who surely had been told not to set foot outside their chambers.

Coming to a double door on the left, we turned into the children's playroom, where years earlier I had been brought to play with the Tsar's third daughter, Maria Nikolaevna, who was my age. Now, upon entering the large room, we found not the tepee, the tom-toms, the toy dog on wheels, or even Aleksei's clockwork train, of which he was so proud, but rather a busy cluster of men gossiping sternly among themselves. There was also a man, his back to us, who was sobbing quietly but furiously as he leaned against the tall green tile stove on the far wall. As I quickly trotted after Papa and Madame Vyrubova toward another door, we passed a group of men — a bevy of doctors and specialists — who glared at us and practically spit on Rasputin. But Papa didn't notice, so I tried to ignore them too. All that mattered, all that my father was focusing on, was the shrieking from the next room.

"Help me!" came the scream. "Mama, help me!"

One of Papa's greatest skills was his amazing ability to concentrate. He could study a single Bible passage for a week. He could search the morose face of an icon for an entire day. And now he focused on the cry of the Heir Tsarevich Aleksei Nikolaevich, reading the tone of pain as intently as if it were a heavenly hymn.

"Not a moment too soon," he muttered, his right hand clutching the gold cross, a gift from the Empress herself, that hung around his neck.

Just before I followed him through the next doorway, I glanced once again at the tall stove. The man leaning against the tiles turned and our eyes caught. *Gospodi,* it was the Tsar himself, his eyes wet and red. My heart ached for him. Was the boy truly on the doorstep of death?

"Mama, I can't! I can't! It's too much!" came the plea from the boy's chamber. "Please make it stop! Please let me die!"

As we entered the next room, a string of prayers fell from Papa's lips, a heavenly chant, a call to God for His mercy. My father shed his peasant coat, dropping it to the floor, and pressed onward, but I stopped, moving against one of the windows, which was covered with large floral curtains. The only light in the room came from the oil lamps suspended before the multitude of icons encased in their large curving *kiot.* Gazing through the soft, smoky light, I saw Aleksei Nikolaevich writhing in pain as he lay on his simple nickel-plated camp bed. It seemed as if his failed body were trying to pull his soul across the threshold of death, while Russia's mighty Empress, Aleksandra Fyodorovna, who was on her knees clutching her son's hand, was trying just as hard to keep him here. Like a mother superior, she was huddled in prayer, begging God for mercy, begging God to save this child who was lost in fever.

"Mama . . . Mama . . . ," he gasped, "will it hurt so much when I go to Heaven?"

With supreme confidence, Papa strode right up behind the Empress, placing his hand directly on her shoulder as if she were nothing more than the commonest of commoners. Startled, Aleksandra Fyodorovna turned, looked up, and, upon seeing him, half swooned to the side, falling upon his thigh like an eager lover. Unable to control herself, the Empress of All the Russias grabbed this ugly peasant's ugly hand and kissed it passionately.

"Thank you, Father Grigori. Thank you for coming," she gasped in relief. "Aleksei fell on his knee, and now he needs you badly. We all need you. Help us, please help us!"

My father said nothing, focusing only on the boy. The Empress, whose health and beauty had been ravaged by years of worry and anxiety, started to beg a question but stopped. I knew what it was. She wanted to know what none of those doctors or specialists in the playroom could tell her: Would the boy cheat death yet again? She started to speak but instead started to sob, and seemed about to faint. Indeed, she might have tumbled over had she not been leaning so heavily on her Friend, her Savior, my father.

Practically brushing her aside, Papa pressed himself up against the bed and stared down upon the pathetic child, who gazed up at him with hollow eyes, eyes that expressed nothing but excruciating pain. Pulling aside a light blanket, Papa saw a leg hideously bloated with blood, twisted and bent up to the boy's chest. Papa made the sign of the cross over Aleksei and placed one of his massive hands directly on the boy's damp, feverish forehead. He then reached down and closed his fingers firmly around the boy's right hand. Papa had healed me from the worst illnesses in just this manner, and I knew he could read it all: the boy's fear, the panic of those around him, the hopelessness everyone sensed, and the boy's pain — the unbelievable pain of the pounding blood that had burst from the veins, swelled the skin, and twisted the limbs.

Without so much as glancing down at her, Papa barked at the Empress, "Leave us!"

Aleksandra Fyodorovna could barely rise, so wrought with worry was she, so pummeled by years of constant fear, the fear that hung like a guillotine over her head every moment of every day, the fear that today the blade might come suddenly crashing down and she would lose her beloved son. She tried to push herself to her feet but could not. She rose, and then sank, and I was about to hurry to her side when a short but muscular figure charged into the room. Rushing right up to her, the man tenderly reached down and took her in his own shaking but loving hands.

"Come, my dear," the Tsar urged gently, his own tears now controlled. "We must let Father Grigori do his work."

"Oh, Nicky!" She wept, clutching his arms, kissing his hands. "I . . . I . . ."

Then Papa offered the greatest of benedictions. "Do not worry. God has heard your prayers. Now leave us!"

Aleksandra tried to contain herself. The strongest of mothers, the mightiest of tsaritsas, attempted to restrain her joy, but she could not. She fell apart, and tears of boundless relief burst from her eyes.

"Thank you, oh, thank you!" she exclaimed, grabbing my father's hand and kissing it.

The Tsar, small tears glistening in his eyes, leaned down, kissed my father's hand, and thanked him too. *"Spasibo."*

"Take care, my Sunbeam," said Aleksandra Fyodorovna, kissing her son tenderly on the forehead. "Rest well, my dearest. Did you hear Father Grigori? You're in the hands of God. Let's all get some rest . . . and we'll come back later. Everything's going to be fine. We'll be back later to kiss you good night."

"Yes, Mama," the boy replied softly, as if the pain was already beginning to pass.

Papa didn't move. He didn't budge. Not as the Tsar escorted his wife from the room. Not as the doctors and specialists were sent away. Not as the bedchamber and playroom were emptied. My father banished everyone, every last one of them except me, and within moments all was quiet and the door to the boy's room was shut. Only I was left because only I understood how to serve Papa, only I, his own flesh and blood, could anticipate his needs. Dropping my coat on a chair, I pushed myself back into the tall floral curtains, where I disappeared. My own deep eyes never left Papa, who kept one hand pressed against Aleksei's forehead, the other clasped around his fingers. Hidden in the vines and flowers of the fine fabric, I stared at my father as he chanted prayers and began the work for which he was both worshiped and reviled, that greatest of Christian gifts, the laying on of hands. But would he be able to perform a miracle yet again?

"Dear God," I prayed quietly, "please grant Papa strength, please let Aleksei Nikolaevich live through the night."

CHAPTER 16

For all my frustrations with my father, I knew one thing for sure: He was a healer. I knew this for one simple reason: Whenever I was ill, his presence, his touch, and his prayers not only made me feel better, they returned me with speed to good health.

The horse with the lame leg — the very first creature he had ever healed — knew that as well, as did the babushka, once bent with arthritis and now walking tall. And the boy run over by the carriage, now living in happiness and good health. Also Madame Vyrubova, who survived the train wreck when the doctors thought her lost. Papa had healed hundreds, if not thousands. Indeed, his powers were not limited to mere living creatures. Back home farmers frequently brought him cumbersome bags of seed to bless, and when he did — holding them close to his heart and chanting heavenly words — they grew into the best fields of rye. Everyone in our province was aware of that. Seeds and plants that Papa talked to would thrive, whereas the ones he ignored would more often than not fail.

My own mother believed firmly in my father's skills. Healers, she said, had always existed across our vast nation, men and women who could bring nature under their control. They were known by the Siberian word *shaman,* and in the 1700s they were found by explorers all the way from the Urals to Chukchi in the Far East. Like Christ, they were special people with a special touch who could make the blind see and the lame walk. It was only recently that modern thoughts — modern *Western* thoughts, my mother always added, with great disdain — had torn the fabric of our ancient Russian beliefs, casting doubts and questions everywhere. Whereas before we took understanding and meaning from the sun and the moon, the trees and the plants, the modern scientists of the last fifty years, almost all of them educated abroad, were trying to explain away our natural world, not in a spiritual manner but a logical and mechanical one, continually dissecting everything into neat little black-and-white packages.

"If your father had been born a hundred

years earlier," Mama had said one snowy afternoon, as her thick fingers made a large, square *pirog* — a savory pie — filled with fish in one corner, wild mushrooms in the next, potatoes and onion in the third, and chopped egg in the fourth, "all Russia would be at his feet. Back then no one questioned the ability or the respectability of a healer. And that's the difference between your father and the modern scientists and doctors — your father seeks to heal people, whereas they seek to cure them."

My mother hated Sankt Peterburg. It wasn't the capital of Russia, she said, it was the capital of the material world, Peter the Great's little window onto Europe which had let in this terrible draft, and made our country ill . . . with two different sorts of consumption. I had read how even our great Leo Tolstoy had said the capital city was "stupefied and deadened by wine, wealth, and lovemaking without love." Yes, call it Sankt Peterburg or Petrograd, the capital had lost in the struggle of the spirit over the flesh, the very struggle my father was determined to fight every single day of his life.

And which the Heir Tsarevich Aleksei Nikolaevich himself was now facing.

I looked past my father, past the small blue robe draped on a bedside chair, and stared at the young boy, lying there on his nickel camp bed. Never had I seen such pain, such a blatant fight between good and evil. And in this child I saw not just an illness but a terrible *metaphora* for all the woes facing the Empire. Here was a young boy afflicted by a sickness brought into Russia by his Western relatives, a disease against which even the best Western doctors were powerless. Only Papa — who'd walked barefoot out of the depths of Russia — and his crude, backward spiritual treatments had offered any hope, let alone comfort. Yes, lying here before me was the body, the vessel, of a small boy, torn between East and West, ancient and modern. Looking at him, one couldn't help but wonder if the sickly dynasty was strong enough to go on or if the time had come for it simply and easily, to die away.

"Help me, please, Father Grigori," Aleksei beckoned, reaching up from the bed. "I hurt."

"I am here, Alyosha. And through me God's will shall be done. He has seen and heard your suffering, my child, and he has chosen to remove your pain."

"Thank you, Father Grigori."

"I have done nothing," said Papa, whose greatest skill was, undoubtedly, his ability to calm people. "It is God Himself whom you must thank."

"Da-s," he said, and closed his young eyes in serene prayer.

My father started chanting and mumbling, and as the words of the Lord fell upon the child, covering him in a blanket of sweetness, I could feel his tension passing. I too closed my eyes, found my lips mumbling, praying, calling to the heavens for serenity and peace, comfort and warmth. I bowed my head and emptied my body of myself. Yes, we have power, all of us, to affect things, just as things themselves have power as well. Like a dream out of nowhere, an image of a blue heart-shaped diamond came into my mind's eye. I could see it as clearly as if I were holding it. I knew what it was. I had read about this gem in our papers, and the ladies had talked of it at the tea table. It was huge and gorgeous, supposedly stolen from the eye of an idol, a terribly famous diamond that had belonged to many doomed personages, including the ill-fated Marie Antoinette, the Hope family of bankers, our Prince Ivan Kanitowsky, and now an American heiress. Death had followed the diamond everywhere and, I was sure, would continue to do so now that it had left Russia for America. So if death could be attached to an inanimate thing, couldn't goodness be tied to something as well? Absolutely, I thought, reaching into my dress and clutching the small Orthodox cross that hung from my neck. Yes, there was hope.

"Death is not here today," I mumbled aloud, not sure how or why I knew this, but certain that I did.

"It has passed us by," muttered my father, mid-prayer.

A shiver traveled my spine, reached a crescendo, and flowed down my arms and out my fingertips. What was it that I was feeling, this glory, this exaltation now surging through me? And where was it coming from?

"It comes from on high," said my father, as if he'd heard my silent question. "*Dochenka maya*, please come here."

I trembled like a schoolgirl called on by a dominating teacher. The fingers of my right hand clutched the fine curtain. Did Papa intend to involve me in some way?

"Come, child of mine," my father beckoned, holding out his hand with its incredibly long, gnarled fingers.

There were so many things I didn't understand about my father. Then again, all that mattered was what he could do right here and now. Papa, I realized, was like Chiron the centaur, who had been wounded by a poisoned arrow but did not die, and who could heal everyone but himself. If only the entire country were here, right in this bed-chamber, there would be no shouts for my father's death, there would be no calling the Empress a traitor. Quite the contrary. She and my father were doing everything they could to save the Heir and the Empire.

Following my father and his unspoken movement, I proceeded around the nickel bed, while Papa continued to the *kiot,* which was filled with a glittering mass of gold-covered and bejeweled holy icons and flickering lamps. As his hand stretched upward, I knew at once which icon he was reaching for, the radiant *Kazanskaya,* Our Lady of Kazan, the painted image covered in a mass of gold, seed pearls, emeralds, and diamonds. Depicting the Holy Mother and Child, this icon had over the centuries become linked with the destiny of Russia. While the original rested in town in the Ka-zanski Cathedral on Nevsky Prospekt, there were many miracle-working copies, of which I could only hope this was one. In our own family this icon was of particular importance for the story of my namesake, little Ma-tryona. In the 1500s a soldier's house had burned entirely to the ground and everything was thought lost, icons and all. That night, the soldier's daughter, Matryona, had a vision of the Holy Mother in the ashes. No one believed her, but Matryona insisted, and in time a spade was got, the girl's mother dug, and the icon was found, completely undamaged. Ever since, many miracles had taken place before this icon, including when it was taken into battle and victory was secured, first over the Poles and much later over Napoleon.

Papa reached up, placed one hand just before the icon, and intoned, "O Most Holy Mother of God, Thou who saved Thine image from harm, we beseech Thee to save us, Thine unworthy ones!"

My father stood there, mumbling and chanting, trembling and shaking. As he called to the heavens to pour forth from and through this religious image, I watched — and felt it, a power, a kind of divine security. Slowly, Papa turned to me, his eyes not blinking, but steadfast and remarkably intent.

"Matryona, daughter of mine," he said, his voice unusually deep and strange, "turn and place your hands over the boy's pain."

I panicked. I had seen death, but only at a distance. I had heard pain, but only from afar. I looked down at my open palms, which were staring blankly back up at me. What were these simple hands and what could they do? Might I hurt the boy instead of help?

Suddenly Papa was touching me on the forehead, saying, "Your wisdom and faith are not here." Next he was pressing his flat hand against my chest and over my heart. "But here."

Startled and worried, I raised my eyes.

"There is no fear here tonight, my Matryona. Trust me. Tonight you must help me reach from the icon to the boy, which you can do. It is time for you to realize your own strengths, of which you have a great many."

As soon as he said it, I realized my father was right. I didn't know if I'd inherited something from him, much in the same way as a singer or painter or sculptor inherits gifts from her parents, or if in fact I had merely observed and absorbed my father's skills. But I felt something, a power perhaps, albeit nascent. Or perhaps what I recognized was simply belief, a trust that these things can be made to happen, that the power of prayer can indeed beckon God to shine down and heal someone.

I turned to the bed and stared at the Heir Tsarevich, who lay there against his sheets like a pallid ghost hovering in a pale cloud, his eyes sunken and rimmed with ashen circles. Several days ago he'd nearly died from a simple nosebleed. Today he'd fallen, and now his leg was horribly bloated and twisted; blood had rushed to the contusion on his knee, filling the entire joint and forcing him to make more room by bending it up. A deep wave of pity surged in me and I wanted to cry out, but Aleksei smiled weakly up at me. He will take his cue from me, I thought, so I must convey my belief and my hope. I must give him my strength so he can find his. So I smiled warmly down upon him.

Behind me, Papa raised one hand again to the *Kazanskaya,* while he clasped me on my shoulder with the other. Oh. So this was how. We were to telegraph the energy from the icon through my father, through me, and down to the boy. I can do that, I said to myself with confidence. I reached down and placed my right hand on the boy's hot forehead and my left gently onto his swollen leg. Aleksei flinched ever so slightly, but I remained sure in my newfound confidence, and a moment later I sensed him already relaxing.

Papa breathed in, exhaled, and intoned the trope, half chanting, "O fervent intercessor, Mother of the Lord Most High, You do pray to Your Son Christ our God and save all who seek Your protection. O Sovereign Lady and Queen, help and defend all of us who, in trouble and trial, in pain and burdened with sin, stand in Your presence before Your icon, and who pray with compunction, contrition, and tears and with unflagging hope in You. Grant what is good for us, deliverance from evil, and save us all, O Virgin Mother of God, for Thou art a divine protector to Thy servants."

Throughout the years my father had studied the Scriptures endlessly, memorizing long passages because he could not read, and this afternoon none could have pronounced the prayer more simply or more humbly. He went on and on, beseeching the heavens for mercy, for comfort, for intervention. And I could feel it, the warmth rushing down my father's arm onto my back, through my body, out my hands, and into the Tsarevich. I closed my eyes tightly and felt the power burning out of my fingertips. It was as if Dr. Derevenko, the Heir's personal physician, had attached one of his electrical apparatuses to me. My entire body began to tremble. Something akin to perspiration began to bubble from my palms onto the boy's skin and sink into his wounded body. One moment I was overcome with warmth, the next I was shivering, icy cold. Papa's words echoed in my ears and resounded through my entire body.

I don't know how long I stood like that, ten minutes or two hours, but I came to understand something that had always been before me but which I had never seen: the infinite power of love. Yes, truly, the power of love to calm and strengthen, the power of love to relax and imbue confidence — and, most important here this afternoon, the power of love to nurture and heal. Such were the lessons of Christ Our Lord, and such was my father's simple and secret weapon. The monarchists, the social democrats, the rich, and the poor were all seeking to use my father, to turn the fabled Rasputin into a political legend of one kind or another for their own benefit. My father knew that but didn't care, for he had found the ultimate truth, this intense feeling of affection and caring called love and the extravagant benefits love could lavish, not just on the heart and soul but on the physical being as well.

After a while Papa turned from the icon and, still chanting, came over to the other side of the bed and touched the boy ever so gently. And I saw it with my own eyes, my father's prayers lifting Aleksei to a place where there was no pain. From my father's mouth the words of the Lord fell upon the Heir, carrying him on a soft cloud to a place of heavenly rest. And like a fever that burst, I could see the pain pass from that small body and move on like a quickly passing storm.

Then Papa took Aleksei on a trip to other lands and other times.

"Close your eyes and hold my hand, dear boy," came Papa's deep, sweet voice. "Now imagine we are strolling through the forest near my home in Siberia. Can you picture it? Can you see the endless pine wood and smell the sweet scent? The trees — they are so big!"

His eyes closed, Aleksei breathed in, exhaled, and replied softly. "I see it all, Father Grigori . . . so many pine trees . . . and mushrooms too! Lots and lots of mushrooms!"

"Yes, that's right! Let's pick some, shall we?"

"Da-s!"

So Papa led the boy via a story to our forest, showing him all the glens and little brooks and the best places to find endless numbers of mushrooms. And when they were done there, when their baskets were overflowing, the snow fell, soft and white.

"Alyosha, would you like to go on a wild troika ride pulled by three of the most beautiful horses in the Empire?" asked Papa.

Aleksei, seeing it all as he lay there with his eyes pinched shut, grinned and nodded, and off they flew through the snow, my father at the reins, whooping and hollering, the bells jingling, and the cold, cold air rushing against their rosy cheeks.

"Here, you drive, Alyosha. I'm going to hand you the reins."

"But . . . but I've never —"

"Of course you can do it! You have power, you have strength! Here they are, take the reins . . . but be careful! Stay on the road! Watch out for the trees! And just look at the snow, it's up to your waist!"

Aleksei laughed aloud and drove them on through fantasy.

After that, Papa took him fishing and hunting, walking and hiking, and finally swimming in the cool waters of our favorite brook. And in all this the boy found peace and comfort and did not that afternoon, thanks to my father, step over the threshold of death.

When Aleksei fell from story into sleep, Papa slipped into prayer and stood there by the bed for hour after hour, mumbling and chanting to the heavens. His strength and endurance were incredible, something I could not even aspire to. At some point I started to sway. My head became light, and I slumped to the floor, pulled my cloak over me, and tumbled into dream, lulled by the deep tones of Papa's voice. I was awakened only by the sounds of the Tsar and Tsaritsa coming back into the room. It was dark of course, our northern sun had already fallen, but it was obvious that a miracle had indeed taken place, for not only was Aleksei's temperature back to normal but his hideously swollen and twisted leg was resting flat on the bed. To everyone's great relief, the boy's color had returned as well, and within the hour he ate two eggs and drank an entire cup of tea with milk.

With the crisis averted, Papa and I were back home by ten that evening.

We decided on poison.

You probably realize that by this time Vladimir Purishkevich, the great monarchist, was deeply involved. Also old Dr. Lazavert, whom I know you have already questioned at length. We were all terribly nervous — we were talking of the sin of murder, after all — but the nightmare of Rasputinism had to be stopped at all costs.

Purishkevich ran his own charitable hospital train, gathering the wounded at the front and bringing them home. Dr. Lazavert worked on this train, as I'm sure you're well aware. It was there, in Purishkevich's private car, that we gathered to make the final arrangements. We decided on the night of December 16 because Dmitri Pavlovich was busy every other night, and we didn't want to change his schedule, lest we attract attention. And, as I've said, we decided on poison. In fact, I clearly remember Dr. Lazavert holding up a small glass vial of potassium cyanide dissolved in liquid.

"We will sprinkle it liberally into the pastries and his wine," said the doctor.

The plan was simple. Promising a party, we would pick up Rasputin after midnight and take him to the palace on the Moika. We would lead him through the side door and down into the basement, into that cozy little dining room. As he waited for the supposed festivities to begin, he would feast on the sweets and wine. Death would come quickly.

I honestly confess I was not in favor of harming Rasputin's daughter as well. Nor did I want to be any part of the plan against the royal family. By that, I mean just what should be done with Aleksandra Fyodorovna and the Emperor, whether or not she should be locked up and he . . . he . . .

Well, that was a matter for the senior grand dukes, you know, the Tsar's uncles. That was family business. Getting rid of Rasputin was mine.

CHAPTER 17

Papa might have been exhausted, but I was famished.

When we entered our flat, my father dropped his coat on the hall floor and walked in a daze to his bedroom, mumbling that he was going to sleep for two whole days. I stood for a moment in the front hall, still trying to absorb my father's actions and all that had transpired at the palace. After a few moments I hung up my coat and headed to the kitchen, where Dunya waited to do what she did best, comfort us with food.

"What would you like, *milaya maya?*" My dear.

"Fish," I replied.

Amazed by my father's special abilities, I sat down at the dinner table and ate every different type of fish we had in the house. One after the other, Dunya brought out cod soup, herring in sour cream, jellied fish heads, and finally a piece of sturgeon fried in fresh butter. The only utensil I used was a spoon, everything else I ate with my fingers, proud of the milky broth and juices that dribbled down my chin. Even though I didn't really want any, I took a piece of black bread, careful to break it with my hands, just like the Apostles. And just like those who couldn't afford utensils, let alone a napkin, I used the dark, sour crust to wipe my chin and blot my lips. When Dunya offered me a sweet warm compote of stewed apples and raisins, I paused in thought. What would Papa do? He hated sweets — "Scum!" he always called them — but was compote really the equivalent of a flaky cream-filled French pastry or magnificent Austrian torte? Not sure, I declined. After all that fish I didn't want to do a thing to darken my soul.

Varya sat opposite, her elbows on the table, her blunt little chin in her hands, and just stared at me. After a few minutes, she brushed aside her bangs and scratched her nose.

She asked, "So what happened, Maria? Is the Heir dead?"

I shook my head.

"Then he's all right? Papa fixed him?"

I nodded.

"*Xhorosho.* I thought he would."

There was nothing to say, no way I could explain to her how amazing the healing had been, so I just ate in silence, my little sister watching me as I slurped up my food, fish by fish. I hadn't witnessed a miracle at the palace, but I had witnessed something miraculous, of that I had no doubt. I had no idea just how Papa was able to beckon the glory of God down from the heavens and into that suffering boy, how he was able to accomplish what no other — no priest, monk, scientist, or doctor — had ever been able to do. But he had and he did. Somehow, the strength of my father's character and belief had not simply enabled Aleksei to find serenity and peace but had inspired the boy's own faith in the power of his body and in his God. No wonder the Tsar and Tsaritsa's trust in my father was unshakable. How could it not be when Papa had saved their son over and over again? As amazing as it seemed, it was now perfectly clear to me that the Heir would have been dead long ago without my father's aid.

Thinking of my own path in life and how I might be able to help others, I wondered if I shouldn't become a bride of Christ. As I chewed on a soft yet slightly crunchy fish head, I considered abandoning this life and seeking the greater glory of God in a women's monastery. I would give up my fancy citified name of Maria and return to the real me, Matryona, the country girl of the far provinces. Yes, I would kiss my father and little sister good-bye, perhaps make a trip home to say farewell to Mama and my brother, Dmitri, and then I would seek out a place to take my vows. I definitely didn't want a place in the capital — Smolny, say — or anywhere nearby. Better something distant, the farther east the better. Yes, definitely something removed from the European influences sweeping our nation like polluted waters. A women's monastery hidden on an island in the middle of a lost Siberian lake would do just fine. There were many monasteries sprinkled across the length of Siberia, all the way to the Kamchatka Peninsula and the Bering Sea, and the best place would be one accessible for only a few months a year, a place where the roads and the rivers were open only during the short summer months. Being cut off from the world would encourage prayer and introspection. Surely my parents wouldn't be against my taking the vows. And since Sasha was gone — what if we never saw each other again? — life as a nun would be far better than marrying here in the capital and becoming one of the petit bourgeoisie, obsessed with the proper address, proper hat and dress, and requisite social standing. I really had no choice, now I thought about it. If I stayed and married here in Petrograd, I could only imagine the money and invitations people would shower upon me, all in the hope of gaining access to my father, which would in turn put them that much closer to the throne. How easy that would be. And how horrid.

I looked up when I'd eaten every last bit of fish, only to realize that my sister was no longer sitting there. When I carried my dishes into the kitchen, Dunya was not to be found either, not at the stove, nor on her little cot tucked behind the curtain. Setting my dishes into the porcelain sink, I glanced at the clock ticking away on the wall. After eleven. Not so late, particularly for this household, but it seemed that sleep in this sleepless city had finally and blessedly come to our flat.

I was just rolling up the sleeves of my dress to start washing my dishes when I heard a slight, discreet movement at the rear door. I stopped still. Someone started knocking gently, a sound so soft it might even have been a mouse scratching at the wood. But, no, I heard the rustle of clothing on the back landing. At this hour I suspected it was probably Prince Felix, who was sure to start pounding until he gained entry — after all, when had a Yusupov ever been turned away by anyone anywhere?

Then it occurred to me that it might be someone else altogether. Praying for this, I ran to the door.

"Kto tam?" Who's there?

The longest moment passed before a deep voice replied, "Me."

A silly grin blossomed on my face. "And what do you want at so late an hour?"

"To come in."

"Why?"

"Because I'm desperate to see you."

"Promise?"

"With all my heart."

I glanced quickly over my shoulder. Seeing no sign of my father or Dunya, I did it. I turned the lock. I opened the door. And Sasha came into our home and into my arms. Without a bit of hesitation, without a single word, we fell into each other's arms. I tilted my head slightly to the side, closed my eyes, and felt what I'd wanted so very much, his lips upon mine. An exhilarating flush of warmth filled my head, my stomach. It seemed to last both forever and yet only a fleeting moment, that kiss, that embrace. All of me seemed to rush into him, and all of him certainly flooded into my entire body. He held me with an intensity I'd never experienced, his strong hands pressing into my back, pulling me against his hard chest. Then I felt his entire body tremble.

"Sasha," I said, finally pulling back, "you're freezing."

"I was desperate to see you. I've been waiting out back for hours."

"How did you get in?"

"Someone came out the back door and I caught it before it shut." He kissed me lightly on my forehead, my eyebrows, my cheeks. "Is everything all right? Did you really go to the Palace?"

"Yes, of course."

"And?"

"There was an emergency," I said, wanting to tell him everything and knowing I would. "I'll tell you later. It was amazing."

Suddenly his lips were fluttering down my neck. And suddenly I was having trouble breathing. My eyes fell shut, my breath came short and shallow. Which is when I heard it, steps from within our apartment.

"Sasha," I said, pushing away from him, "you really shouldn't be here, not now, not so late."

"But —"

"My father will kill me if he finds

you here."

And someone was up. I could hear it clearly now, the sound of someone walking about.

"Please, let me stay. I'd love to meet your father."

"Maybe tomorrow."

Suddenly I was afraid. Not just of what Papa would think if he walked in here and saw Sasha, but of everything else. I still hadn't had the chance to tell my father about my surreptitious visit to the Sergeeivski Palace, how I'd been forced to flee through the watery cellar, or, most important of all, the warnings from Elena Borisovna.

Gently nudging Sasha out the door, I said, "Sasha, you can't stay here now. I'll see you tomorrow."

"Yes, good night, my sweet," he said, with one last little kiss.

And he was off, my delectable Sasha. I locked the door behind him and then listened to him make his way down the dark, steep rear stairs — his clothes rustling as he left — and then nothing.

I took a deep breath and turned away from the door.

I really did need to talk to Papa. What if he was gone by the time I woke up? What if something happened to him, even tonight? Or to the Tsar or the Tsaritsa? What if the grand dukes acted in one decisive swoop — perhaps as early as tomorrow — first, assassinating my father, second, locking the Empress in a monastery, and, finally, forcing the Tsar from the throne, maybe even killing him too? *Bozhe moi,* I was never going to be able to sleep until I talked to my father and made him understand just how serious the situation was. How could he not see it? I cursed myself for not speaking of it earlier, but in all the confusion and desperation at the palace the only thing that had mattered was saving the Heir. There hadn't been a moment to tell Papa about the threats being made against him and the Emperor and Empress. And thinking of the high treason floating throughout the city, I was as stirred as if I'd drunk four glasses of tea. I had to talk to Papa before he went to sleep. He had to do something. At the very least, he should summon Minister Protopopov. Never mind us, but perhaps a special troop of soldiers should be dispatched this very hour to protect the royal family.

Putting Sasha out of my mind, I quickly made my way through our apartment, expecting to find Papa wandering about. When he wasn't to be found, I went right up to his door, which was shut tight. Had he already gone to sleep? Leaning forward, I could hear his deep voice mumbling and moaning. No, he was lost in prayer, perhaps continuing his work for the Heir, as he often did from afar. I imagined him out of bed, prostrate before the icon in the corner, crossing himself and touching his head to the floor over and over again. I knew from experience that rousing him from his entreaties to the Lord was more difficult than waking him from his deepest sleep. But I was so worried about the dangers I had no choice, so I carefully turned the doorknob and pressed open the door. The room was dark, of course, with the only light coming from the tiny red oil lamp hanging in front of the icon he most valued, his simple, unadorned copy of the *Kazanskaya*. Papa's voice was indeed deep and full of passion, but he wasn't praying. Peering in, I realized with a horrible start that while Papa was indeed prostrate, it was not before a piece of wood with its holy depiction of the Virgin Mother and Child. Rather, he was lying face down on our very own Dunya. They had both dropped their clothes on the floor and crawled into Papa's narrow metal bed, and beneath the blanket that barely covered their moving naked bodies, I could clearly see my father holding our housekeeper by her soft parts. So involved were they that they didn't even notice my intrusion, and so shocked was I that I couldn't even gasp, for I had stopped breathing.

Behind me I heard the distinct squeak of a floorboard, and I spun around in absolute terror. Varya, dressed in her nightgown, was making her way toward me. I nearly slammed my father's door.

"Is Papa still up?" asked my sister. "I want to kiss him good night."

In total panic, I held my fingers to my lips. "Shh! He's asleep!"

Hurrying toward Varya, I grabbed her by the arm and spun her around. What had I just seen? My heart pounding, the only thing I knew for certain was that tonight was not the time for my younger sister to learn what I now knew, that our dear house-keeper, who was like our second mother, was in reality just that.

"We can't disturb Papa," I snapped.

"Hey, let go of me!" Varya whined. "That hurts!"

"Come on, Papa needs his rest . . . and so do we! You have to go to bed."

"But —"

Like an angry schoolmarm, I dragged Varya back to our room, where I practically shoved her into bed.

"Now go to sleep, Varichka," I said, heading out as quickly as I could lest she see the tears welling in my eyes. "I'll be back in a few minutes. I'm just going to finish the dishes."

"Oh, all right!" She was yawning as she crawled under the covers. "But I hate it when you push me around like that."

Back in the kitchen, my tears fell one after another into the dishwater. Did this mean that Papa didn't love our mother? Was he going to leave us? What about the sanctity of marriage he so often preached?

"To hell with him!" I cried aloud, slamming my fist into my thigh.

Biting my lower lip, I thought of the many stories told back home over the kitchen sink, of how my parents were married when Papa was twenty and she a few years older. I had come to understand that my mother, like all peasant wives, had been chosen not so much for her beauty, which was limited, and certainly not for her wealth, which was nonexistent, but for her strength and ability to manage farm life, which were exemplary.

Through the cracks in the family stories, however, I had also come to understand that while my mother always loved Papa, in time she had turned away from him. Now that I

304

thought about it, I remembered how things had changed between them after Mama had had an emergency hysterectomy. Had the operation that saved her life in fact killed something else — namely, her need for amorous attention? Mama always claimed she tolerated my father's long absences from home because she supported his religious life — but that was a total lie, wasn't it? And what kind of lie was my supposedly holy father — who spoke so often of the blessings of love — living as well?

Right then I hated them all — Mama, Papa, and especially Dunya. Dunya, who was always so sweet to us but who was nothing more than a conniving wench who'd wormed her way into our home and into my father's pants. A fresh wave of tears burst from my eyes. Everything felt dirty and horrible: this apartment, my entire family, and me. I wanted to run away, flee this place and this life.

And then I heard it again, more knocking at our rear door. Oh, God, I thought, flooded with a kind of bitter joy, Sasha was back. Shaking the dishwater from my hands, I took a towel and dried my eyes. I was just about to reach for the door and pull it wide open when it came, an all too familiar chant that in this case was more like a threat. In an instant I knew it wasn't Sasha.

Half muttering, half growling like a cat, a woman's voice called, "Chri-i-ist is ri-i-isen!"

I had no doubt it was Madame Lokhtina, the former beauty of great society and influence who had abandoned husband, daughter, and fortune, all to become Father's greatest — and most annoying — devotee. She was the one I had discovered attacking Father, ripping away his pants, hanging on to his member, and demanding sin. What in the name of the devil did she want this late, and what was she even doing here in the capital? The last I'd heard she had been walled into a cell at the Verkhoturye Monastery, where soup and bread were slipped to her through a small hole.

Lest her muttering turn into a scream that would wake the dead, not to mention the entire building, I had no choice but to unlock the back door and crack it open. Staring into the darkness, I saw not even a remnant of her former delicate beauty but rather a haggard, filthy woman in a long torn coat of homespun. She leaned on a tall staff decorated with little ribbons, while on her head sat a most strange hat made of wolf fur, torn and muddied, that in a strange way resembled the headgear of a nun.

Around her neck hung a multitude of little books with crosses that represented the twelve Gospels.

She leaned forward like a mole, squinting and half whispering, "Christ is risen! *Christ is risen!* CHRI-I-IST IS RI-I-ISEN*!"*

"Da, da," I replied quietly, hoping to appease her. "Christ is risen." Madame Lokhtina was known and dreaded for this, her habit of walking down any street and barging into any room, screaming these words. Father had commanded her to stop and later taken to beating her, all to no avail. Indeed, the more he struck her, the louder she screamed.

"Yes, go ahead!" she had pleaded whenever she was thrashed. "Strike me! Beat me!"

Our newspapers wrote that my father had driven her mad — why else would a woman of such good breeding now be living on alms, her feet wrapped in rags in the winter and bare in the summer? The truth, however, was that Papa had healed her of neurasthenia, from which she had been bedridden for five years. After her recovery she had forsaken the material world and become the truest of believers. There were even some, including several highly placed bishops, who wanted to bless her as the holiest of the living, a *yurodstvo* — holy fool — revered in my country for choosing to suffer in the name of Christ.

"Is the Lord of Hosts at home this eve?" she inquired, eyeing me most suspiciously.

Without even hesitating, I lied for the second time that night. "Unfortunately, *nyet.* Papa left not too long ago."

"Do you know where he has gone?"

"Well, I'm —"

"Not supposed to say, eh?"

"I . . . I . . ."

The forlorn Lokhtina stared at me, and I was afraid she was going to burst into more of her hysterics, but she asked, ever so quietly, "Do you perhaps know, my child, if he has gone out for *radeniye?*" Rejoicing?

"Yes, absolutely," I replied, without thinking.

As soon as I said it, I saw a distinct look of appeasement melt across her grimy face. That's when I realized what I'd told her. I hadn't implied that my father had gone to dance with the Gypsies, or that he'd gone off to drink at the Restaurant Villa Rode or at the Bear, or even that he'd been whisked away to some fancy party with Prince Yusupov. No, in their own secret code, I'd just informed Madame Lohktina that my father had gone to participate in the principal *Khlyst* ritual, when members washed away sin with sin via the act of *svalnyi grekh* — group sinning — an act that was widely rumored to be nothing more than frenzied *grupa seksa.*

"Ah, *ochen xhorosho, ochen, ochen xhorosho.*" Very good, very, very good, said the filthy woman before me. "The flying angel," she continued, referring to the one who passed news and warnings from one ark to the next, "was afraid your father would refuse us again."

I had never seen Madame Lokhtina so quickly pacified. I had never seen the faintest trace of a smile upon her face, either. And yet she had a pleased look as she turned and started back down the rear steps.

It suddenly occurred to me what I must do. The *Khlyst* community was a closed one, deeply secret, almost impenetrable. And yet right here and now it was not my door but theirs that had been opened. Did I really want to do this?

"Wait a minute!" I called after her.

Madame Lokhtina turned and stared strangely at me. "What is it, my child?"

"I have been learning the greatest secret of the group," I ventured.

This powerhouse of religious hysteria stared at me, her eyes shrinking into suspicious slits, and said, "Which is?"

"How to nurture Christ within oneself."

"And where did you hear such things?"

Even I couldn't believe the words that came out of my mouth. "At the last *radeniye.* I am expected again tonight."

And this woman, who was but a crumb of her former self, said, "Well, then, you had better get your coat and come straight away with me, because we're both late. And tardiness is the one thing 'our own' cannot abide."

CHAPTER 18

I was so mad at Papa that I hoped he checked and saw that my side of the bed was empty. Just let him boil in worry, I thought as I followed Madame Lokhtina through a back alley and onto a side street.

But while being devious felt like the best revenge, what was I getting myself into? What I really wanted, of course, was to be with Sasha. And yet, wiping the last tears, now frozen, from my eyes, I glanced all around and realized he was not about. I really and truly had sent him on his way. Resigned, I trudged on after my father's most fanatical devotee.

In Russia there had never been such a thing as a conservative priest, much less a liberal one. There was only one Orthodox Church with only one liturgy, just as there was only one tsar. In fact, any Russian knew that to be anything but Orthodox was heresy and strictly punishable by beating or lifelong imprisonment or both. By law there was no deviation from any of the official church doctrines. Last year it had taken me hours to try to explain this to a girl I'd met, the daughter of an American diplomat. She claimed that in her country religious opinion could and often did vary from church to church, which I myself barely understood. Something like that could never happen in Russia. In our country, *pravoslavni* actually didn't mean just Orthodox, it meant the "correct worshipers." The Catholics and Lutherans, even the Muslims, were always from different countries and only barely tolerated here. Beneath them came pagans like the Buddhists, lower yet, of course, the Jews. And at the very bottom were the schismatics, those Russians who dared to seek another path.

Because there was officially only one God and one tsar, one orthodoxy and one Russia, anything different — any splinter group that preached a different liturgy or outlook — was called a sect. Supposedly, there were hundreds of sects scattered all across Siberia. It was only out there, at the back of beyond, that one could escape the government's reach, build a free life, and nurture any kind of independent thought, let alone a religious one. Sometimes even Siberia wasn't far enough. If caught, a sectarian could be whipped and lashed; in the old times, it was said, their nostrils were cut off. After Peter the Great had initiated church reforms — he placed the church under his control, encouraged men to shave, and required his subjects to cross themselves with three fingers, not four — the Old Believers broke away from the state church, fleeing all the way through Siberia and, finding themselves still hounded, across the Aleutian Islands to our most distant territory, now owned by the Americans. Other secret sects hadn't gone so far; they could be found hidden along forgotten rivers and in distant villages. Though no one admitted to membership or even firsthand knowledge, one heard regular whispers of the *Skoptsy,* who believed in castration as the way to deal with sexual feelings, the *Dukhobory,* who were known as pacifist "spirit wrestlers," the *Subbotniki,* whose religion fell somewhere between Christianity and Judaism and who, it was said, practiced necromancy, the *Molokans,* who rejected the divinity of the tsar by drinking milk on fast days, and many others. Not long ago I'd heard a group of women talk right in our apartment about whole villages where personal property was condemned as sinful and whose residents lived as one large family. Supposedly, the peasants owned and worked the fields jointly, and both the monarchy and capitalism were condemned. Even more shocking, there were no priests, only people of the people who conducted church services.

But while every Russian knew of the sects and swapped titillating tea-table gossip about them, no one openly admitted to being a sectarian of any kind. That was why I was so struck by Madame Lohktina's claim of a *Khlyst radeniye* taking place tonight, right here in the capital. Could it really be made up of a group of princes and dukes, countesses and baronesses? As I followed her through the dark, I probably should have been afraid, but it never crossed my mind. Instead, a strange sense of exhilaration began to seep into me.

As she scurried along, Madame Lokhtina suddenly burst out, saying, "Nazareth was not unique. No, not unique at all!"

Because no one knew what would set her off, Papa had always told me to avoid her lest she launch into some tirade. But tonight I didn't care. In fact, I wanted to hear it all, see it all.

"What do you mean?" I asked.

"I'm talking about the birth, of course.

314

The one there in Nazareth, when God was born a man!" She shook her head as if trying to shake away some evil thoughts. "It didn't just happen once, you know. It couldn't."

Trying to keep her talking, I said, "Of course not."

"Exactly. The birth — it's being repeated all the time. Once you submit, once you recognize the power of the Holy Spirit, that's when it happens. A new Christ is born! A new Christ who can heal the sick and see the future! A new Christ who can save us all on Judgment Day!"

"Yes, I've learned that's one of the principal beliefs of the *Khlysty* —"

She spun on me like a crazed animal, grabbing me by the arm, her eyes afire. Terrified, she looked behind us for someone, anyone, who might be following us down the deserted street.

"Shh! There are things — names — you must never mention! Never!" She pulled off one of her tattered gloves, pushed up my sleeve, and sank her cracked fingernails into my naked wrist. "Never!"

"Yes." I winced.

I tried to pull my arm from her painful clasp, but she wouldn't release me. Indeed, she drew me closer, pressing her lips close

315

to my ear. I cringed as her dank, steamy breath poured against my cold skin and spilled like old tea down my collar.

"Some used to call us the Cod People, but our true name is this." She checked the street again, to make sure we weren't being observed, and then pressed her dry, cracked lips right against my ear and whispered, *"Khristovshchina,"* the Christ faith, "that's our real name, though you must never speak it."

"Of course not."

"It was only the dark ones, the evil priests, who changed our name. They sought to darken us, to blacken us with rumor and innuendo, so others would stay away. And yes, it was the priests who branded us with that name." As fierce as a drowning person, she pulled me close again. "They called us the *Khlysti*" — The Whips, the Flagellants. "But they lie! They say terrible things and they say we cut off the breasts of virgins and eat them! The priests lie to protect their positions and keep their gold gowns and pearled hats!"

"Perhaps," I said, as scared of her as I was of her blasphemous words.

"It is truth!" she nearly screamed.

This time it was I who firmly took hold of her. Latching my arm beneath hers, I tugged her along.

"We must hurry."

"I tell you the truth. I do!"

"I know, I know. But we're late and . . . and someone will notice us if we stand here much longer."

Madame Lokhtina flinched at the thought and glanced furtively up and down the street, searching the deep night for secret agents.

"Look!" she gasped. "I saw something move, a shadow! Someone's back there, someone's following us!"

I looked carefully but saw nothing, only a deserted street. "Come on, we must keep going."

Finally, she started moving, and as we pressed on she clung to my arm and babbled away, saying, "I will tell you the secret of tonight's activities, my child. Do you know it? Do you?"

"Well, I —"

"It's all about cleansing, of ridding yourself of darkness. Just remember, if you have a glass of dirty water there is no way to turn what is foul into clean. Even if you add some pure holy water, the water in the glass will be tainted. Satan is so powerful that only a drop of him can ruin all! So what can you do? You must first empty that glass!"

That made sense, I thought. I myself had never felt so dirty and in need of purification as I did now.

"You must cast away that soiled water, no matter how little or how much is in the glass! And only when you have flung it away, only when you have emptied the vessel, is there cleanliness and innocence, and then — and only then! — is there a sacred place for the freshest water to come in and be stored without contamination."

"I see," I replied, understanding not just in my head but in my heart as well.

Arm in arm, we scurried along, two women, one young, with boots crunching in the frost, and one old, her rag-swathed feet sweeping through the snow. When she tugged my arm, we turned right at the next street. A half block later we ducked down a side alley and wound our way through the middle of a block. Emerging on a major thoroughfare, we continued to the left. And so it went for at least a half hour. With a smile on my face, I thought how Papa would lock me up for this, being out so late and walking the dark streets with just another woman. But I didn't care. It all felt so liberating.

From time to time, Madame Lohktina would growl under her breath, "Christ is ri-i-isen! Chri-i-ist is ri-i-isen! Chri-i-i-i-ist is ri-i-i-isen!" And then, bubbling like a nervous brook from her lips, "Alleluia! Rivers, great rivers! And Christ, the Lord Sabbath! I have fear and love, great love! Help me, give a hand, help me! *Allelu-iaaaaaaaaaaaaa!*"

Suddenly, she jerked me to the right, into an alleyway wide enough for only one person. She stuffed me into this black hole, then peered back out, searching up and down the street. There was no one, of course. The last people I'd seen were several blocks back, a group of wounded soldiers huddled around an open fire.

Smashing me against the wall of the narrow passage, she pressed past me, then snatched me by the hand and pulled me on.

"Bistro!" Quickly, she commanded.

I could barely see, and half stumbled, half ran as I was dragged along. We went around one corner, another. As if we were entering a cave, the passage became smaller and darker with every moment.

"Steps!"

That's indeed what came next, a waterfall of steep steps I nearly tumbled down and would have, had Madame Lokhtina not caught me and guided me. We turned one last corner, descended one last set of stairs.

Finally, the two of us huffing, we stood before a heavy wooden door, against which she rapped once, then thrice, finally twice.

A voice from behind the door called, "Who flies this night?"

"Bozh'i-Liudi." God's People, she said.

"What did the prophets predict?"

"That Christ would descend upon us."

A heavy bolt was thrown aside and a thick door pulled open. We blew in like a cold gust, and the door was slammed behind us. Gazing around, I saw a handful of candles burning on the stone floor, and a stout man, whose head was covered with a white hood in which eyeholes were crudely cut. On his body he wore nothing but the plainest white flaxen gown, which hung all the way down to his bare feet. Reaching under his hood, he pulled out the end of his long gray beard and tugged on it. First he carefully studied Madame Lokhtina. Satisfied that she was one of theirs, he nodded his approval and pulled her past him, shoving her down a dark hall. When he turned to me, however, I immediately sensed his confusion, even fear. Almost at once he started shaking his head. Turning me to the side, he pulled away the heavy scarf covering my hair and examined my profile. Of course he didn't recognize me.

"Nyet, nyet, nyet!" came his deep, confident voice.

Almost at once his meaty hand emerged from beneath the gown and grabbed me by the shoulder. With his other hand, he reached for the heavy iron bolt and began sliding it open. In a panic, Madame Lokhtina leaped from the shadows.

"She is his!" she screamed.

The heavy man didn't care who I was or where I'd come from. All he knew was that I didn't belong down here, and with great speed and force he proceeded to heave open the door.

"Wait!" screamed Madame Lokhtina. "You don't understand!"

Of course he understood. I was not one of theirs. And I was not to be admitted, no matter what. As he pulled back the door, another gust of winter chill cascaded inward. Dear God, I thought, as the man grabbed me by the collar and made ready to hurl me out. I was fairly confident I could find my way home, but at this hour of the night I could only hope to do it safely and without incident.

Suddenly a second hooded man appeared out of nowhere, bellowing, "Wait!"

In the snap of a second I was jerked back. Once again the thick door was heaved shut and the iron bolt slammed into place. I turned around and stared at another man in a white hood and flaxen gown, this one not as tall or big as the first. Right behind him stood Madame Lokhtina, whispering in his ear. I heard nothing but one magical word.

"Doche." Daughter.

Yes, I was indeed his.

The shorter man nodded decisively, stating, "It is permitted!"

A smile on her dirty face, Madame Lokhtina burst forward and grabbed me by the hand. "Come with me, child!"

As I was pulled past the second man, I felt him staring at me from beneath his hood as if he knew me — and I, assuming he was one of my father's followers, was sure he did. When he nodded distinctly and politely to me, I couldn't help but wonder if he'd eaten fish soup at our table.

Dragged along by Madame Lokhtina, I followed her down a narrow brick passage lit by an occasional torch. Suddenly she stopped. In the flickering smoky light of one of the torches, she probed a wall with her filthy gnarled hands. When her splintered fingernails came across one particular brick, she nearly glowed with delight.

"Chri-i-ist is ri-i-isen," she crooned as she

pressed on the brick. *"Chri-i-ist is RI-I-ISEN!"*

Like magic, a hidden door in the wall gave way, opening into a large chamber. Madame Lokhtina grabbed my right hand, squeezed it, and took me through, entering the hidden world of the *Khlysty.* As my eyes swept from side to side, my body flushed with a weird kind of excitement. Here before me, buried in a lost cellar beneath Petrograd, were some thirty men and women, all dressed in long white gowns of flax and virtually nothing else, no pants, no dresses, no shoes or boots. In the sweet flickering light of beeswax candles, they swayed from side to side as a small choir chanted, "Our hearts are filled with joy, for seeing Christ has risen!"

In reply, Madame Lokhtina beat her chest in a cross and intoned, "Yes, indeed, He has!"

Still clutching my hand, she tugged me across the room. No one seemed to notice us as we traversed the space. Indeed, all the believers were totally focused on one man, thin and bearded, his smile broad and happy, who stood at the front chanting a prayer. He was their leader, I presumed, and the head of this ark or, in the terms of the *Khlysty,* the local Christ.

"In here," commanded Madame Lokhtina. "We must remove our clothes and put on holy garments!"

As she pulled me into a small side room lit by a single slim candle, I flushed with worry for the first time. Tossed on the floor were shoes and boots, pants and dresses. Off to one side, hanging from a hook, were a handful of white flaxen gowns. Dear Lord, I'd been only too happy to escape our apartment, but now what? What had I got myself into? All the old stories and rumors came flooding back. What if they were all true? What if the breasts of virgins were lopped off and eaten? What if virgins were pinned down and impregnated by all the men? What if the blood of virgins was drunk?

Bozhe moi, I thought in complete panic, what if I am the only virgin down in this hidden place?

"Get undressed! Hurry, child, they are waiting for you!" pressed Madame Lokhtina.

Waiting for *me?* In a flash it was perfectly clear: I had no choice, there was no escaping. My hands trembling terribly, I reached slowly for the top buttons of my dress, only to glance over to see Madame Lokhtina frantically undressing. As eager as a debutante to join a mazurka, she dropped her staff, tossed aside her absurd headgear, and started ripping away her dress. A moment later I spied her bony naked body darting around the small chamber. Oh, Lord, help me, I prayed as she clumsily tugged one of the gownlike shirts over her head and spindly neck.

Forgetting about me, Madame Lokhtina rushed from the room. Hearing the choir sing louder, faster, I peered around the corner and into the main chamber. The local Christ was calling and shouting out in great glee.

"Brothers! Sisters! Let us call down God!" he commanded as he lifted both hands to the heavens.

"Oh, Lord the Spirit!" screamed one woman.

"Oh, God the Father!" shouted a man.

"Oh, Holy One!"

"Come to us, Dear One!"

"Present Thyself!"

It was then that I saw not only several of the revelers studying me, their brows creased with disapproval, but also the first hooded man, the heavy one. Sealing the secret door, he turned his angry eyes upon at me. In one brusque movement, he pulled off his hood, revealing a fat, gray, and hairy face that looked none too pleased to see me in my regular clothes.

A deep voice to my side suddenly commanded, "You must cast away your European clothing and garb yourself in *sermyaga!*"

Gasping, I jumped back. Standing just inches from me was the second hooded man, the shorter one.

Jerking away from him, I replied, *"Da, da!"*

Retreating to the side room, I knew I had no choice. I had to undress and put on one of their coarse peasant gowns. If I didn't, they'd know for certain I wasn't truly one of them — and then what? What would they do to an interloper? Far better that I try somehow to blend in. I huddled in a corner and started to shed my clothes. Oh, God, I thought, fearful that the second hooded man would come in as I undressed, terrified that he would corner and molest me. I now saw what an utter fool I'd been to come here.

Dressed in one of their plain flaxen gowns and shaking from head to toe, I emerged from the side room a few minutes later. Feeling my naked body rub against the loose rough cloth, I felt totally exposed in front of this group of sectarians and clasped my arms tightly across my chest. They wouldn't attack me, would they? The very idea of sacrificing myself in order to be proclaimed their *Bogoroditsa* — their Mother of God — was revolting. Surveying the room, I tried to spot Madame Lokhtina, hoping to find shelter in her protection. But when I heard a sob and saw her begin to whirl up at the front, I knew it was useless.

A strong hand grasped me from behind, the fingers sinking into my shoulder. I stifled a scream. It was the second of the hooded men.

His voice hushed, he ordered, "Do not tremble so!"

I tried to pull away but he wouldn't release me. Tears came to my eyes. Glancing to the front of the room, I saw the local Christ begin to whirl and cross himself. My heart started pounding, for the *radeniye* had begun. A huge whoop went up from the celebrants, and the choir started chanting faster, louder.

"He will come!" shouted the local Christ as he whirled and whipped himself with a rag.

"We are ready!" shouted a man, jumping forward and starting to spin as well.

The hooded man pressed himself closer, whispering in the din to me, "Do not worry. There's nothing to be afraid of. You are one of us now, and that is good. We are all one family!"

Bozhe moi. I could hear the lust in his hushed voice, sense it in his close presence, feel it in the warm breath that spilled over me. What did he want?

"Do not worry, Maria, I am here," he said. "Change will come soon, and soon you must run from the city, this Western seat, without looking back!"

I cowered in terror.

A woman screamed, "He will come to the People!"

Another shouted, "He is of us!"

"We are of Him!"

In the flickering candlelight the entire congregation leaped into the middle of the room, formed a large circle, and started slowly moving from right to left. The choir half cried, half sang some special song. In response, the throbbing congregation cried to the heavens. Someone started screaming. Two men slapped their knees to the beat of the chant. The local Christ shouted an incoherent prayer. Bit by bit, the circle of celebrants began to move faster and faster.

The hooded man took me by the arm. "Come, we must join them!"

I was shaking more than ever, and the tears rolled freely from my eyes. "Please, no! I can't! I . . . I . . ."

He stopped and gently, gingerly, touched me on the shoulder. "But there's nothing to fear!" He grabbed the top of his hood and started to pull it up. "Maria, I wouldn't let anything happen to you!"

First his chin appeared, then that sweet mouth. I couldn't believe it. And when I realized who it really was, when I saw him standing before me, I collapsed sobbing in his arms. It couldn't be.

"Sasha!"

"There's nothing to worry about! I'm here," he said desperately, wrapping his good arm around me and holding me and kissing me on the head. "Sweet one, my Maria, I won't let anyone hurt you!"

"But how . . ." I tried to talk but couldn't. "I mean, you're here. . . . How . . . what . . . oh, I thought . . . I thought — !"

"Everything's okay, even wonderful!" he said, with a huge grin.

"But how —"

"You mean you didn't know?"

"Know what?"

"That I'd be here, that I belong here? And who I am, and — don't you understand? Isn't that why you're here? Don't you know? I would have told you — I wanted to — but I couldn't. Secrecy is my greatest commandment."

"Sasha, what are you saying?"

"I'm a flying angel. I travel from ark to ark, carrying news and warnings to and from other groups. That's why I was going to your village when we first met, why I asked so many questions about your father, and that's why I had to flee so quickly — to carry the news of the attack on your father to the other groups."

"You mean you're not a revolutionary?"

"Of course I am! What does revolution mean but to turn, to whirl, to twirl? And that's what we must do, turn everything around. We must get rid of the foreigners. God and tsar, they are all that matters. Your father is remarkable, for he not only abhors wealth and possessions, he has done the impossible, he has made it to him, Tsar *Batushka.* Your father connects us as no other peasant ever has to the Almighty's Own Anointed!"

"But . . ."

One of the celebrants shouted, "Oh, the Spirit!"

"Descend upon us!" yelled another.

They were all singing now. And all dancing, too, moving, gyrating, always circling right to left, crying to the heavens, begging for mercy, delivery, love. One person whipped another person with a rag, the local Christ whipped himself, and Madame Lokhtina, sweat streaming down her face, shouted gibberish.

"And your arm — what happened? How were you hurt?" I asked.

"There are two arks here in Petrograd, and when I was visiting the other one, we were raided by the police. I shouldn't have come to your house — that put your family in danger — but I needed your father's healing . . . I needed you."

I hadn't realized how abandoned I had felt, how lonely and ordinary. But now . . . now he was here, and I kissed him. I fell into him and kissed his lips and mouth as deep and hard as I could.

Then Sasha grabbed me by the hand and pulled me forward, saying with a big smile, "We must dance!"

Yes, I was dirty and wanted to be cleansed. I wanted to be rid of everything but this moment. So dance we did, joining the group in joy and ecstasy. We all held hands and spun and cried out. I stared into Sasha's lovely brown eyes and saw them staring back. We turned and twisted. And as I moved and twirled I felt my worries and fears and impurities begin to lift from my shoulders. I stepped faster, spun more quickly, and, yes, I felt everything start to fly away, as if I were shedding something filthy and confusing.

Someone dropped from the group, falling into the middle on his knees and whipping himself with a wet rag. Sasha's head fell back, and he bellowed out something in Indian or in the language of Jerusalem.

"Rente rente funtritut!" he cried at the top of his voice. *"Nodir lisentran entrofit!"*

I had no idea what he was saying, but I understood what he meant, what he was searching for, for he was seeking nothing more than that which all the *narod* wanted: freedom and love and spirituality, the sense that no man was above another, and the absolute knowledge that every man of every level had the capacity to cast away his sins and become at the very least Christlike. I wanted all that too. As I spun and cried out, as I shook and trembled, my sweat began to fly from my brow and my flaxen gown became soaked with perspiration. Someone in the middle twirled and whirled so fast that he flew to the side, falling on his knees, screaming.

"Oh, the Lord! He is close!"

"Oh, Brother! Oh, Brother!"

"Alleluia!" shouted the local Christ, completely drenched with sweat and twirling faster than ever. "I feel it! He is coming!"

I broke loose and started spinning and turning, my gown twirling wide, my hair flying. I felt every dark thought, every doubt, every sin, seeping from my being, emptying through my pores. Sweat gushed from me, washing everything impure from my body and soul. Suddenly a gigantic whoosh — a kind of spiritual beer — poured into me and lifted me up. I raised my hands and felt something divine rain down from the heavens and swim through and around me, a power greater than any I had ever felt. What was it? What godly force was overtaking us all?

Out of the corner of my eye, I saw Sasha spinning and smiling, his face turned to the heavens. Yes, he was here, we were together, all would be well.

"Oh, Spirit Lord!" sobbed someone.

"Alleluia!"

"Rejoice, for He has come!"

And then Sasha was grabbing me with his one good hand and pulling me along. My body had stopped spinning, but my head could not.

"Oi!" I shouted, tumbling into him.

"Come, my love," he gasped, pulling me along.

I closed my eyes, feeling like a cloud blowing through the sky — yes, a cloud, blowing right into him.

"Brothers! Sisters!" cried the local Christ. "I sense it! The Holy Spirit has come! God has poured Himself into me!"

A woman screamed. A man collapsed on the floor.

Half running, Sasha led me into the side room. We went there, into that little space, and while the rest of the congregation spun and sang and cried out, we began kissing. He pressed me against the hard brick wall, and his soft lips flew across my mouth, my ear, my neck. My body flushed with a desire I had never known or even expected, and I wanted him as I never wanted anything else. Every bit of inhibition had been spun away, and I felt nothing but love and desire, heat and want. He dove downward, burrowing his face between my breasts, rubbing, pressing, kissing, and I clasped him and pulled him as hard as I could against me. This was our future, our destiny, and together we were crossing over a bridge of passion to everything wonderful. I shoved him back, and without a moment's hesitation I grabbed the length of my flaxen gown and pulled it up and over my head, exposing my naked self as I never had to any man. Pulling at his collar with his good hand, Sasha tore open the entire front of his gown. I clawed at the thatch of hair on his chest, groped his firm stomach, and, for the first time, caressed a man's firm, determined desire.

And as the rest of the congregation collapsed harmlessly on the floor of the main room, Sasha and I fell into each other in joy and love and celebration.

CHAPTER 19

I woke alone the next morning.

As much as I wished it otherwise, as much as I still sensed his firm body in my dreams, Sasha was not lying by my side. Rather, I was at home and in bed by myself. Opening my eyes to the bright light, I saw neither walls nor ceiling, only this: his naked body pressing into mine. Pulling up my night-dress, I gingerly ran my fingers over my naked belly. His seed was there, within me. A soft smile spread across my lips.

When he'd dropped me at the rear door late last night, Sasha had embraced me, saying, "Take care, sweet one. I'll see you soon."

"When? Tomorrow night?"

"Yes, I'll try."

"Promise?"

"Absolutely," he said, kissing me on the forehead.

Now climbing out of bed, I felt no shame

for having given myself to Sasha. Just yesterday I would have been terrified that Papa might find out, but today I didn't care, not a bit. Nevertheless, there was no need for him to find out, was there?

It hadn't occurred to me just how late I'd slept, and I couldn't tell from the low dark clouds in the December sky, but when I looked at a clock I saw that it was nearly one in the afternoon. Given the healing at the palace and then my late-night adventures, it wasn't really a surprise. What did astonish me, however, was to learn that Papa had already risen and had been seeing petitioners, one after the other, since nine that morning.

Stepping out of my room was like stepping into a bazaar. No wonder, I thought. It was Saturday, and Saturdays were always Papa's busiest. Today, December sixteenth, would be no different. Women of every age and fashion were buzzing through our apartment, some of them old and dressed in black, others young with abundant curves, some made up with Parisian rouge, and others pale and homely. Our dining room table was strewn with today's gifts — candies and flowers, fruits and nuts — while the samovar was steaming before a near-continual line of supplicants in search of winter's antidote, tea. The telephone seemed to ring nonstop.

Making my way into the washroom for my morning toilet, I noticed right away a sense of nervousness, of desperation.

"In the Duma there's talk of nothing but *revolutsiya,*" said one woman quietly, standing in the hall, eating a biscuit and sipping tea.

Her friend pressed close to her and muttered, "Just terrible. . . . Did you hear what Maklakov, the Duma deputy, has been saying around town? He's saying it won't be a political *revolutsiya* but one of rage and revenge of the ignorant masses! He keeps shouting, 'Beware the peasant with the ax!' "

"*Bozhe moi!*" gasped the first, crossing herself, biscuit in hand.

Frightened, I hurried past the two women. Once I'd washed and brushed my hair, I peered into the salon, searching for my father. And there he was, standing before a very proper lady with a feather boa and another woman in a worn cardigan, the first holding his right hand, the second kissing his left. Why, I couldn't help but wonder, were these women — not just these two, but all of them here today — so willing, so eager, to give up control and submit to my father? Were they that needy, that scared, that desperate? On the other hand, Papa, his eyes settling on nothing and no one, seemed not to notice any of the attention. In fact, he looked frightful, his hair more disheveled than ever, his blouse wrinkled, and the sash around his waist loose and sagging. Spotting me, Papa pulled away from the two women and started across the salon. Never had I seen such dark rings beneath his eyes.

"Hello, my little bee," Papa said softly, kissing me on the forehead. "Did you rest well?"

Averting my eyes, I nodded. Did he have any idea that I'd spied him in bed with Dunya? Better yet, did he even suspect that I'd sneaked out last night? Amazingly, the answer to both was, I knew, no.

"Papa, I'm worried."

He shrugged and looked past me. "Faith has been lost."

"But people are saying the worst things. People right here in our apartment are talking, and . . . and . . ."

"You think I don't know it will soon come to an end? There are enemies everywhere — yes, even here within our home."

His passivity shocked me. Never had I heard or seen my father so demoralized. Had he had a vision during the night, or had he simply come face-to-face with common sense? Then again, was he beyond the brink of exhaustion?

No matter my anger and disappointment in him, I knew at least that I had to warn him, so I said, "Do you remember Elena Borisovna, the one whose grandson you healed?"

"Certainly."

"Well, she said —"

He pressed the long hard index finger of his right hand to my lips. "Shh, my sweet little bee. I hear and follow the words of God and no one else."

"But —"

Again he kissed me on the forehead. "Go and eat a bowl of steaming hot kasha — don't forget the crispy onions! — and then some fish. Clear your soul of worries. Eat, and then prepare to go out. You and your sister must meet your cousin Anna this afternoon."

"But, Papa, I . . ."

He walked away with all the authority of a tsar who'd just muttered the imperial *bit-po-semo* — so be it. For a moment I was tempted to run after him and grab him by the sleeve. I wanted to hit him and yell at him, even to confess my adventures. Instead, guarding my secrets and my passion, I turned and slowly made my way through the handful of petitioners. For the first time, I sadly realized that my father and I were not only traveling separate and divergent paths but our paths were destined never to cross again.

Toward three in the afternoon, Varya and I were indeed forced into an excursion with our cousin Anna, who was newly arrived in the capital. Much to Anna's delight, we went straight to Nevsky Prospekt, where we visited the numerous shops of Gostiny Dvor and then, crossing the street, the tall arcade of Passazh. Much to my dismay, we took dinner at the small apartment of Anna's close friends, who had moved to the capital some five years earlier. We didn't return home until after ten that evening, and when Dunya greeted us at the door I couldn't even look her in the eye.

My back to her as I hung up my cloak, I asked, "Where's Papa?"

"He has a visitor."

"Still?" said Varya as she slipped off her boots.

"Your father has had a very busy day," our housekeeper replied as she handed us our *tapochki,* for she would not allow us to go about in our stocking feet in such cold weather.

When I peered into the salon, I saw that it was empty, meaning, of course, that Papa had escorted his guest to his small room with the sofa. This in turn told me not only that my father's visitor was surely a woman but probably a blonde — and almost certainly buxom as well.

Irritated, I demanded, "Who's visiting Papa at this hour? What's her name?"

As if she thought nothing of it, Dunya said lightly, "Sister Vera."

Shaking my head in disappointment, I headed off toward the kitchen. Her name might be Vera, and she was probably someone's sister, but I doubted if she was a sister of truth.

"Maria," called Dunya, "where are you going at this hour?"

"To make some tea. I need to stay up so I can talk with Papa."

"*Nyet, nyet, nyet.* It's much too late already."

"But it's important!"

"Whatever you have to say can wait till morning."

"But —"

"Off to bed, the two of you — scoot!"

Freezing there in the hall, part of me was ready to explode at her — didn't she know

I understood what was going on between Papa and her? — while the other part wanted to fall into her arms and tell her not only about Elena Borisovna's warnings but about Sasha as well. Instead, I went off to bed, sure of only one thing — that it would be best for all of us to quit Petrograd by the light of tomorrow's sun. Perhaps Sasha could follow, but Papa, for his own safety, needed to leave the capital as soon as possible. I was sure that if he lived for a while in the distant woods he could find what he had lost, the very thing the depravity of the city had stolen from him: his hunger for true spirituality. In the past several years, Papa's face and body had become so fleshy and full, sated by bottomless wineglasses and endless feasting.

Oh, God, I thought as I stood in my room, unbuttoning my dress and letting it fall to the floor. I didn't want to be here. I didn't want to be observing my stupid father and his ridiculous actions. And I certainly didn't want to be under the sharp eye of our fat housekeeper. I didn't belong here anymore. I wanted to be with Sasha. I wanted to tell him my worries. I wanted his advice. I yearned for his arms around my shoulders, his tender caress, his sweet kiss.

Sitting down on the edge of the bed in my

underlinens, I realized that my mind and body were numb. I wanted nothing more than sleep . . . and yet how could I dare to close my eyes at a time like this? If I drifted away, how could I warn my father about the grand dukes? Better yet, how could I keep Papa from hurting himself, from doing something stupid and dangerous, like going to the Gypsies to drink and dance? It occurred to me that I should take a blanket and sleep on the floor in front of the main door. No, I thought, Papa could still slip out the back. Perhaps I should nail both doors shut. Or perhaps I should telephone the palace and beg to speak with the Emperor himself and plead for his help. *Oi,* finding myself lost between three doors, I didn't know where to turn or what to do.

As she crawled into the other side of the bed, Varya said, "You've been crying a lot lately. What's the matter?"

"I'm just a little worried, that's all," I replied, blotting my eyes. "I . . . I need to talk to Papa, and yet I can't bother him. But if I go to sleep, I'm afraid I'll miss him."

"You mean you're worried he'll go out and you don't want him to?"

"Exactly."

"Oh, that's easy," said Varya, clambering back out of bed.

"Wait!"

"Hush, I'll be right back."

"You can't disturb Papa in his study!"

"Don't worry, I won't. What do you think I am, some kind of *durachka?*" Cute little idiot?

There wasn't much I could control in the world, so few things over which I had any influence, my sister being one of the very few exceptions. Just then, however, I was so exhausted I was practically helpless. I should have hurried after Varya to make sure she wouldn't do something stupid like walk in on Papa and the supposed Sister Vera, but as the seconds ticked by, my energy trickled away. Fortunately, I heard Varya's light steps returning a few short minutes later. In her arms were Papa's tall black boots — nothing fancy and only slightly polished, the leather creased and softened from near-endless wear. They were the kind a peasant would wear for years and years, not in the fields but on Sundays or into town to trade grain. Even though Papa had been given fancy velvet breeches and hand-embroidered blouses and wore them often, his tall country boots were the one thing he had never abandoned for big-city footwear and never would.

With a big huff, Varya blew her bangs

upward. "I hid his special fur coat once when I didn't want him to go out, but it didn't work. He just took his old wool one. But he always wears these boots, and he'd never go out without them."

"Molodets." Smart girl, I said.

"And he always shouts when he can't find them."

Of course he does, I thought with a smile. Whether he got up in the middle of the night, determined to search out some entertainment, or rose in the early morning and wanted to go to the *banya,* I'd certainly hear him pacing around and shouting for his boots.

Appeased, I took the boots from Varya and tucked them just under my side of the bed. With the last of my strength, I shed the remainder of my clothes and slipped on my nightdress. As I crawled into bed, I leaned over the lumpy mattress and kissed my sister on the forehead, then turned off the light and snuggled under the covers. Rolling onto my stomach, I reached under the edge of the bed and brushed my hand over the soft leather. Like the mighty River Tura that flowed through our village, I felt an overwhelming sense of relief flood my body. Tonight at least we were all safe. Within an instant, sleep carried me away.

CHAPTER 20

Oddly, I didn't dream of Sasha but of my mother's *pelmeni* — meat-filled dumplings — that were a staple of any Siberian diet. Mama always made them with not just two but three types of meat — beef, pork, and lamb — ground together with garlic and salt and pepper. She made them by the hundreds and kept them frozen in a bank of snow just outside our rear door. Throughout the long winter she would pluck them like dill weed, dropping a dinner's worth into the large kettle of boiling water that roared nearly every night on the fire. I loved mine slathered with our home-churned butter and a dollop of sour cream so fresh it was still silky sweet. More recently, even though it wasn't at all Siberian, I'd taken to following the aristocrats and sprinkling them with a bit of that French import, vinegar.

I dreamed, too, of the last time all of us Rasputins were home and gathered around the dinner table as one. Our parents had drunk vodka, while we children, as a very special treat, sipped the birch-tree juice we had gathered that afternoon in containers of bark. And honoring the joy of being all together, Mama had dropped two special *pelmeni* into the pot, one filled with salt, the other hiding a one-kopeck piece. With delight Varya had bitten into the coin, thrilled by the omen, certain it meant her grades would be good. I was glad to spy my mother secretly slipping the salt-filled dumpling to my brother, for when simple Dmitri bit into it, he hooted with delight.

"Good luck for one year!" he shouted, a smile spread across his wide, pimply face. "Good luck will follow me for one year!"

And when I woke with sweet memories, I wasn't at all surprised to open my eyes to darkness. I had no idea what time it was — night or day — but when I rolled over and groped for Papa's tall boots, my hand came up empty. With a gust of panic, my hand slapped everywhere and found nothing. When I'd gone to bed, I'd tucked the boots right there on the herring-board parquet floor, hadn't I? A horrible premonition swept through my soul.

From somewhere in the flat I heard movement, and through our cracked door I saw a sliver of light. Mother of God, I realized, Papa had sneaked in here and found his boots, and now he was getting ready to go out. In the flash of a second, I was completely awake, throwing aside the thick covers, leaping out of bed, and rushing barefoot from our room. What time was it? Where was Papa going?

I blew down the hall as fast as a fearful wind. Papa's door was half open, the room glowing a soft red from the icon lamp, but he wasn't there. Where in the name of the devil had my father got to? And where was Dunya? Turning, I moved on, poking my head into my father's study and finding it empty, then hurrying through the dark and abandoned main salon. Holding up the edges of my nightgown, I dashed to the front door, which was shut tight. Looking at the hooks lining the wall, I saw Papa's fancy fur was gone.

From the kitchen came sounds of shuffling. Perhaps Papa was avoiding the security agents by sneaking out the back? Wasting no time, I passed through the dining room and into the kitchen, where the single overhead bulb was burning. But there was no one. And then, from behind the curtain, I heard subtle rustling.

"Dunya?" I called.

"Maria, is that you?" she replied from her cot. "My child, what are you doing up now? Don't you know it's the middle of the night?"

"Where's Papa?"

"Gone out."

"Gone out? Where? When?"

There was more rustling and a groan as Dunya pushed herself to her feet. A second later, the curtain was pushed aside. Clutching her nightdress over her ample bosom, Dunya glanced at the clock and then at me.

"Maria, my dear, you need to go back to bed. It's —"

"I need to speak to my father!" I demanded.

"Milaya maya devochka," my dear young girl, "it's not even after midnight, and you've only been asleep for an hour. Now, really, you must return to bed. It would do no good to have you get sick!"

"Did Papa go out alone?"

"Nyet."

Oh, God, I thought. "Did someone come fetch him? Who? Who did he leave with?"

"What's the matter, Maria? Why are you so nervous?" Like a calming mother, Dunya ran one of her hands through my hair. "Everything's all right, my child. He just went out with Prince Felix, that's all."

"Oi," I moaned, jerking away from her.

"What's the matter? Everything's fine. The two of them have had plans for tonight for quite some time. There's nothing unusual about it, really. I was lying on my cot and heard everything. The prince came to the back door here and rang the bell, your father answered, and they left for the Yusupov Palace. Princess Irina is to be there. They only left a minute ago —"

A minute ago? I lunged for the back door and charged to the top step.

"Papa! Papa, wait!" I screamed.

There was no reply, not even a hollow echo. They'd already left the building, but maybe there was still time. If I hurried, if I was quick enough — if, if, if. In that instant I was tearing back to my room, casting aside my night clothes and pulling on my dress.

"What's going on?" asked Varya, sitting up in the dark and rubbing her eyes. "What time is it?"

"It's late . . . I'm going out," I said frantically. "Papa just left, and I have to catch him!"

"Oh," she moaned as she rolled over and went back to sleep.

Moments later I was grabbing my cloak and scarf and gloves and heading through the kitchen.

351

"What on earth are you doing, Maria?" demanded Dunya, standing in front of the door like a mother bear blocking the exit from her cave. "You can't go out at this hour! And certainly not by yourself!"

"I have to catch Papa. I've got to tell him something, I've got to warn him!"

"*Nyet,* I forbid it! It's too late, it's too cold! Your mother would kill me for letting you go."

Nothing had changed, and yet everything had. My task now was not to follow what someone decided was best for me but to take care of what needed to be done. I had no choice.

"Out of my way, Dunya," I said, with firm determination.

"Wh-what?"

I pushed past her, meeting no real resistance. Throwing open the door, I hurried to the steps and started down, my feet moving as quickly as a ballerina's. Behind me, Dunya's voice sang out like an angel of mercy.

"It's cold out — be sure to cover your head!" she called.

Well trained, I did just that, tying my scarf over my head and pulling my gloves on even before I reached the outer door. Flying outside, I burst into our courtyard, finding it deserted, cold and dark. A handful of lazy snowflakes descended on me as I turned one way and the other and then just stood frozen in confusion. Had they gone through the front archway and to the street, or had they sneaked out the back and through the alleyways as Fedya had done just the other night? My heart told me it was the latter, and I dashed toward the rear of the courtyard. I was just about to scream for my father when I saw something move in the dark depths of a corner. At first I thought it was one of the security agents huddled there out of the wind. But instead of a man in a long black leather coat, a smallish man with a beard ran out of the shadows toward me.

"Maria!" gasped Sasha with a nervous smile. "Perhaps I shouldn't have come, but I couldn't wait another —"

"Did you see my father?" I interrupted, totally ignoring his soft eyes and outstretched hand.

"Well, actually —"

"Was he with anyone? A younger man with a little mustache?"

"Yes, I . . . I think so."

"Bozhe moi!"

"What's the matter, what happened?"

As soon as he asked, I knew that if I didn't stop Papa from leaving, he would never return, and I begged, "They went out the back, didn't they?"

He hesitated a moment before nodding.

"Come on, my father's in danger!"

From the worry on his face, it was clear that, while Sasha understood nothing, he understood it all. I grabbed him by his good arm and pulled him along, the two of us darting out the back and through the maze of alleyways. We charged along the same path I had taken when I'd followed Fedya the other night, hurrying down one discreet passage, turning left at the next. In the smallest of snowdrifts I saw two fresh tracks, the larger certainly belonging to my father, the smaller undoubtedly that of the lithe prince. There were no other immediate tracks, at least none that I could see, meaning that while they weren't followed by an assassin, neither were they tailed by a security agent. And of course I understood: This was why Prince Felix was leading Papa out the back and down these lost alleys — so no one would see them, no one would know. But know what, the true nature of their relationship or the dangers ahead?

Oh, Papa, I thought as we ran, you can't be so stupid, can you? Are you nothing but an ignorant peasant after all?

Holding hands, Sasha and I bolted around the last corner. But we were too late. At the far end of the arching passage a motorcar painted military gray roared to a start and took off like a leaping tiger. Breaking away from Sasha, I started running as fast as I could. By the time I reached the street, however, the motor was speeding around a corner, and the last I saw of it was its black canvas top and rear windowpane of mica.

Feeling completely helpless, I stood there in the cold night air. What should I do, just return to our apartment and wait? Telephone the Empress — and say what, that I was desperately worried about my father? No, though I was on the verge of tears, I knew exactly my next step.

I called over my shoulder, saying, "Sasha, I've got to get to Prince Felix's palace on the Moika Kanal."

"No, Maria, that's not a good idea. Why don't you —"

"You don't understand, I have to!"

"But —"

Glancing up and down the narrow snow-swept street, I searched for a horse cab. "I've got to find a driver."

Understanding how determined I was, Sasha came up and brusquely kissed me on the cheek. "Wait right here."

"Why? What are you going to do?"

"When I came there was a motorcar parked in front of a restaurant back there. Just give me five minutes."

He was off that very instant, dashing to the left, down the street, and around a corner. I didn't know if he was going to try to bribe the driver or steal the car, but the moment he disappeared, I knew this was wrong. I couldn't involve him. Who knew what was going on tonight and just how dangerous it really was, but this was family business. I had no choice. My mind made up, I turned in the opposite direction and made my way quickly down the block. As I hurried along, I glanced back only once, desperately sad but relieved there was no sign of him.

Seconds later I emerged on Goroxhovaya Street, which to my dismay was deserted. Were this the middle of the day, the terribly straight street would have been full of horse cabs, their drivers, huge men with bushy beards wearing thick blue coats and square red hats, perched up front. But of course this was the middle of the night. When I searched up and down the street, there was nothing, no cabs, no sledges, certainly no motorcars. A squall of snow suddenly burst from the skies, and the flakes fell large and heavy on my head and shoulders, dusting me like confectioners' sugar. Was it hopeless?

Then I heard it, that most famous of Russian sounds, the jingling of troika bells. And not just heavy brass bells but silver ones, their chime fine and sophisticated in the still night. Any family of significance had their own troika with silver bells precisely tuned so their vehicle could be heard coming, as this one was. Or was it going? I looked one way, another, searching for a sound that seemed to bounce out of every street and off every building. My heart began beating faster, for with each moment the bright sound grew. Suddenly, a magnificent sleigh pulled by three horses burst out of a side street, the middle horse high and proud, the side horses lean and fast. In a flurry it turned my way. The coachman was cloaked in a heavy fur, and when I saw the peacock feather sticking like a flag from his big black hat, I knew I was right, this was a private sleigh.

Waving my arms madly, I leaped into the street. At first the troika didn't slow and barreled down on me, snow flying from the horses' hooves, the bells ringing away. Finally the burly driver spotted me, this speck in the street, and pulled back on reins as thin as leather threads. I didn't budge until the three horses, steam spouting from their nostrils, slowed to a prance and then a stop just steps from me.

"I need to hire you!" I said, running around the side.

The driver stared down at me like an amused bear ready to swat a pathetic bee. "This is a private sleigh, young lady."

"I have an emergency —"

"Sorry, I'm no Vanka," he said with a chuckle, referring to common horse-cab drivers, all of whom were so nicknamed. "Besides, I've just dropped off my master and am returning to the stable. My night is through."

When I saw him ready to crack the reins, I shouted desperately, "Two hundred rubles for an hour of your time!"

He froze, looked down upon me, his grin wider yet, and said, "And where does such a young thing as you come upon such great money? That's more than I make in months!"

"I'm Rasputin's daughter," I said, more proudly than ever. "Take me to the Yusupov Palace and back, and I swear there's two hundred rubles in it for you. Agreed?"

He thought for only a moment, then calmly said, "No doubt you'll find the sable blanket in the rear seat very warm."

I clambered in the back and we took off with a jolt. Speeding along, we were halfway down the block when I heard a desperate plea calling through the snowy night.

"Maria, no!"

Pushing myself up, I peered out the back of the troika. Sasha was running after us like some sort of crazed man. I kissed my hand and held it up to him in loving farewell.

And then I shouted out, not to Sasha but over my shoulder to the driver, calling, "Faster!"

The night of Rasputin's death, I remember, it was just two or three degrees above freezing and a damp snow was falling. I know for a fact that Maria thought it was up to her to save her father, that she thought she was his last hope. And perhaps she was. What she didn't know was that we knew her every move, nearly her every thought, which meant that every step she took was in fact a misstep.

And another strong memory, yes, most definitely: I remember staring down at Rasputin's body as it lay in the snow. He was wearing a fur coat and a beaver cap. And, too: His coat was flung half open and he wore a blue silk shirt embroidered with cornflowers, a thick crimson cord around his waist, and . . . and, oh, yes, black velveteen pants and high black boots, all of which was very grand for a peasant, very grand indeed. Someone told me later that the Empress herself had stitched those cornflowers on his shirt with her very own hand.

To tell you the truth, you've never seen such a trusting victim. Right up to the end Rasputin didn't suspect a thing. I kept thinking he would. After all, he was famous for his second sight.

You know about that telegram, don't you, the one from the Grand Duchess Elizavyeta, the Tsaritsa's sister? She congratulated us! The very day after the murder, she wrote, "All my ardent and profound prayers surround all of you for the patriotic act." Can you imagine, she, a nun, congratulating us for committing an act of murder? That was how widely hated, how dangerous, that bastard Rasputin was.

Actually, you know, the only thing I keep coming back to, the only thing that haunts me, was that poor girl, Maria. You can't imagine the shock on her face. I see that in my sleep, her absolute horror. The blood, too. She was covered with blood.

CHAPTER 21

Everyone in the city knew the palaces of all the grand dukes and nobles, including, of course, that of the most princely family, the Yusupovs, who after the Tsar were said to be the richest in Russia. Their sprawling palace at 94 Moika held, according to gossip, a gilded theater, picture galleries that held treasures of the world, bowls of uncut jewels, and room after room, some five hundred in all.

When the troika rounded a bend in the canal and the majestic yellow façade of the palace came into view, I wondered where in the name of God my father could be in there, in which wing, on which floor. Or was he even in there at all? If by chance it was all a ruse, if Prince Felix meant my father mortal harm, could he have driven him elsewhere? Peering ahead, I spied lights burning in a corner room. I only hoped it was really a party, that Papa was in there, dancing and drinking his Madeira. But how would I get in to find out? No matter whose daughter I was, there was no way I would be admitted, not at this hour and not in my plain dress. Even if I made a scene at the front door I wouldn't be allowed entry, nor would my father, if indeed he was there, be able to hear me.

Pointing to a side alley, I shouted up to the fur-covered driver, "Pull in there!"

In one giant arc the troika came swooping into the narrow street, slowing to a comfortable stop.

"Wait here," I said to the driver as I climbed out of the rear. "I'll be back in fifteen minutes."

"Now wait a minute, young lady. I wasn't born yesterday. How do I know you'll return . . . and how do I know I'll get my rubles?"

"We live at sixty-four Goroxhovaya, third floor. If I don't come back, go there and ask our housekeeper, Dunya, for the money. On the name of *Xhristos,* I promise you'll get paid."

As he shook his head and rolled his eyes, he said, "Fifteen minutes, no more!"

"Fair enough."

Pulling my cloak tightly around me, I hurried off. Within a few quick steps I emerged onto the street, turned to my left, and crossed to the granite sidewalk along the canal. Just ahead the Yusupov Palace, so massive and severe, nearly as formidable as a prison, rose up in the snowy night.

Oh, Papa, I thought, are you in there?

As if in reply I heard it clearly in my mind, a silent plea: *Yes, Marochka, sweet daughter of mine. Come quickly, quickly!*

Suddenly a sense of forgiveness flooded through me, and at that moment I knew not only how much my father needed me, but how deeply Papa and I were connected, how much of me was simply him, both literally and spiritually. The next moment, however, I felt a shock of mortal fear rip through me. Something terrible had already transpired against him. I knew it for certain, for I could feel his pain in my soul.

Shuddering, I hurried forward, following the edge of the frozen Moika. On this end of the palace sat a courtyard, which was separated from the street by a short stone wall and gate. And while I saw neither motorcar nor carriage parked inside, I did spy a small service door tucked in the side wall of the palace itself. Up ahead I could see but few lights on in the expansive building, most of them in the corner closest to me. That made sense. Palaces as huge as this were usually divided up, one wing for the parents, one for the younger generation. Yes, those lighted rooms were undoubtedly part of Prince Felix's apartments; who else would be up so late? Even as I approached the structure I heard revelry of some sort — music, actually. Pausing, I heard a song blare through the double-paned window. Was the prince hosting a soirée of some sort? Were those the sounds of a small band? I couldn't really tell. I could see shadows within, some movement, but nothing more specific, for heavy draperies framed the sides of the windows and lace curtains covered the center.

Hugging the wrought-iron railing along the embankment, I hurried on, scanning the façade of the palace, which rose some three or four stories. There had to be more than fifty or sixty large rectangular windows facing the street, and all but a very few were dark. Reaching six tall white columns that framed the entry, I saw the doorman sitting just inside, snoozing away.

I crossed the narrow road and went right up to the palace itself. Along the base of the structure was a series of half-moon cellar windows, and I peered in one after the other, finding them not only dark but covered with thick iron bars. Standing on my toes, I reached up to the metal sill of one of the ground-floor windows and tried to see in but could not. The room inside was black, and the heavy curtains were drawn tight against the cold.

Wasting no time, I headed toward the corner where the lights burned. With some sort of soirée going on, Papa was more than likely there. These early hours — it had to be near one in the morning — were his favorite for drink and dance, and the possibility of merriment relieved me a bit. Perhaps I was all wrong to worry. Hoping so, I neared the windows and could hear the music more clearly. In fact, I recognized the tune, one of the most popular of the day, "Yankee Doodle." I heard words in what I knew was the English language and surmised that the music wasn't coming from a small band but from one of those new machines that only a prince could afford, a gramophone. Even as I listened, the tune came to a scratchy end and started over.

The only windows filled with light were the last two or three ground-floor ones, and I stood again on my toes and tried to peer up into one of them. The fine white curtain was so sheer it was nearly transparent. The first thing I could make out was a brightly lit sconce on the right wall, second was the barely discernible image of someone crossing the room. I could see nothing more. And above the loud music I could hear nothing, no laughing or talking.

Then I heard a scream, not one of pleasure or delight but deep and coarse.

My entire body went rigid with panic. That had been no princess in distress, no fine lady either. It had been a man — my father. I recognized his shout immediately, for the tone of his distressed voice resonated deep within me. I jumped up, tried to see in the window, but couldn't. The only thing I could see was the blazing sconce on the wall, and the only thing I could hear was the cheerful fast-paced words of "Yankee Doodle."

Then the end happened faster than I could have imagined: A single shot rang out. But it didn't come from behind the lace curtains of the ground-floor room. Rather, the blast seemed to circle my feet, followed immediately by another scream, this one less powerful and infinitely more desperate.

"Papa!" I cried aloud.

Bending over, I saw faint light emerging from an arched window in the cellar. I fell to my knees, clung to the heavy iron bars, and tried to see in but couldn't, for the window was covered with heavy drapes. In my heart of hearts, however, I knew exactly what had happened: Papa had been led to the palace, taken down to some basement room, and then . . . then . . .

I tugged like a crazy woman at the window grate, but of course it didn't budge. I turned to the right, the left, peering helplessly up and down the street. What could I do? Who could help? Even if I shrieked to the heavens, it wouldn't matter.

Then it flashed before me, the image of the tiny service door tucked in the side of the palace. All at once I was on my feet, tearing down the snowy sidewalk. The courtyard gate was locked, so I ran right up to the short stone wall, gathered up the folds of my skirt, and clambered over. Slipping as I swung my feet over the top, I fell onto the ground inside. Frantic, I scurried to my feet and rushed like the maddest of fools to the small door. It never occurred to me that it might be locked, it never occurred to me what I might find within if I did gain access to the palace — or what I would do.

When I reached the unremarkable door, I pulled on it with all my force and it did indeed come flying open. All at once I found myself standing on a small landing inside the Yusupov Palace itself. Carefully pulling the door shut behind me, I stood there quite still, gasping for breath. I'd gotten inside, now what? To my left a set of rather steep, narrow stairs curled around and up to the main floor; to my right they curled downward. I was just about to rush to the cellar when I heard a door open below. All at once an abundance of deep, even jubilant voices came bellowing upward. It was a group of men, and the next moment they started up the stairs, their heavy boots beating the wooden steps. I didn't even consider fleeing outside — what if I couldn't get back in? — and instead clambered ahead of them, my feet moving quickly and softly.

As the stairs turned and curled upward, the sounds of "Yankee Doodle" grew ever louder. Within a half flight I came to a door that I slowly pushed open, to emerge in the smallest and oddest of rooms, not much more than a landing, really, and hexagonal in shape. Stranger yet, each of the six walls was actually a door, and to make matters more confusing, each door was covered with mirrors.

Standing there in my cloak, I froze. Which door led to safety?

As the pounding steps from below grew closer and closer, I lunged at one doorknob and twisted it. Nothing. It was, I realized, a false door. I tried another. It too was false.

Flushing with panic, I tried a third. The knob twisted, I pulled the door open, and I was immediately struck by the overwhelming beat of the American march from the gramophone. I was about to step through the door and into a salon of sorts when I thought I heard footsteps in that room. Was someone in there? Fearing discovery, I let go of that door and leaped at the next. To my great relief, the next one opened as well, revealing a shallow closet, into which I quickly pressed myself. I didn't even have time to pull the door fully shut behind me before the men emerged from the stairs. Through a slim crack I saw them all, and I was not surprised that I knew most of them.

"Thank God that reptile is no more," said a handsome young man, emerging and passing just inches in front of the closet.

It was, of course, Grand Duke Dmitri Pavlovich, the Tsar's own nephew, dressed smartly in military uniform. Behind him came his dearest friend, Prince Felix, who was nervously brushing his small black mustache.

"Why in the devil didn't he eat the pastries or at least take some wine?" demanded the prince, his voice shaking. "You don't think he knew about the cyanide, do you? I mean, he couldn't have, could he?"

"It doesn't make any difference, he's gone now. And obviously very mortal, after all."

Huddled in the closet, I nearly fainted. So I'd been right about these two. I'd been right about their hatred and their intent. And now my father was dead. Good God, why hadn't I warned him sooner? Why had I waited even a minute or two, let alone all these hours?

A man dressed, I thought, in a lieutenant's uniform followed next. Then came a fourth, this one dressed in plain clothes. I didn't recognize either of them, but the fifth, a bald man with a reddish beard and pointed mustache, wearing a khaki military jacket, was entirely familiar. It was none other than Vladimir Purishkevich, who was known across the country from his portrait, which regularly appeared in the journals.

"We shall celebrate, gentlemen, the end of the Elder," said Purishkevich, "and give thanks to God that the hands of royal youth have not been stained with that dirty blood."

Oh, God. Oh, Lord in Heaven. What had happened down there? What had those men done to my father?

Wanting nothing more than to attack them, I nearly burst out of the closet right then and there. Instead, I held myself back and only leaped from the closet once the five men had disappeared through the mirrored door and into the salon. Shaking so terribly I could barely walk, I charged back down the stairs. Reaching the very bottom, I came to a heavy oak door, which I hurled open. The first thing that hit me was the smell of fresh paint. The room, a sophisticated *bonbonnière,* had obviously only just been completed, yet it looked straight out of an ancient Russian palace, with its low arched ceiling, a thick carved column, heavy moldings, and walls painted dark brown and red.

"Papa?" I called into the dimly lit space, softly and hesitantly.

Stepping in, I entered an otherwise cozy room. My eyes scanned this way and that, somehow taking it all in: a warm fire burning quaintly in the granite fireplace, a gorgeous ivory crucifix placed on the center of the mantelpiece, a hand-carved chest, red brocade curtains draping from the small windows, and a tea table covered with an assortment of petits fours, little pink and brown pastries that had obviously been chosen because they complemented the colors of the room.

The first thing that crossed my mind was how stupid these men had been. My father would never have touched any of those little cakes. Of course, poison had always been the favorite weapon of the higher-ups, for well-bred people hated the mere thought of soiling their hands with death. But if these children from the higher stratum of society thought they could kill the infamous Rasputin by feeding him poisoned pastries, that proved how little they knew or understood my father and his convictions.

In the flash of a second, I pictured Prince Felix offering my father the plate of petits fours and heard Papa's disdainful response: "I don't want any of that scum. It's too sweet, it darkens the soul!"

Seeing the untouched glasses of wine, I was perplexed. If they had dropped poison into the glasses, why had my father avoided that as well? Had he had a vision? If he had indeed refused the wine, I was sure Prince Felix had flown into a panic and the rest transpired quite quickly.

My voice quivering, I called again. "Papa? Papa, are you here? It's me, your Marochka!"

Taking another nervous step forward, I saw that the room was actually divided into two parts. The front half with the fireplace was more like a tiny dining room, while the back served as a sitting room. Looking through the arch into the rear, I saw a settee and, on the floor in front of it, a white polar-bear skin. And crumpled next to the white hide lay a dark figure.

"Papa!"

He didn't respond, didn't even flinch. With tears gushing from my eyes, I rushed to him, dropping to my knees. He was rolled on his side, his front facing away, and touching him carefully I felt something warm and sticky.

"God, no!" I wailed, staring at my sodden-red fingers.

I held my hands above him, slumping onto the floor. And then, without even thinking, I did exactly as we had done at the palace when Papa had healed the Heir. Simply, I splayed my fingers wide and laid my hands directly upon my father. Emptying my soul, I closed my eyes and pointed my head to the heavens.

"Dear Lord, please have mercy! Please don't take him! Please, Heavenly Father, give him back to us!" Bowing my head over my father, I beckoned, "Papa, come back! It's me, Maria, your Marochka — come back to me!"

And he did just that. He returned.

Whether it was the Lord Our Father who infused life back into him, or whether Papa himself was able to summon the last of his strength, I didn't know. But he gasped terribly, spit some blood from his mouth, and then — with one horrible tremor — started breathing once again.

"Papa!" I called, bending down and smoothing his hair.

"*Dochenka? Dochenka maya?*" Little daughter? My little daughter?

"*Da, da,* Papa! It's me, your Maria!"

"*Oi,*" he moaned. "I just saw my own father. He was right here. Did you see him?"

I shook my head but had no doubt of my father's claim. Papa was dying and had crossed over to the other side, where he'd been greeted by his loved ones. Only my pathetic pleading had pulled him back to us, the living.

Moaning deeply, Papa said, "Felix . . . he betrayed me . . ."

"Yes, Papa, he shot you! I know. But I'm here now. I'm going to take care of you. I'm going to get you out of here!"

"*Da* . . . must leave . . ."

So the prince and his group had tried to poison Papa by offering him tainted sweets and wine. When that hadn't worked, Prince Felix had simply shot him. In any case, somehow my father still lived, but if I didn't get him outside and find help, he would certainly bleed to death from the bullet wound.

Invoking the age-old fear of every Russian peasant, I said, "Papa, you have to get up. The prince and the grand duke are going to come back — and they'll kick and beat and whip you!"

As if he'd seen it a hundred times in his worst dreams, my father's eyes widened in panic, and he reached up to me with one weak hand, begging, "Help me, Maria!"

As far as I could tell, my father had been shot in the stomach. As he struggled to rise, I clutched him around his back, helped him first sit up, then climb to his knees. With each movement he bit his lip and groaned.

"Are you all right?" I asked as he struggled to his feet.

He nodded hesitantly. "We must go . . . *bistro!*"

The first few steps were the most difficult. Papa stumbled badly and moved only with great effort. I feared, of course, that we might make it to the stairs but not up the steps. Fortunately, each movement seemed to get easier. Passing through the heavy oak door, we made it to the bottom of the staircase, where we paused, bathed in the distant rhythm of "Yankee Doodle," which had been started over yet again. All would be lost if any of them came back down.

"We only have to go halfway up, Papa. That's all. Just lean on me. There's a side door, and a troika is waiting for us."

He nodded. *"Xhorosho."*

I took a step up, and Papa, clutching the railing, did likewise. I moved higher, and he did as well. And so we proceeded, bit by bit, up and up. Within a few long minutes we reached the side door, which I kicked wide open. A flood of freezing air poured over us.

"Breathe in, Papa! Take in some nice night air! That's it, doesn't it feel good?"

Although he could barely swallow even a bit of air, he nodded. *"V'koosno."* Tasty.

We stepped directly from the palace into the flat courtyard. Glancing toward the gate, I wanted to pull my father along faster. I wanted to cry out for Sasha. I wanted a doctor. There was hope, always hope. Papa had been horribly wounded when that madwoman stabbed him, his entrails pouring out of his body. And yet he'd survived. Now he'd suffered just a single bullet wound, so couldn't he . . . he . . .

"I see it so clearly now, Marochka," muttered my father. "I see my mistakes —"

"Shh. It's okay, Papa. Just keep going. Don't stop. That's it, one foot after the other."

"I forgot. I became vain."

"Shh. Just keep moving."

"My mistake was simple. It wasn't me. Not me who healed people. Not me who . . . who . . ."

"Of course it was, Papa. You've helped hundreds, even thousands, of people, people who were horribly sick, people who were dying! Even the Heir Tsarevich — you saved him! I saw with my very own eyes how you stopped his bleeding and brought him back!"

"*Nyet!* It wasn't me who saved the boy, it was God! I was just the vessel. And I forgot that. I forgot I was just the earthly vessel for the Lord Almighty to do His work!"

I looked up and saw we were halfway to the gate. "That's it, Papa. Just keep walking, one foot after the other."

"*Da, da, da* . . . that's what I did wrong. I became vain. I . . . I took personal glory in my achievements."

"Don't stop, we're almost there!"

"But it wasn't me . . . it was Him, Our Father, who saved the boy and all those other suffering souls. It was God who healed them, not me! They were His miracles, not mine, yet I took advantage of it all. The power, the money, the women . . . I had it all, took it all! And now I'm being punished . . . punished for my vanity!"

"No, Papa, that's not true! You gave to so many — you gave and gave! Think how many you helped, think how much money you passed to those in need!"

All of a sudden my father stopped and grabbed his stomach. "Ah!"

Wincing in terrible pain, he tumbled into me, and if I hadn't clutched him just then, he would certainly have fallen over.

"Just a little farther, Papa," I said, holding him by the shoulders and begging him onward. "We have to keep moving."

"I . . . I . . ."

He could say no more. Nor could he move. Was it the bullet biting into him? Had it shifted about inside?

"I'm here," I coaxed. "And you're going to be okay. Just a little bit farther. Just a few more steps!"

"Ohhhh . . . ," he moaned.

Oh, God, I couldn't lose him now, could I? We'd made it out of the palace, we'd come this far. If we could just make it to the troika, if we could just —

"I . . . I —"

"Calm down, Papa. Catch your breath. We'll rest here for a minute."

"I . . . I fear that my time . . . has come," he said sadly, looking up at me.

"No, Papa, you mustn't give up!"

"When it . . . it . . ."

"Shh. Don't talk. Just be quiet and catch your breath."

"When it does, my sweet daughter, you . . . you must let me go."

Tears welled up in my eyes as I held him. How could I ever let my father go? Overwhelmed, I stared up at the dark heavens above me. It was starting to snow again, the flakes fat and heavy. Was this how it was all to end, here in a courtyard of a princely home? I'd had a vision of something like this, but why, dear God, why hadn't my gifted father?

Papa asked, "Child, comfort me with a poem, will . . . will you? How about that one I like so much? You know the one, by that writer, that . . . that fellow all you girls are crazy about."

I nodded and tried to steady my voice, as I recited, as softly as a prayer, the words of the great Aleksander Blok:

"To sin shamelessly, endlessly,
To lose count of the nights and days,
And with a head unruly from drunkenness
To pass sideways into the temple of God."

"Yes, that is nice, very nice . . . yes,

sideways." With no small effort, Papa grabbed me by one hand. "My sweet, dear, beautiful girl . . . I must tell you a secret."

Biting my lip and trying my best not to break down sobbing, I merely nodded.

"I know for sure that that is Heaven," he said, weakly pointing to the sky. "But now I . . . now I see also that this" — he looked around — "is not earth but hell."

"Papa, no. You mustn't talk like that."

He nodded. "Yes, this . . . this is hell."

Mopping my eyes with the sleeve of my cloak, I stood paralyzed in fear. If only the world could see him now, Rasputin the devil, for who he really was: my father, a *muzhik* who, unarmed and unsuspecting, had been shot like a mad dog. How easily he had been brought down . . . and how easily he had brought himself down. But I couldn't crumble, not now.

"Papa, listen to me. I have a troika waiting just around the corner. I'm going to fetch the driver, and the two of us will come get you."

My father's body went rigid with one huge spasm, and he cried out in pain. I held him around the waist and shoulder and felt his entire body quiver horribly.

"Yes . . . go," he finally muttered.

"I'll hurry!"

Carefully letting go of my father, I started to pull away. He began to teeter to the side, and for a moment I thought he would collapse right then and there in the side courtyard.

Raising his reddened eyes to me, Papa commanded, "Go!"

I gathered up my cloak and started to run. I just had to get the driver to bring the troika right here, and then the two of us would gather up my father and whisk him away. We just had to be quick. I had to be quick.

Dashing to the stone wall, I started over. Oh, Lord, I thought as I lifted my feet, I can climb over, but what about Papa? How would we get him —

I heard it quite clearly then. Just as I landed on the other side of the wall I heard someone shouting the alarm.

"He's getting away! Hurry!" yelled a voice that was much, much too familiar.

Turning around, I saw the small service door flung wide. And standing right there in the doorway, the light pouring from inside and over him, was . . . was . . . but how could it be? How did he — ? No, this was impossible.

"Sasha?" I muttered.

My entire body flushed with horror. Yes, it

was indeed my sweet Sasha. Only he wasn't coming to my rescue. No. He was . . . was . . .

"Hurry!" he shouted over his shoulder into the palace. "Bring a gun. You've got to shoot him again!"

I felt like a tiny bird that had flown full speed into a large pane of glass and then, stunned, fallen to the ground. What invisible reality hadn't I seen before? What hard truth was I facing now? The betrayal was too much, I couldn't comprehend what I was witnessing. And if I hadn't been in such shock, I would have cried out in horror. Sasha hadn't come to our rescue, but to make sure of my father's death?

"Where, Prince, where?" shouted Purishkevich, that infamous monarchist with the famously pointed mustache.

"Out there!" replied Sasha, pointing directly at my father.

I tried to call to my father, to beg him to run, but nothing came out of my mouth except a horrible piercing cry. I watched as my father glanced back and laid his eyes on the man who I thought was my lover — but who was, in fact, one with my father's murderers. Oh, dear God, what had I done? What web of deceit had I fallen into?

Finally, I managed to scream, "Hurry, Papa!"

His face awash with terror, Papa hobbled on, hurrying toward me, pleading, "Run, Maria! Get away! Save yourself!"

I couldn't move. Behind my father I saw Purishkevich struggling to load a revolver. First one, then a second bullet dropped from his shaking hands into the snow. Frustrated and furious, Sasha ripped the gun from Purishkevich and raised it high. And then Sasha — none other than Sasha! — took careful aim at my father.

"No!" I shrieked. "No!"

The very next instant Sasha fired, shattering the night. Before I knew it, something went screaming through the air not far from me. Sasha had missed! Papa, I realized, was still struggling onward!

"Run!" I called to my father.

But before Papa had taken three more steps, Sasha was again raising the gun. How could this be? How could the sweet young man I had kissed so passionately and given myself to now be so consumed with anger? How could his face be twisted with such hatred?

To my horror, this time Sasha took longer, straining to steady his wavering arm. And then, when my father was only some twenty paces from me, Sasha fired a second time — and again missed! With every bit of his strength, Papa pressed on, half stumbling, half running.

"Please, God, give him strength!" I sobbed.

But then several more figures burst from the palace, including Prince Felix and none other than Grand Duke Dmitri Pavlovich, that young dashing member of the royal family, a pistol in hand. My entire body shuddered. The grand duke was an Olympic athlete, a trained soldier, a seasoned hunter — and a Romanov bent on eliminating the "stain" of my father from the dynasty. When I saw him take confident, godlike aim at my father, I knew there was no hope.

The grand duke fired . . . and the bullet struck my father in the back, causing him to halt in his tracks. Slowly and with great effort, my father turned around, his hand rising slowly as if to make the sign of the cross. With great care, the grand duke fired again . . . the second shot struck my father directly in the forehead . . . and I screamed through the night as Papa tumbled to the ground, his hot red blood quickly melting away the cold white snow.

EPILOGUE

April 1917
Four months after Rasputin's death
"And then what happened?"

Wiping my eyes, I raised my head and stared across the wooden table at him, at Aleksander Blok, the man who'd once been my favorite poet and who was now my interrogator.

"I'm sorry, what did you say?" I asked.

"What happened next?"

How, I wondered, had the world been turned so on its head? I gazed around, craning my head and studying this columned room, St. George's Hall, buried in the heart of the Winter Palace. Just weeks ago this had been the elegant throne room of the greatest monarchy on the face of the earth. Now it had been trashed by angry revolutionaries. And there it was again, I thought as I looked toward the dais, a distant noise coming from behind the grate. So the looting of the palace continued unabated. Yes, I thought, beware the peasant with the ax.

How strange. Just when I had begun to understand my own father, he had been killed. And just when I had found someone to love, that young man had betrayed me as had no one else.

"You understand Sasha's real identity?" I said, looking up through a mist of tears.

"Yes, of course, Prince O'ksandr of Novgorod. A great friend of Prince Felix and Grand Duke Dmitri."

And, I thought, a dabbler in the sects of Russia, particularly the *Khlysty,* which was why, of course, Prince Felix had first drawn Sasha into the plot against my father.

Blok dipped his pen into some ink, took a deep breath, exhaled as if in pain, and said, "I need specific information of that night."

"Why? What do you care for truth?"

This man, one of our greatest purveyors of words whom many called the heir to Pushkin, flinched. Sure, I had just insulted him, but so what? His religion was using fine words to slice apart the complexities of the world and thereby expose the truths and the lies. Yet did I think my story, no matter how honestly he recorded it, even embellished it, would ever see the light of day? Never.

"You will write my story, but do you think it will actually be seen by any but a few officials? Do you think people in general will be allowed to read it?" I shook my head, and as confident as only a Rasputin could be, said, "Absolutely not. I'm quite sure these pages will be buried away and disappear."

Aghast, Blok looked up at me. "Why in the name of the devil do you say that?"

"Because the real truth of Rasputin is not what your people need, it's not something they can use to justify what they've done or something they can now use to fuel their revolution."

"But —"

"Everyone is running around saying that first my father was poisoned, next he was stabbed, and then he was shot, but still he lived. He lived, and nothing killed the holy devil Rasputin until he was thrown into the frozen waters of the Nevka and died by drowning. But none of that's true! I saw him killed! My father was murdered, first shot in the stomach and then in the back and finally in the head. Even the most cynical of revolutionaries wouldn't believe that even the great Rasputin could survive a bullet wound in the head. After all, he nearly died at the hands of a small syphilitic woman, so he was obviously as mortal as the rest of us."

Blok stared at me, not daring to contradict my words.

I said, "You know, of course, why Prince Felix and the others started this awful story? It's perfectly obvious, isn't it?"

After a long moment, he finally nodded. "To maintain the myth of your father."

"Exactly. There was no way a Yusupov could say that they had simply shot a peasant in the back as he tried to run away. Nor could they say that a defenseless and unarmed holy man from Siberia was easy to kill. Either statement would have enraged the *liodi*." I continued, my voice full of anger. "So to make sure that the murder wouldn't inflame the common folk, they made up the whole story of how difficult it was to kill Rasputin, the mad monk. And then they threw in the final tidbit, that my father died not by poison, or being stabbed or shot, but from drowning. You understand why that's so important, too, don't you?"

Blok nodded, albeit slowly.

"Then go on, tell me. Tell me why."

"Because . . ." Blok pushed back his chair and rose, moving away from the table. "Because if your father were still breathing when he was thrown through the ice and into the freezing water, he could never become a saint."

"Exactly. Their story not only confirms his supposed evilness, it entirely prevents him from being worshiped — ever! — simply because *liodi* believe that those who drown can never be canonized."

Blok turned and looked at me with eyes so sad, so tired, that I knew I had actually done the impossible and punctured a hole in his revolutionary zeal. This was exactly why, I knew, Blok and his cohorts would never allow the real story of the real Rasputin to get out, for it would make the revolution look like the black joke it was.

"You're sure of this, that your father was finished off by a bullet to the head?" he asked.

The crack of the gun, my father's horrible groan, the sight of him falling into the snow. Could I be more sure?

"Absolutely positive. And it wasn't Prince Felix or Prince O'ksandr or even Purishkevich who killed my father in the end. It was that splendid marksman, Grand Duke Dmitri Pavlovich."

"Dear Lord."

As would any Russian, Blok immediately understood the ramifications. Earlier the virulent Purishkevich had given thanks to

God that the hands of royal youth had not been stained with blood. But in the end, of course, that was exactly what had happened. Purishkevich wasn't referring to Prince Felix, certainly one of the most noble young men in the country, but not royal. No, he meant Grand Duke Dmitri Pavlovich, an immediate member of the ruling monarch's family and a direct grandson of the great Alexander II.

It was all just as I had been told. "My father's death was supposed to be only the beginning. The grand dukes next meant to kill the Tsar, toss Aleksandra Fyodorovna in a convent, and install one of their own, the young, handsome, and modern Grand Duke Dmitri Pavlovich. But *russkiye liodi*," the common Russian people, "would never have accepted him as a pretender to the throne if they knew that he, a grandson of the Tsar Liberator who had freed the serfs, had killed one of their own, a true *muzhik*, in cold blood. And the grand dukes' plot probably would have succeeded if it hadn't been so cold, if the bread riots hadn't broken out, if —"

"Of course." Blok shook his head. "And you haven't told anyone this?"

"No, absolutely not."

"You're positive?"

"Not even my own mother. I haven't been able to tell a single soul . . . until you."

"And why is that? Why haven't you come forward?"

"Because they threatened me, because . . ."

The memories came flooding back, and I turned away. As if it had happened only moments ago, I remembered it all perfectly clearly, how I had rushed, sobbing, to my father's body. No sooner had I fallen in the red snow, however, than a group of men had charged around me. Within seconds they were hauling me away, dragging me into the palace. I had screamed and cried, kicked and twisted. When someone struck me in the face, I had turned and seen Sasha.

"Shut up!" he shouted. "I'm sorry, but we had to do it. Your father left us no choice!"

I cried out again, and suddenly I felt the cold barrel of a gun on the back of my head, and Purishkevich was yelling into my ear, "Shut up or I'll shoot!"

Looking back one last time I saw Prince Felix hysterically crying out and kicking my father's body.

"Papa!" I pleaded, helplessly.

And when Prince Felix had fallen against the corpse and started beating and slugging it like a madman, I turned away, unable to bear it. . . .

Now staring at Blok through a thick veil of tears, I said, "They kept me locked up in a coal bin for hours before tossing me out. And I'm still not sure why they let me go. All I can think is that Sasha — Prince O'ksandr — arranged it. When they did release me, however, they said that if I told anyone, they'd kill not only me but my sister, my brother, and my mother. All of us. They promised to eliminate all the Rasputins, to *liquidate* us."

"Dear Lord."

"That's why I've kept silent these four months since Papa was killed." I shook my head, trying to rid myself of the vision of that night. "It was all so horrible. Prince Felix went crazy, beating and kicking my father. Was it some repressed feeling in him? Had he both desired my father sexually and hated him too? Yes, surely. As I look back, I think Prince Felix earlier that fall must have confessed himself and his feelings to my father, who in turn was only trying to heal the prince of his 'grammatical errors.' "

"And Prince O'ksandr?" said Blok, shaking his head as he wrote something down. "Do you have any idea what happened to him?"

"No. None."

"But you do understand what role he

played in this, don't you?"

Nodding, I wiped my eyes. "I've since learned that he's from a very noble though not very wealthy family in Novgorod, a family that dates all the way back to the days of Prince Rurik. And when Prince Felix found out that Sasha had secret connections to the *Khlysty,* he got Sasha to snoop around for anything they could use against my father. When they couldn't find anything, they didn't just stop. No, they kept pushing and digging . . . and they decided that Sasha, the youngest of them, should use his charms to try to get information from me, Rasputin's daughter."

"And this, I presume, is why you've returned to the capital, to look for Prince O'ksandr. Correct?"

I wanted to tell him, but when I stared into Blok's eyes I couldn't decide if it was safe to confess.

"Well," pressed Blok, "is that correct?"

His eyes just looked so sad, his soul so vulnerable, that I couldn't help but nod. "There's something I need to tell him, just one thing he needs to know."

"But do you have any idea where he is?"

"I know that while Prince Felix and Grand Duke Dmitri were exiled for their part in my father's murder, Sasha was imprisoned by the Tsar. I thought he would have been freed after the revolution, but I've heard from someone who heard from someone else that he was in the Shpalernaya Prison, and . . . and that he might be suffering from typhus."

Aleksander Blok stared at me with something akin to horror as if I were a vision, a harbinger, of things to come. And yes, I was quite sure I was. People lost, people looking, people dying . . . all this wasn't just in Russia's future, it was already here, already playing over and over like a tragic dirge.

"Of course, if he was really there, the chances of his still being alive aren't very great," I continued, fully aware that Shpalernaya was the worst of the worst. "There should be lists, people should be helping one another, but people aren't talking anymore. Have you seen how frightened everyone is? I wish someone would help me, but who's ever come to the aid of a Rasputin?" I shrugged. "You don't have any idea where he could be, do you? You haven't heard anything?"

Blok shook his head.

It was just as I thought, this revolution would come to no good. The Provisional Government was not in control, and Kerensky wasn't powerful enough to maintain order. There were already rumors that the Bolsheviks were plotting a putsch. In the end, everyone would probably realize what everyone already knew, that Russia needed someone to rule her with an iron fist. So there probably would be another tsar, one more mighty than the last, though certainly not a Romanov.

But I'd had enough of it all, this poet and his interrogation. I didn't care what Blok wanted; I would be kept no longer. So I got to my feet, turned, and started for the large doors at the far end of the hall.

I hadn't gone more than ten paces when Blok suddenly barked, "Stop right there!"

I turned and gazed into the eyes of our great poet — our defeated poet. "What?"

"You said you returned to the capital to tell Prince O'ksandr something, but you haven't said what. I can only assume it's something terribly important. What is it? What does he need to know?"

With eyes nearly as intent as my father's, I stared right back at him. "I want him to know that I'm planning to leave not just Petrograd but Russia, and I'll never be back." Somehow I knew it was safe to tell Blok the rest, so, gently touching my stomach, I added, "And I want Sasha to know that I'm pregnant with his child — yes, he is the father of a new generation of Rasputins. The *shaman* back home in our village believes it will be a girl, so if by chance you ever see him, tell him that too. Tell him he is the father of this Rasputin's daughter."

Blok watched the young woman cross the large room defiantly, her figure tall and confident, her stride direct and determined. He didn't doubt that Maria had spoken the unfettered truth of her father's life and death. It was amazing how much she knew and understood. Almost everything, actually.

But he had to remain focused. The old order was gone, the new had arrived. It was not about these little personal tragedies but the future and what it would bring. Right now a great storm had swept across Russia, changing and electrifying everything. He knew they were in the middle of it, these days so dark and turbulent . . . but then? When the storm passed and the skies cleared, would the transformation be complete? Once he had been so sure, now he was not.

Blok gazed across the huge throne room and watched as Maria Rasputin reached the tall gilded doors, slipped through one, and pulled it shut behind her, disappearing into history. So be it, thought Blok, as he took his pen, dabbed it in his pot of ink, and jotted down notes for the report he would write on Matryona Grigorevna Rasputina for the Thirteenth Section. He already knew he wouldn't mention that she was with child. Indeed, he decided he would deem her harmless and of no further interest. Odd, he thought, how her openness, her story — the truths she so freely gave — in turn protected her from other truths, albeit very painful ones. No, he was glad he hadn't told her.

Laying down the pen, Aleksander Blok took a deep breath and ran both hands through his thick wavy hair. Rising, he headed from his simple oak desk toward the pair of doors just to the left of the dais. It had been through these doors that the tsars had entered St. George's Hall. And as he walked, Blok's eyes fell on the exquisitely carved wooden grate located next to the dais, open on this side but covered on the rear with a silk curtain. Not only had trumpeters, tastefully unseen, once stood behind the fancy grillwork heralding the royal entry, but advisers and ministers had huddled there unseen, overhearing all that transpired before their tsar.

Blok, who'd noticed Maria glance at the

grate several times, wondered if she had suspected.

Taking hold of the large gilded door lever, he pressed down, pushed open the door, and entered a much smaller albeit regal room, the plaster walls painted a pale blue, the cove ceiling covered with detailed plasterwork that was akin to filigree. Here the tsars had gathered before making their grand entry. Now, however, the atmosphere was decidedly somber, for on this side of the grate were two armed guards and their prisoner, a severely ill man who sat securely tied to a chair, his mouth covered with a thick white cloth.

"Remove the gag," ordered Blok.

One of the guards, a broad-shouldered man with a bushy mustache, reached down and all but yanked the cloth away. The prisoner, his face covered with a shaggy beard, coughed sharply and gulped in a large breath of air.

He did indeed look horrible, thought Blok, staring down upon the young man, who'd been captured and imprisoned the very day after Rasputin's murder. True, mused Blok, the months of deprivation and interrogation, even torture, had left the young man as pale as a winter field and as thin as a shaft of wheat. Even worse, a deep red rash was crawling up his neck, he was having trouble breathing, and, by the perspiration beaded on his forehead, it was obvious he was running a high fever.

"Prince O'ksandr?"

"Y-yes?" came the dazed reply.

"To be honest, Prince, the Provisional Government doesn't quite know what to do, whether to treat you as a national hero or a common murderer."

"Please . . . just let her go."

"Don't worry. I can see she's harmless. She's already left, and I'll make sure she's bothered no more. The commission will be interested in her observations, of course, particularly of the last night, but I'll keep certain things confidential."

While Blok didn't know whether or not Maria had suspected anyone was lingering in this room, he was sure she had never guessed it was her Sasha.

"So will you release what she told you about her father, or — as Maria said — will it be buried? Will the people ever be allowed to know the real Rasputin?"

"That's a complicated question with a simple answer: No." Blok slipped his hands into his pockets and turned and gazed out a window. "Before the revolution the stories of Rasputin served the anti-tsarist movement very well, just as they now serve the revolution, the more exaggerated the better. Rasputin soiled the image of Tsar Nikolai as no one else could, and once *liodi* stopped seeing the Tsar as a demigod, the revolution was both easy and inevitable. Otherwise, Rasputin, not to mention the Empress, are guilty of only one thing: exceedingly well-intentioned but horrible judgment. In other words, Maria was absolutely correct. To allow any of what we really know about Rasputin and the former imperial family to become public knowledge would be political suicide, even today. The man himself continues to serve the revolution best in myth."

"But that myth is so dangerous — rather like a stick of dynamite. Even behind the prison walls there's talk of civil war."

"Of course. Russia is a very big bear — a wild one, at that — and we have many difficulties ahead. Perhaps we're doomed to a second revolution, as so many suspect." Blok folded his hands behind his back and gazed down at his feet. "You heard what she said, that she's pregnant with your child?"

Staring into his lap, he nodded ever so slightly.

"So maybe instead we should charge you

with treason. After all, rather than extinguish the Rasputins, you've ensured that they will live on."

"She's not . . . not like her father. She has a very pure soul — and a real gift with words." His hands still tied tightly behind the back of the chair, Sasha did not look up. "Prince Felix sent me to infiltrate the *Khlysty* and his family — to find his religion, charm his daughter, enter his home — all in the hopes not of simply getting information but of unearthing scandal. Scandal that we could plant like dangerous propaganda. After all, don't you think fear and rumor and innuendo are —"

"More powerful than the mightiest cannon? Yes, absolutely."

Sasha looked up, his brown eyes pleading. "It's better that she move on with her life, so please . . . please don't tell her I'm alive."

With a shrug, Blok turned on his heel and started out. "Don't worry, I won't." Reaching the door that led back into the throne room, he took hold of the lever . . . and then turned and stared back at the pathetic young man. "After all, it's obvious you haven't got much longer."

As Blok left the room, he heard the young man begin to weep gently, perhaps as much out of relief as anything else. But there was no need, thought Blok as he returned to his desk, to tell Maria that the father of her unborn child was alive. There was no need because Prince O'ksandr would soon be dead, for it was obvious the typhus was well along. What did he have — a week, two at the most?

Yes, he thought as he sat down at his desk, one more death. In the greater scheme of things, this young man, no matter how highly born, was insignificant, just another soul. But how was this to end and when would the cleansing of the country be complete? How many more millions would have to die before the war against the Germans would be over and the revolution within Russia would stop roiling?

And when would the River Neva stop flowing red?

Blok glanced at the extensive notes he'd taken of Maria's story. He'd fill out the report tonight and have it typed up tomorrow. But what were they, really? Just more words, more paragraphs? Pushing aside those papers, he came to yet more words — Prince O'ksandr's testimony taken yesterday — and reread the opening lines:

Believe me, I'd tell you if I knew. But I really have no idea how Rasputin was introduced to the former imperial family, and I will swear to my death that I took no part in it. I've heard rumors that he was eager to penetrate the palace, that he did so via dubious means, and that he was assisted by one of the former grand duchesses — I think the one from Montenegro. It seems quite possible, but of all that I have no firsthand knowledge.

No, I didn't become involved in the plot to murder Rasputin until much, much later.

As he scanned the remaining pages, Blok realized that while the prince's words all seemed truthful, the Thirteenth really had no choice. No matter how long or short Prince O'ksandr had to live, if he got out, the truth of Rasputin might get out too, and then — well, no, no need to risk anything. Turning back to the front page of the prince's confession, Blok wrote in large letters, PRISONER TO REMAIN AT SHPALER-NAYA INDEFINITELY.

WHAT HAPPENED TO THE CHARACTERS BASED ON REAL PEOPLE?

Rasputin had long predicted that, in the event of his own death, the royal family would soon perish. Indeed, not even three months after Rasputin's murder, Nicholas and Alexandra were pulled from the throne by the February Revolution. Exiled to Siberia, the imperial couple and their five beloved children were secretly executed in July 1918. Their hidden grave was not found until after the fall of the Soviet Union in 1991.

The highborn aristocrats involved in Rasputin's death were sent into exile before the Revolution and, because of this, escaped those tumultuous days unharmed. For the duration of his life, Grand Duke Dmitri never commented on the murder of Rasputin. Having fled to Europe with no fortune, only a title, he married an American heiress and died in 1942; his son, Paul Ilyinsky, was for many years the popular mayor of Palm Beach, Florida, and died in 2004. Prince Felix perpetuated his own version of what happened that night and wrote several memoirs; he and his wife, Princess Irina, lived in relative comfort in Paris until his death in 1967. The monarchist Vladimir Purishkevich died of typhoid fever as civil war raged around him.

Anna Vyrubova, Alexandra's closest friend, was arrested and interrogated at length by the Thirteenth Section. When questioned about a possible sexual relationship with Rasputin, she swore under oath that these rumors were nothing but lies and she was in fact a virgin. A small cadre of physicians examined her and, much to the surprise of the Thirteenth Section, immediately confirmed her claim. Eventually freed, Madame Vyrubova was later re-arrested by the Bolsheviks, only to escape and disappear into hiding. Several years after Lenin seized power, she managed to flee across the ice floes to Finland, where she took her vows. She lived in seclusion until her death in Helsinki in 1964.

Rasputin's most notorious and fanatical

devotee, Madame Lokhtina, was arrested by the Thirteenth, interrogated, and released. Dressed in torn filthy clothing, she was last seen in 1923 at a train station poking at people with her staff and begging for food.

Alexander Protopopov, Russia's last Minister of Internal Affairs, was imprisoned and shot, his body dumped in an unknown grave.

The great Russian poet Alexander Blok was indeed drafted and brought in by the Extraordinary Commission to transcribe the Thirteenth Section's interrogations of those who knew Rasputin. While he welcomed the overthrow of Nicholas II, he was soon greatly disillusioned by the Bolsheviks. His epic poem *The Twelve* was published within a year of the Revolution, and while many consider it one of his greatest works, it also proved to be among his very last. His spirit and health shattered by what he saw around him, he died in 1921, at age forty-one, of complications from hunger and syphilis.

Grigori Rasputin's ever-devoted wife, Praskovia, mentally retarded son, Dmitri, and youngest daughter, Varvara, were all driven from their Siberian village by the Bolsheviks. Praskovia is believed to have died soon thereafter of unknown causes.

Dmitri was later captured by Stalin's hench-men and thrown into the brutal Salehard Camp, one of the many gulags of Siberia, where he died of scurvy in 1937. Rasputin's treasured younger daughter, Varvara, dis-appeared completely, though it is rumored she died unnoticed in Leningrad in the early 1960s. Edvokia Pechyorkin — Dunya — who served Rasputin as both housekeeper and mistress, vanished into the flames of the Revolution.

As for the real Maria Rasputin, she fled to Siberia after the Revolution, where she impetuously married Boris Soloviev, an of-ficer with a shadowy reputation. They escaped from Russia during the civil war — the only members of the Rasputin family to do so — and eventually found their way to Paris. Soon after her marriage, Maria gave birth to one daughter and then another, and when her husband died in 1926, Maria danced and sang in a cabaret to support her little family. Later she found work as a lion tamer in both London and Los Angeles, and the crowds flocked to see the daughter of the "Mad Monk" perform her magic over nature's wild beasts. While on tour with the Ringling Brothers Circus in Peru, Indiana, she was mauled by a bear, which forced her to quit the circus and take a job as a riveter in a Miami shipyard.

Finding peace far from Siberia, Maria lived out her old age in a bungalow tucked in the shadows of the Hollywood Freeway, where she lived on Social Security and the occasional babysitting job. While she never published any poetry, she wrote several memoirs and co-authored a cookbook, which includes recipes for both Jellied Fish Heads and her father's favorite, Cod Soup.

Maria died in 1977. The Rasputin descendants continue to live in the environs of Paris.

CHRONOLOGY

1894

Nicholas II succeeds Alexander III

1914

War breaks out against Germany
St. Petersburg is renamed Petrograd

1915

Grand Duke Nikolai Nikolaevich is removed as Commander in Chief
Nicholas II appoints himself Commander in Chief, leaves for the front
Alexandra's power and role in the government grow rapidly

1916

Rasputin murdered by Yusupov and others December 16

1917

February: Massive demonstrations break out over food shortages
Riots turn into revolution and mutiny

Nicholas II abdicates February 28

The Provisional Government attempts to restore order

March 4: The Provisional Government forms:

- The Extraordinary Commission of Inquiry for the Investigation of Illegal Acts by Ministers and Other Responsible Persons of the Tsarist Regime
- The Thirteenth Section, charged with investigating the Dark Forces (all who knew Rasputin are incarcerated and interrogated)

August: The former imperial family is exiled to Siberia

October: Second Revolution breaks out as Lenin and Bolsheviks seize power

1918

Nicholas, Alexandra, and children are secretly executed July 16

1919

The report of the Thirteenth Section, nearly 500 pages long, vanishes

Maria Rasputin escapes from Russia

1920

Russian Civil War ends

1977

Maria Rasputin dies in Hollywood, California

1995

The entire report of the Thirteenth Section is auctioned at Sotheby's in Paris

GLOSSARY

ahmeen amen
arzhin .71 meters
banya Russian sauna
batushka the dear father
bistro quickly
bit-po-semo so be it
bizmyen permission to kiss the tsaritsa's hand
bog God
bogoroditsa the Virgin
bozhe moi my God
bozh'i-liudi God's people
chai'naya teahouse
da yes
derevenschina naïve country girl, yokel
devochka young girl
devushka girl
doche daughter
dochenka maya my little daughter
dorogaya maya my dear
Dukhobory a religious sect known as pacifist

"spirit wrestlers"

durachok cute little fool

durak fool

dyadka uncle, fellow, bodyguard

dyavol the devil

fortochka small transom window

garderob-sheek coatroom attendant

gospodi good heavens

gospodin mister

grupa seksa group sex

izba peasant's log hut

kammerfurier court log

Kazanskaya The Virgin of Kazan, one of Russia's most revered icons

Khlysty a religious sect known as "the Whips"

kiot large icon case

konyechno of course

kosovorotka Russian shirt, fastened alongside the collar

kroogli durak round idiot, complete fool

kto tam? who is there?

leemoan lemon

liodi common people

malenkaya maya my little one

milaya maya my dear one

ministir minister

molodets excellent, a smart one

Molokans a religious sect known as "the milk drinkers"

muzhik peasant
nyet no
narod the masses
ochen very
pelmeni Siberian meat dumplings
pirog a pie
podstakanik metal holder for tea glass
pravoslavni Russian Orthodoxy
proshchaitye farewell
prospekt prospect, boulevard
prostitutka prostitute
radeniye rejoicing
radi boga for the sake of God
rasputitsa a season of horribly muddy roads
rasputiye a crossroad
rasputnik a debauched person
reeba bez vodii a fish without water
revolutsiya revolution
russkiye Russian
sevodnya soopa nyetoo today there is no soup
sermyaga peasant clothing of heavy cloth
Skoptsy a religious sect known as "the castrators"
slava bogu thanks be to God
spasibo thank you
starushka a sweet, old woman
strannik a (wandering) pilgrim
starets a religious elder, a man of God
starii xhren an old piece of horseradish

Subbotniki a religious sect whose beliefs fall
   between Christianity and Judaism
svalnyi grekh group sinning
takzhe also
tapochki slippers
telega a cart without springs
vershok 4.4 centimeters
v'koosno tasty
vranye fibs, the art of creative lying
xhama rogues
Xhristos Christ
Xhristovshchina the Christ faith
xhorosho good/fine
ya spala kak ubeetaya I slept like the dead
ya tebya lubloo I love you
ya Vas slushaiyoo I am listening to you
zakuska appetizer

ABOUT THE AUTHOR

Over the course of the last thirty years, **Robert Alexander** has studied at Leningrad State University, worked for the U.S. government in the former U.S.S.R., and traveled extensively throughout Russia. Since 1990 he has been a partner in a St. Petersburg corporation that operates a warehouse and customs clearance center, dental clinic, and Barabu, a chain of espresso shops.

Born and raised in Chicago, Alexander now lives in Minneapolis. For more information, visit the author's Web site at www. rasputinsdaughter.com.

The employees of Thorndike Press hope you have enjoyed this Large Print book. All our Thorndike and Wheeler Large Print titles are designed for easy reading, and all our books are made to last. Other Thorndike Press Large Print books are available at your library, through selected bookstores, or directly from us.

For information about titles, please call:

(800) 223-1244

or visit our Web site at:

www.gale.com/thorndike
www.gale.com/wheeler

To share your comments, please write:

Publisher
Thorndike Press
295 Kennedy Memorial Drive
Waterville, ME 04901